I0570895

Eleanor Tibbett

The Revenge

*Do you not see how necessary a world of pains and troubles
is to school an intelligence and make it a soul?*
—JOHN KEATS

Eleanor Tibbett

The Revenge

Miles Wortman

DE STAEL

ELEANOR TIBBETT: THE REVENGE
© 2020 Miles Wortman. All rights reserved.

DeStaël Press

Without limiting the rights under copyright above, no part of this publication
may be reproduced, stored in or introduced into a retrieval system, or trans-
mitted, in any form, or by any means (electronic, mechanical, photocopying,
recording, or use in motion pictures and otherwise), without the prior written
permission of the publisher of this book.

ISBN 978-1-7328003-3-5 (Paperback)
ISBN 978-1-7328003-4-2 (Ebook)

Book design by Morgan Crockett | Firewire Creative

Printed in the United States of America

DE STAEL

For all the world's exiles refugees and immigrants

On rough seas

Behind bars and barbed wire

In deadly deserts

Beyond terror

They yearning to breathe free

To find peace for their families

To create bright shining futures

As did our forebears

In forgotten times

Also by Miles Wortman

Leaves: Tales of Development

Zoo Story

The Road to Help: The Revolution in Charity, Philanthropy and International Development

Notable Family Networks in Latin America (with Diana Balmori & Stuart Voss)

Government and Society in Central America, 1680–1840

Latin America

———•————————————————————•———

*Many thanks to G. Robin Schore and Myrna Chase Wortman
for their helpful suggestions.*

Introduction

———•———————————————————•———

THE LIFE OF ELEANOR TIBBETT, the Eleanor Tibbett we all know so well today, her presence everywhere, in tabloids, financial pages, on TV talk shows, and at benefits, that life began at 42. The epitome of the successful 21st century woman, this "most-admired woman" so mild-mannered, smart, worldly and with such a keen business sense. Attractive, not artificially glammed up like so many others, but primly so, modest and proper.

She rules, if that is the word, from her legendary tower office at the foot of Manhattan, with a 360 degree view of the city, to the south, the freighters, cruise boats, and sailboats crowding Hudson Bay and Lady Liberty, to the north, the Freedom Tower, the lights of Broadway up to Central Park. She is one of the nation's notable personalities, someone that politicians turn to for advice and support.

She cares for the poor and oppressed, for women's rights, and social equality. She gives her time, her endowments and her participation on charity boards. Widely admired and frequently sought after, when she speaks it is not with the exalted, self-important pretense of so many leaders, no sound-bites, empty phrases, and loud declarations, but quietly and decisively. She is truly a model for all women.

And yet so little is known of her past. You read about an Oprah or Clinton or Gates and there's so much detail and gossip. Grist for the tabloids. Don't you think it curious that this celebrity, this mogul we all know and admire, has no history to speak of? In this town, if you're big, you're grist for the mill. Paparazzi hound you. Neighbors are hassled. And writers print lies.

Google her and what do you get? A few mentions of real estate holdings, newspaper opinion pieces on her next move, a donation for some veterans' charity. Direct quotes? Nothing. Photos? Rumors? Nada.

How did Eleanor Tibbett become *the* Eleanor Tibbett? How did a quiet and shy girl emerge transformed through pain, tragedy and suffering into success? Hers is a unique American story filled with mystery, deaths, disappearances, and betrayals, that of a woman hiding within herself, observing, learning and preparing, whether she knew it or not.

The tragedies of the past Tibbett, those hidden from all of us, begat the second life, the one on display today. But the past is for the present. It always is.

Part One

1.

Bobby White

———————•———————

AT DAWN, BEFORE THE BIRDS BEGAN CHIRPING, before the click of the coffee maker or the drone of early morning traffic and before the early spring sun lighted the pastel drapes, came the Knock, first faintly, then stronger. Eleanor White stirred, moving just enough to wake Joey. He rose, went to the window and saw the uniforms. One man. One woman. Army mufti. He said simply, "I think they're here about Bobby."

2.

Joey White

———————————————————

SIX MONTHS AFTER THEIR SON'S FUNERAL and the European trip, an autumn evening, he watching football on the wall-size TV, bourbon in hand, a near-empty bottle by his side. She reading quietly in the corner under an elaborate reading lamp, copper tubes twisting all about and ending at three bulbs, the lamp her father made for his young daughter so addicted to reading. She sips chamomile tea. A small gold-framed picture beside her shows two young boys wrestling on the lawn. A faint odor of roasted chicken lingered in the air. A slice of untouched apple pie sat on the table, a fork astride it like an oar in a rowboat, awaiting its turn.

At half-time, he took another swig. The tinkle of ice. She looked at him briefly. He caught her glance. He kissed her on the head. She pulled away. He stumbled out into the quiet suburban evening. It is not a pastoral scene, despite the vain attempt of landscape firms. It is a Hollywood set, an architect's drawing, a Potemkin attempt at the idyllic life. He weaved his way up Rose Drive, past the Zabriskis, whose nightly screams entertained the folks walking their cockers and retrievers. He crossed Magnolia to the Callins with their perfectly-trimmed treeless lawn.

A wisp of wind disturbed the quiet air. Car traffic hummed softly in the distance beyond the subdivision. He took the fork to Petunia Place to Carol and Sid's, Carol who always winked at him in the supermarket and Sid always asking Eleanor if there was anything he could do for her, "anything." A car passed by, its timing slightly off, he noted.

He strolled on, head down in a mindless journey. He heard a knock in the distance. The development had banned electric chimes. The Board insisted on traditional bronze knockers, the type that echoed through the air announcing outsiders, one of the subdivision's rules, along with keeping dogs on leashes, garbage out Wednesdays and Saturdays, and restrained Christmas lighting. The knock on each door was the sound on every door, but the knock, this time on the Callins' door caused him to pause.

No more toys, soccer balls, frisbees or plastic jungle gyms. Childless streets save for the Zabriski kid who remained at home, not really a kid, but a guy stuck in the nest, working at odd jobs and spinning his hog around town. All the others were gone, their laughter and screams like a chorus once resonating through the air now memories, subjects of brief, modest conversations of aging parents, strolling with pets, passing by and exchanging greetings.

At the end of the cul-de-sac, he paused and turned back, trapped at the end of the secure neighborhood, as American as apple pie. Weak street lamps lighted the walk as in a fog.

Bobby, his son, had died bravely, taking fire while the platoon moved to outflank the enemy. That's what they said. He took fire for the good of the nation. "Your son was a real hero," they said. He will get the Distinguished Service Cross. And a personal letter from the President.

Joey White was a car man, born to the job, as they say. Mild-mannered and polite, a kind smile, a shoeshine, and a slight laugh at awkward customer jokes. He saw their garb and gait as they entered the dealership, the cut of their hair, the look on their faces, and, like a seer, he foretold the model, color and price. The salesman's salesman. A young, nervous couple wanders into the showroom, hesitantly, lost as in a jungle. They look about in awe, virgins in the market, he, hands in pocket, she with a neat pleated dress. For them, a 15G sporty hatchback. The parents with two prams and a pouting five-year-old. For them, a van or a crossover. The forty-something guy with pressed jeans and shaved head. No ring. A striped 2 door with six on the floor and 350 big ones under the hood. The aging widow. A two-door gas-efficient cheapo, big enough to get in and out but suitable for long drives.

Joey did not manipulate or judge. He was a presence to lives passing through, matching desires and needs, budgets and goals. No emotion. No reflection. A natural, just the kind of guy you'd want to hang out with, a guy born to the job, a salesman's salesman. Light chinos and an open shirt, his uniform. He looked you in the eye, listened to your wants and he just knew. "First you sell yourself, then you sell the company, then you sell the car," that's what old man Shrankman taught him. Whoever the customer: the long-haired, tattooed rebel, the housewife looking for adventure, the mid-level manager needing a mid-level vehicle. All had their ideas. Color? Conservative grey, mild silver, young yellow, or shocking red. Seating? Leather or upholstery. Which for the office car park? Which to show in the driveway like a piece of fine furniture to offset the ranch house? Long-term lease? Low down-payment? High trade-in?

And when he saw the eyes sparkle and the hands shake, he went for the sale, the one-time price reduction, an attractive financing deal, the loan that might be paid in simple, easy monthly installments, the price break for the "last car on the lot." And after the sale, the add-ons, the tire flaps, undercoating, extended warranty, high-end audio with power amps, GPS, and theft insurance. "You only live once, you know."

Then, he proclaimed, "you're getting a great deal here," not because he was selling but because he was giving a great deal. He never said, "this is the car I drive." He never lied. Just a natural. He had risen through the ranks until Carl Shrankman had no choice but to offer him a partnership. And then, when Shrankman retired, he bought the GM dealership in the center of Lincoln Gardens, the corner of Broadway and Ashford, next to what was once the ice cream parlor and now the Starbucks, across the street from what was once the A&P and now the Whole Foods. Still, Shrankman Autos. Everyone in Lincoln Gardens knows Shrankman Autos. License plates with Shrankman frames cover the entire state.

Joey was success without the attitude. He drove his Chevy sedan and Buick van. Certainly no Cadillac. Who wants to buy a car from some rich townie while you're struggling to make the payments, figuring out if the monthlies fit in with the mortgage, the taxes and the budget? The district GM guy insisted he drive a Cadillac. Gave him a Caddy license plate. But Joey knew better. He was one of the guys. At the diner for breakfast. At the club. At church. A call me at any time type of fellow.

Quiet. Low-keyed. No judgments. Guys would drive onto the lot with rusting, stinking jalopies filled with empty beer cans, dog hair and condoms. They'd track mud onto the spotless white tile floor, but Joey didn't blink. A natural, born to sell, that's what Shrankman had said. Joey would offer them a fair trade-in and when they bargained, he offered a little more. All part of the game. His customers, his neighbors, the members of the club, the Episcopal parishioners, and school parents, he knew them all, knew how they voted, what they wore, what they would never wear, their style, their engines, and their colors.

He hired their kids, trained them as salesmen, taught them the tricks, ("First you sell yourself, then you sell the company, then you sell the car") and when they showed up with drink on their breath or were late, he gently reminded them who they were, citizens of Lincoln Gardens, people providing a service and if they couldn't do that, then they better move on but if they thought that they could, he'd work with them.

A few years back, some guys came by with a deal to switch to Toyota. But no, he was going to play it safe and stay American. He knew Toyota was coming on strong, but GM was the American car, ingrained in the heartland, with customers as dependable as the morning sunrise. *See the USA in a Chevrolet! As American as Apple Pie.* He was doing well enough. Why get greedy?

The Chevies, Pontiacs, and Caddies were not bad cars and they certainly had improved over the years. Automatic tranies, power steering, air conditioning, convertibles, leather seats, minivans and big strong engines that could carry a family of six cross the USA with the dog and all the luggage you'd need. Sure, the cars would need shop-time every now and then, change the oil, do a tune up, fix a recall, but that was the price you paid. "Bring it back any time, and we'll fix you up."

GM was America, gave its workers strong wages and benefits, sponsored football, drove the country, or so they said. Yes, he complained to Detroit, the doors didn't close exactly right, didn't have the nice click like the Germans or the Japs, and the recalls didn't help at all. But that was always the case ever since Henry Ford himself. Who was to know that the world was changing, that "they" would want dependability, cars that didn't break down, smaller cars, non-American tiny things made by workers paid nothing somewhere overseas? Who was to know?

He walked back towards home, along the quiet streets past silken, azalea-edged lawns. Bright blue recycling bins sat at the curb overflowing with empty Chardonnay and Bordeaux bottles, Bud Light and Coke cans, Tide containers, and mayo bottles. A tree here and there but few and far between. This neighborhood was clean. Antiseptic. Television screens blinking against the stars. A rabbit crossed his path. What was he thinking, this car man, filled with liquor, this life of recalls and rebates, radiators and regulations? He inspected his lawn, wandering about unsteadily, pulling weeds haphazardly. He looked back down the lane, turned and entered the house.

I'm sorry, but we did all that we could. I must explain, I would suggest that, I'm sorry, seeing your son would do no good, I promise you. Best to have a closed casket. We will arrange for the funeral, of course, send an honor-guard. Just tell us what we can do to help. He gave the ultimate sacrifice, and his country will remember him always. To the end.

There were always ups and downs, but you handled them. That's what one does. Business was rocky, to be sure, lease payments fell behind, and more and more customers drifted away to the Germans and Japanese. And then there was Craig, lost Craig, the other son, the boy always in trouble who one day just picked up and left for who knows where? They called the police. After all, the boy was underage, but there were no phone calls, no credit card charges. Nothing. They had gotten over that. Certainly, they hoped the boy was alright. He would find his way, somehow, some way. Someday. There was always Bobby, the good son, the type you could be proud of, handsome, strong and solid, just like his father.

Until the Knock when it all seemed to crumble.

There was this woman, the wife of the town handyman. Slim and pretty, with long, blonde and slightly disheveled hair announcing her disdain to the world, she of the sly laugh, a dimple and a stare right into his face. They came to price the pickup, the handyman and his wife, a slight smell of alcohol on their breaths. He, shaved head, muscular arms and angry stare. She, just watching her man stroll the showroom and laughing disdainfully at the compacts, scoffing at the ragtops. He took the truck for a test drive. She remained behind on the bench, her legs crossed, her dress rising above her knees. Joey brought her coffee. She flirted, the salesman was used to that, just another customer trying to make a deal. And when her husband returned and spotted her leaning slightly towards Joey, he grabbed her arm and dragged her roughly to the street.

The next day, she came back. Alone. Around closing time. She asked for a drink. And that was that. The beginning. And the end.

Joey closed the door and muttered, "I'm back." Eleanor didn't respond. He poured another bourbon, threw in some ice, and shuffled up the stairs to Bobby's room. He glanced about, at the mementos, trophies, diplomas, pictures of friends, all untouched since the Knock, as if some day he might return.

Why did Bobby join up? It was a mystery to him. No family in the military. They were patriotic, but not overly so. No flag on the lawn and all that. Sure, Joey gave his best Chevy for the July 4th parade but that was as far as that went. No failed love for Bobby either, no crisis of the heart or rejection. He was a good average kid, who got his Bs at Lincoln Gardens High and a little trouble on the roads as kids do, harmless stuff, underage drinking, speeding down empty country roads, late-night knocks at the door with the town cop bringing him home. Girls called at all hours. He certainly could have gone to college, money enough for that, and he'd probably get a football scholarship from State. He was a fine running back, and the coaches came asking. Bobby wasn't interested. He just went and signed up without explanation. Eleanor and Joey never showed much emotion, and, he supposed, neither did their sons. Their warmth was shown through looks, brief shoulder touches and understood jokes. They were Episcopalian with mid-western manners. American restraint. It seemed like a good life, almost a perfect life. A comfortable home with soft, white puffy furniture against white walls, like a field of cotton, some plants here and there, a house open to teenagers to lie around or come and go as they pleased. A full fridge, the pizza number on a magnet and plenty of snacks in the cupboard.

And then, Bobby went to war. And the town asked, "What is going on there? What did he flee? What did *they, those two boys,* escape? What was the problem?"

Joey returned. Eleanor kept reading. He wandered from room to room, without thought or purpose, his head weary from drink, to the guest rooms now visited only by a dust mop, to the pool room where friends once gathered, and back to the bottle.

"You're drinking too much," Eleanor said quietly.

"Yes, I suppose I am."

"You know what I think?"

"Why don't you tell me again?" he retorted.

"They called from the showroom. You left early again today."

"Yeah, well. Not much to do. The place takes care of itself."

"And you, who takes care of you?"

"Fuck off." He slapped her head, not hard, just a slight touch. She ignored the touch. He emptied the bottle. "I'm going to bed."

3.

Sam Devlin

———————•———————

OVERWEIGHT, TIRED AND BORED, the cop sat in the small office reading the day's paper and glancing at the TV. Police work in the 'burbs: sitting and waiting. No thrills or mysteries. Speeding tickets, drunken brawls, zoning violations. Mostly just driving about, having coffee at the diner and spending evenings by the phone in case Fido went missing. Tedium.

The phone rang. "Lincoln Gardens Police, Sam Devlin speaking," he said lazily.

"Sam, this is Eleanor White. My husband just killed himself."

4.

Eleanor White

———————•———————

THEY ARRIVED WITHIN MINUTES. Officer Devlin and Chief of Police Dan O'Reilly. Eleanor sat quietly in the corner, her head in her hands. O'Reilly put his hand on her shoulder. "I told them to make this as easy as possible, Eleanor."

"I appreciate that."

"You've had a tough ride. You really don't deserve this."

"Thanks, Dan." She looked into his eyes. "I hope you will, how can I say it . . . ?"

"You don't have to say anything."

A car pulled into the driveway. "That will be County. We had to call her."

"Yes, of course," Eleanor said. "Whatever you need to do."

A tall African-American woman walked through the open door. "Miss White, Chief O'Reilly? I'm Cindy Williams." She flashed her badge. "I investigate felonies."

Eleanor nodded. "My husband killed himself," she murmured.

"I know. Just formalities. We have to do this." She was matter of fact. No smile. Direct. A cop. "If you don't mind if I look around?"

"Feel free."

The detective climbed the stairs and flashed her badge. Officer Devlin stood by the corpse. "A suicide," he said.

"We'll see," Williams replied. She pulled out a small, red notebook and began writing.

"He had his hand on the pistol and the pistol in his mouth," Devlin said

"He had? You change anything?"

"No. Not really."

"Not really?"

"Yeah, well. I took the gun out of his mouth or what was left of it. It was kind of disgusting. Trying to protect the wife, you know."

She jotted notes. He looked at the pad.

She asked, "where was she when he . . .?"

"Downstairs."

"And you took the gun out of his mouth?"

"Yeah. I took the gun out of his mouth. So what? Look, this couple lost their son to the towel-heads. Joey was a good guy, town leader and all that. Started drinking after the death. Cut and dry. What a shame."

"Yeah," she said with a flat voice. "Where'd the gun come from?"

"Don't know," Devlin said.

"Well, why don't we just find out? Maybe this chick decided she got tired of him." She scribbled in the red note pad as she spoke.

"Listen, detective. What did you say your name is?"

"Williams, Cindy Williams."

"Call me Sam. Everybody does. Cindy, I know these people, they're what we call pillars of the community."

"I get it," Williams said. "But still, the gun?"

"I'll go find out," he said flatly.

"Thank you. I'd appreciate that," an edge in her voice.

Devlin pulled O'Reilly aside. "She's making a case of this. Young, angry and suspicious. Not one of us."

O'Reilly picked his nose. "I'll handle it. You watch the front door."

"Eleanor," the Chief said. "A few questions. I'm sorry."

"That's quite all right. Whatever you want."

"The detective, she wants to know where the gun came from."

"That gun?" She stared into the carpet. "I was so much against it. But the guys in the neighborhood and even at the club said we had to get one, being so famous and people knowing we had money. Everyone has one, I guess."

"Yep, it's usually a good thing."

"I didn't like it, but Joey insisted. It's been around for, I don't know, seven, eight years. Remember those break-ins? First the drugstore and then some in the neighborhood. A couple of car jackings. That's when we first got it. We went to the shooting range to learn. I hardly paid attention."

"You've got a license."

"Yeah, sure, we both do."

"When was the last time you handled it?"

She shrugged. "I just don't know, Dan. I never used it. It sits in the bottom drawer beside the sweaters." She stared into the room. "I do handle it once in a while when I go through the clothes, spring cleaning and all that. And we do have to clean the thing. That's what they told us."

"But you haven't touched it recently?"

"No, Dan. Why would I?"

"That's all I need to know. You come down to the station tomorrow. We'll take a statement. Best not to go in that room until we have another look through. Just a formality. There will have to be a coroner's hearing. I'll try to make this easy, but you never know."

"I appreciate that."

The ambulance arrived. House lights burst on, doors opened, neighbors wrapped in robes strolled towards the house. Officer Devlin led them away. "It's Joey," he told them. "Best to leave her alone."

They retreated, a slow ebb, talking among themselves. *Another tragedy. How could this happen to them of all people? Are they damned? What will she do now?* One by one, house lights flickered off.

5.

Cindy Williams

———————————•———————————

"**I** WANT TO KEEP THIS OPEN, give it some time."

County prosecutor Kurt Rabe rocked back and forth in his chair, head in hand. "Cindy, let's not make a big deal out of this."

"You're the boss, it's your call."

"That's right."

"And you don't think white chicks kill their husbands?"

"Do we have a motive?"

"No, not yet. Maybe she's nuts. Yeah, I'm sorry they lost their kid, but maybe it sent her over the rails. Maybe she had enough."

"Anything in the house that might hint at a crime?"

She pulled out the red notebook. "That house? Clean as vanilla ice-cream. No dust, can you believe it? Just lots of books. I mean there were books on the table and bookshelves all over the place, sort of like a library."

"That's evidence, I suppose?"

"Just weird. You don't see that many books in a house. In a library, maybe, or some teacher's house. But these people sell cars, for God's sake."

"You still have that little red pad."

"Yeah, it helps. Just in case something comes up in the future."

"You're diligent, I give you that."

She ignored the compliment. "I spoke to her friends."

"And?"

"That's the weird part. She got around but wasn't, how do you say it, 'one of the girls.' Kept her distance."

"She works, Cindy. My guess is the women of Lincoln Park, they take care of the kids, the home, make sure everything's right for when hubby comes home."

"Yeah. Rich bitches."

"Cindy, you right for this investigation?"

"Yeah, I'm OK. It's just these people, they're well off. Big houses. Big cars."

"So what of it? We got our job to do."

She flipped through her notes. "Anyway, the ones that know her don't really know her, it seems. She's polite and all that. She takes part in the town and school events, but she doesn't play."

"What does that mean?"

"You know girls. They like to play. Go shopping, to the movies, for lunch, that's what these people do, but not her."

"She's got a job," he repeated.

"Nobody really knows her. They all say the same thing. She's quiet. Very polite. Too polite. They explain it as being the wife of the car man. An excuse, I guess. She never opens up, or so they say."

"No crime in that."

"They even talk about those books. They think it strange. But they all agree the two were fit for each other. So I ask them about Joey and they say he was a nice enough guy. I even asked about affairs. You know, something going on the side? But nothing." She shook her head. "It's just she's here but not here. Books and car stuff. That's all there is."

"So?"

"Too clean. Too perfect. There must be something going on somewhere. The banker says they were the best customers he's ever had. She pays promptly and if a guy misses his car payments, she calls and tries to work something out. Too antiseptic, America ain't like that."

"Let's close it up. We've been getting calls from all sorts of people, the Mayor, the Minister, and the Chamber. Hell, even the guy who runs the tavern called to say how much Joey was drinking. No motive. No evidence. Only the testimony of a cop who took the gun out of the guy's mouth. This case is closed."

6.

Lincoln Gardens

———————•———————

SOME WOULD HAVE BEEN DESTROYED, taken to bed, drink, pills, depression or long, sullen walks of self-contemplation without resolution. How did she handle it? The investigation, the yellow tape strewn about the house, and the constant questions. The invasions, the taking of the bed linens, the bottle, the gun, and the search of the house again. And again.

And there was Detective Williams, calling and asking questions. "Any sign he was going to do this? Why didn't you get him help with the drinking? Sorry to trouble you, but you having money problems? Your love life. Was that OK?"

Someone thought Eleanor should call her lawyer. "Why?" she asked. "There's nothing to be done."

And then the inquest in which the whole bloody affair was gone over. Williams argued to keep the case open. No one listened. Suicide was the verdict.

The funeral came and went. Eleanor sat in the same pew as she had for Bobby, the boy covered with American flags and guarded by uniformed soldiers. Now Joey's, a plain and austere ceremony, like an afterthought. She followed the service quietly, praying with the rest of the congregation, repeating the psalms, and listening to the sermon. Not a tear shed.

Whispers and gossip spread throughout Lincoln Gardens, in the pews, malls and cul-de-sacs: How does she do it? She is so brave. No tears, can you imagine that? Is she on drugs? Where is her pride? Doesn't she have feelings? Do you think she's alright? I'm concerned for her. I'd offer help but she doesn't seem to want it. I wonder why? Do you think she's flipped? Something must have broken in her. I think she must be in trouble. Did she call you? No, not me, I thought maybe she called you? Doesn't have close friends, does she? Relatives? No sign? What can we do? Imagine, first that Craig, then Bobby then Joey. I couldn't bear it.

7.

The Blonde

———————————•———————————

A FTER THE KNOCK, AFTER THEY BURIED THEIR HERO SON, they tried to recover and to renew life. They flew to Europe and wandered about. They strolled the Seine, sipped café on the boulevards, saw the Mona Lisa and the Rodins. They ate at five-star restaurants. The ache remained as well it might. In Rome, they prayed at Saint Peter's, and toured the ruins. They returned home to an empty house, haunted with memories and filled with relics.

The pain. Joey had never drunk much and Eleanor hardly a drop. Now, he stumbled home, needing a drink and then another, not hungry, saying little, and heading straight for bed. She hated arguments, the screams and shouts from her harried childhood. She avoided conflict. It solved nothing, she felt, only leading to more anger.

So she said nothing. And then one day, tired of waiting, she drove to the showroom. No, she was told, he had gone, they didn't know where but, you know, they figured he was going for a drink. It was his usual routine these days, leaving at lunch and not returning. He used to call in but recently, not even that.

The next day she returned and sat outside, waiting patiently until he drove off. She followed down the street and across the tracks to a modest, run-down house. A straggly lawn, two broken-down trucks in the driveway and a pretty, young blonde with disheveled hair, waiting in the doorway, a drink in her hand, a tilt to her hip, and a broad smile on her face.

She told no one, not even Joey, but returned to her books, covering betrayal with words from other worlds. As she always had.

8.

Detritus

———•————————————————•———

FRIENDS AND NEIGHBORS OFFERED HELP. She politely refused. Alone, after the wake for Joey, she disposed of the memories, the clothes, the pictures, and all traces of Joey. Then came the lawyers. Then the will. Then the dealership. Then the house sale.

In the late afternoons, in sleepless nights, and in early morning before the sun struck the drapes, alone, she dealt with life's chores. Cleaning up.

The home buyer thought the furniture tasteful, beige couches with slight hints of color in the faux artwork on the walls. He took the contents of the house. Still, twenty years of papers had to be dealt with, records crammed into old, grey rusting file cabinets, sitting row by row in the basement, their drawers stuck and off-track.

She knew those files. After all, it was she who handled the mundane paperwork, years of contracts and agreements with GM, parts suppliers, security vendors, and cleaning companies, tax forms, vehicle registration notices, zoning permits, business licenses, certified letters, and warranties. Lawsuits, lawyers, and accountants. Files and files, most worthless, a life of expired, archived trash.

Her friends never knew that side of her, the thankless backroom chores of a car-man's wife. How could they? She never mentioned them. Golf outings, school functions, and lawn parties were for chitchat. She was the car-man's wife, smiling at little jokes, conversing, serving and attending. Being a "good" member of the community.

Day after day, she kept on until the deed was done, sorting papers, some pushed to one side, recent taxes and car warranties. She threw ancient contracts into black bags. The things of life. Piles and piles. She skimmed them all, hour after hour, coffee after coffee, with coughing bouts from the dust and detritus. She, determined to end it all fast, like a responsible person which she always was. She did not ask for help. She did not tire. One line kept repeating over and over in her head: "Because I could not stop for death."

Did she gain purpose from destroying the past, hoisting those bags as black as death itself, up to the street? Is that what drove her?

She came to the last file cabinet, rusted, slightly warped and leaning against the wall. The drawer resisted but with a strong pull gave way. She scanned the ancient crumpled files, corporate agreements no longer of value and long-expired city permits. She spotted an unlabeled file, its tab stiff and clean unlike the others, but without writing. She pulled and it sprung open. Small notes fell to the floor, perfumed pink and flowery papers with female handwriting.

Eleanor squatted and gathered them together. Under a dim fluorescent light, she read the words: how they can't continue like this. How she missed Joey. She felt like a whore cheating on her man. She had to see him, can't see him, can't keep away. How can this keep going on and on, how late at night she cries and cries, no more, no more, no more.

She read and reread. She took them to the living room, lit a fire, and made a cup of tea. Slowly, one by one, she tore up the notes and threw the fragments into the flames. Sparks rose briefly. She sat back in her chair and sipped.

9.

Mysteries

———————•————————————•———————

CINDY WILLIAMS CAME BY THE HOUSE. "I just want to make sure you're OK."

"That's very nice of you, but I'm fine. I thought the investigation was finished."

'Oh yes. No need to worry there. All the Ts are crossed and the case filed away. You can proceed with your life."

She looked straight at the detective's deep ebony face and saw a line cut across her cheek. "You're very pretty."

"Thank you."

"Frankly, I've never met a black woman detective before."

"Yeah, well. I guess I'm sort of an alien in this town."

"No, I didn't mean anything. I apologize."

"'Tis nothing. That's just the way it is."

"How did you get that scar?" Eleanor asked.

"Excuse me?"

"That line on your face."

Williams eyes shot at her. "A small accident."

"Doesn't look small. Without it, you'd be perfect, just perfect."

Williams turned and walked about the room, looking about. "These books, you read them all? Quite a collection."

"Yes. I enjoy reading, solves lots of problems."

"Mysteries, do you read mysteries?"

"Mysteries?"

"You know crime thrillers."

"No, not much. I've always thought they were a bit crass, manipulative. I tend more to novels. You read much?"

"Just a little. I like Chester Hines and Walter Mosley. You know them?"

"Only by reputation."

"Agatha Christie? Patricia Highsmith?"

"No. I steer away from them.

"I guess you're too smart for crime novels?"

"I don't understand."

"You seem to be a smart lady and if you can figure out a crime novel, it would be rather boring."

"I don't know. Just not my taste."

"So you have read them?"

"I guess, a long time ago."

Williams wrote in her red notebook. "Any you'd recommend?"

"Miss Williams, I don't want to be rude, but what is the meaning of your visit?"

"No reason. Like I said, I wanted to make sure you're OK. You've gone through a really rough patch."

"I'm fine."

"That's an interesting lamp," Williams said, staring at the twisting copper tubes. "I've never seen anything like it. An heirloom?"

"No, my Dad made it for me years ago. 'Cause I loved reading so much, he wanted to give me as much light as possible."

The detective walked about, fingering the books. She stared into space. "You know, I've known many crafty people, smart guys who knew all the angles, who could cover up anything. They got away with hustles, drug deals and murders. I investigated and investigated and came up short. So many times."

"Must be frustrating," Eleanor said.

"Yeah, well, I knew they did it and they knew I knew and they knew there was nothing I could do about it. But I keep everything here in my little red books, just in case, ya' know? But always, always, I keep finding one thing. You know what that is?"

"Miss Williams, I have no idea what you're talking about," Eleanor said angrily. "You solved the cases, did you?"

She turned towards her. "Nope. Never solved the cases. But I do go back and visit these guilty low-lifes, and there they are, sauntering through life. And they see me coming and they put on a good face, smiling and all that, but I see what's become of 'em. There's always a problem, a deep and infected wound that just don't go away. God's punishment, I call it.

"And if it ain't God, it's instinct or nature or something more animal than human. You probably know 'cause you're so smart. Some of these guys can't help themselves. They keep doin' crime until they get caught. Others don't but they still got memories of their evil acts to their brothers and sisters. Black or white, man or woman. They become alcoholics or bums or just fat, ol' solitary creatures who just keep livin', looking over their shoulder, looking for that black woman with the line down her face, me reminding 'em of that act of the devil that ripped any humanity they might 've had from their souls.

"Well, I wouldn't know," Eleanor said.

"No, you wouldn't, would you? As you say, things go bad, you go to your books. I apologize if I offend. You must be suffering terribly."

She nodded.

"I mean, first, one son wanders off, what was his name?"

"His name was Craig."

"Was? Is he dead?"

"Dead? No, I don't think he's dead."

"But you said . . ."

"I know what I said. Miss Williams, please."

"Anyway, you've had it terribly rough, first Craig leaves, then your other son dies, and then your husband. I don't know if I could stand it."

Eleanor stood and crossed the room, looking out into the quiet driveway. "There used to be so many there."

"Ma'am?"

"Cycles. Soccer balls. Playthings. The driveway was such a mess. It was like a world out there, children becoming adults. I don't know how many tears were shed from childish falls and then broken hearts."

"I feel for you."

Eleanor turned. "About what you said. I think I understand. Maybe I killed them."

Cindy Williams paused and stared at her. "Maybe?"

"Yes, now that I think of it. I'm sure I did."

"Your thoughts have cleared?"

"Yes," Eleanor whispered again, "I killed them."

"Why don't you tell me how?" She opened the pad.

"It's good talking to a woman. I think you'd understand."

"I do. Believe me."

"He was so withdrawn. Didn't seem to have any emotions. We are not demonstrative people, you know. And, then, somehow, I guess I didn't show enough love. I just wasn't there for him, for them. I was, well, you know."

"No, I don't."

"I guess too cold."

"So you killed them."

"Yes. One left me and the other just left and got himself killed."

Williams turned back. "Who are we talking about here? Craig, your husband? I don't understand."

"No," Eleanor turned angrily. My husband's name was Joey. Craig was my son."

"Oh my, I am sorry, I thought . . ."

"I know what you thought. So, now, is there anything you need from me?"

"Well," the detective stammered. All right then, I'll be on my way."

"I'll be seeing you around."

10.

Books

"CINDY, YOU WENT BACK?"

"I just thought I'd do a little more checking. I mean, I asked her friends and all that and nobody had heard from her. I found that strange."

"But not your problem, is it?"

"I don't know, Chief. My family comes undone. My husband kills himself. I've buried him and all that and what do I do? I sit alone in this big house. Don't call on friends. Don't answer the phone. Don't go to Church. Sounds mighty strange."

"Cindy, you're fishing in a dry pond. You're young and you think you can figure these things out. But this ain't TV, is it? It's real life. Maybe the woman has gone nuts and closed down, turned away from life."

"I know real life, Chief, you don't have to sass…"

"Yeah, I know, I'm sorry, but you're still young."

She looked at him, shaking her head. "She's smart, really smart. I start talking about people getting away with murder and the guilt it causes and she changes the subject and traps me into an embarrassing error."

"You give her too much credit."

"Do I? She's smart. Really smart. Look at all the books she reads."

"Books prove nothing."

"She killed her husband."

The DA shook his head. "Makes no difference no more, does it?"

"Does. If she's gotten away with murder."

"Which she hasn't. That's what the court says."

"Well, I'm not sure." She waved her red notebook at him.

"You'd better be. Move on or I'm going to have to, you know… "

"Yeah, OK. I'll drop it. But I don't like it. Smart, white woman, rich house, big lawn, all this money and a dead husband, just doesn't sound right. If it were Motown, she'd be in chains."

"But it isn't Motown, is it? Stay cool, move on."

11.

Harry Tibbett

W HERE WAS THE SORROW? The mourning? The tears, grief, depression and all those steps to recovery that must follow? You might have asked where was the happiness, laughter, thrills, regrets, screams and cries of the prior life? There was always a flatness in Eleanor, a pall like a muffled trumpet playing a low-register B flat.

The child Eleanor Tibbett ran the cash register. Sitting erect on an old wooden stool, awaiting the next customer, a book on her lap, the seven-year-old took money from burly Midwestern workers who winked, joked and patted her on the head. She'd smile and call them mister. Not disdainful, mind you. They were customers, as her father always said, good people who supported their family, spending the money earned in hard labor at the mill. Regardless of who they are, he said, they deserve respect. "You certainly are a pretty, little thing," they would say, over and over. "Aren't you cute, the way you handle money. You sure you've got that change right? Let's count it together. Yeah, I guess you're right."

Harry Tibbett, Eleanor's father, owned the town hardware store, Tibbett's, like his father before him. "Tibbett's is the town. The town is Tibbett's," that's what everyone said. He loved that store, the daily chitchat, the center of everything.

"A community," his father would say. "We are all in this together, through thick and thin. If they don't have money, just write it down, they'll make it good. They're all good people. You just ignore the chitchat, OK? Not right for little girls."

The dark, narrow store with creaking wood floors stocked a jumble of the town's needs, nuts and bolts, patches to hem torn pants, glues, solders and flux. Sam says he wants a drill. "What happened to the old drill, Sam? Run into a metal stud? We'll fix you up." In the good times, Harry walked the floor, checking the inventory, arranging, metric screws to the left, American to the right. Nails down the aisle. "Keep them close but separate. All in their place." He lined up paint cans by size and color so that Sam and all the other Sams would find what they needed right away. Swedish matches and Chilean fertilizer. Cast iron skillets for the ladies and marbles for the kiddies. The newest stuff, power painters, ratchets, electric sanders, all out in front, not just to sell but to provide the stuff that helped men remodel, fix, or just mess about in the basement. His tools were as good as Sears, solid steel, lifetime guaranteed. W-D 40? Eveready batteries? Fire extinguishers?

After school, Eleanor ran to the store and jumped on the stool. While other girls played with dolls or soccer balls and while her baby sister Joan chortled away at home, she watched her Dad sweep the floor, straighten the shelves, laugh with the customers, negotiate salesmen and manage the help. They were partners, Eleanor and Harry, Eleanor learning the business, listening to her Dad's advice, not saying much, just taking it in, like a smart girl sitting in the front of the class.

"When the sales guys come in hawking their stuff, you let them sit awhile. You want their stuff but you don't show it. Offer 'em a cup of coffee. A magazine. You treat 'em with respect 'cause they're workin' to make a living just like you and this is their sad ol' territory and they're struggling going from town to town, but that don't mean nothing where business is concerned. Business is business. You make the best deal you can and then you pass that deal onto your customers. 'Cause if you don't. And the store down the road makes a better deal, you'll lose your customers in a flash. They'll be saying 'how come I can get that hammer for a dollar less in the next town?'"

The men sat in the backroom, playing dominos, smoking, having a beer with her Dad, and telling dirty jokes, talking about girls, the new Bonneville, the high school team, the boss, the "I'm gonna quit that place and get me a real job." She took it all in, listening to the loud cracks of the dominoes striking the table and recording it all with a plain, poker face.

At day's end, Eleanor counted the day's take, filled out the deposit slip, and stuffed it in the canvas bag. Hand in hand, father and daughter walked towards home. They paused as she shoved the bag through the bank slot and then moved on, he talking about how the day went, how'd they need to stock up on this or that or how they don't make flashlights like they used to, and after dinner, she to her homework late into the evening under the twisting copper lamp, with three bright 60 watt bulbs, that her father had jerried together. Night after night. Paradise.

She was eleven when the mill closed, the mill that supported the valley for almost a century, the mill that produced the steel for war efforts, farmers' tractors, truckers' trucks, and America's cars. Then, the bypass was built, the "miracle mile" outside of town, with McDonalds and Sears, Walmart and Pizza Hut, KFC, and Home Depot. The large box stores provided credit to its customers, cheaper goods, and the convenience of shopping next to the supermarket and the movie theater.

Tibbett's Hardware declined. The Sams of the world stopped coming, unemployed and struggling. A grey layer of dust fell over the shelves. "Harry, you got any more two inch galvanized?" "I'll order them." Not a good answer. He stocked cheap knick-knacks at the cash register, plastic toys and candy and folksy old-fashioned soaps, small magnets and flimsy screw drivers meant for do-it-yourselfers who never did anything themselves. To no avail.

Sales dwindled and the bell above the door rang less. Harriet's Fine Clothes across the street shut down. The diner closed early, after lunch, and then permanently. Ol' Tibbetts, the friendly hardware store, continued on, an island amid For Rent signs on a Main Street no longer main, a place where old-timers stopped by to shoot the breeze and maybe pick up a box of detergent or a mop or a battery.

Harry stood around, waiting for the guys to come by for dominoes and beer, but after a while, they didn't have the time. Or the money. Or the joy. And

Harry disappeared into the storeroom for a nip. First a little nip at lunch. And then through the day.

Eleanor rummaged about. In the store room, back behind rusting varnish cans, she discovered crumbling ledger books, accounts of an earlier time, of her granddad's shop. She entered into the past, reading of other times, India ink on lined pages, a pound of wheat for a hammer, two day's labor for a wooden plank, $4 credit to Farmer Norton for cattle feed, paid off in weekly twenty-five cent installments, paid in full in sixteen weeks, no interest, $8 credit to Rick Bishop for seed, payment halted after three weeks, a big X next to his name.

How does a young girl react to a failed father, her idol and source of strength? How does a man react to his own failure, he who inherited the family business, a mainstay of the town, who trained his daughter to take over the shop, only to fail, not real failure for this is an American story where rapid change destroys the most stalwart, but failure in his own eyes?

"Eleanor, sweet Eleanor," he called from the storeroom, not feeling "up to it," to the now pubescent girl at the front counter, the girl who knew the price of every widget, tool, and implement, who knew whom to trust for credit and who not and why not, and who ran the dying business alone, closing at night, taking the meager returns to the bank and leading her sodden father home to more drink, fights, slammed doors, desperate silences, and tearful apologies.

Screams through the night, shaking walls, and slamming doors crashed into the soul of the young girl. The cries of her fearful mother, hiding in the bathroom with baby Joan. The swing on the fist that missed the mother and struck Eleanor slightly but enough to shatter her soul. The knock on the door from the neighbors. The flashing police lights. The uniformed officers walking through the house, "just checking everything out." And then at dawn, the sodden, scruffy figure of a fallen man, collapsed on the living room sofa. The maternal hugs. The "don't worry, everything is going to be all right. You just get ready and go off to school."

How does a young girl respond, one whose adoration for her fallen father knew no bounds? She plunged into books, stayed late at school, squirreled away in the town library, and straggled on the way home. She searched for silence and isolation building a rigid shield to repel all attacks.

How does a girl react? With a heart of stone and a fear of risk, an impenetrable, reptilian soul.

If this tale ended with the suicide of Eleanor's husband, it would suggest a singular lack of luck. But Eleanor was smart, attractive and, until just a year or two earlier, a success in life, married to the man who ran the town's car dealership, and with a good son. True, she was now alone, but also a creature of scars and turpitude, a woman with a life of experience as sad as any. A life of survival.

But how much can one person take before they break? Before something goes off? Who pulled the trigger? Joey? Eleanor? Or the fates that threw down so much bad luck?

For this is an American story, one told by thousands of Americans with failed businesses, war casualties, illnesses, divorces, addictions and crack-ups. And if there is something that we have learned time and time again, for Americans with the fortitude and luck to revive, repair and bounce and begin again, there are second acts in American lives. And maybe even third or fourth.

Part Two

12.

Craig

———•———————————•———

A HOT DUSTY TOWN IN NORTH TEXAS, four by four, that's blocks not miles, off the interstate, the "time has passed by" sort of place. Sneeze and you'd miss it. A one-pump gas station, a few shops and a diner. A boarded-up post office.

A lone waitress cleaned the counter, removing utensils and putting down fresh napkins. She hummed as she worked, checking empty tables, and watching the clock. The door crashed open. He stumbled in and fell onto a stool. He wore a crumpled and soiled shirt and torn blue jeans. Just like every other guy around these parts, she thought, except for the large red welt on his cheek, a slice of raw meat.

She stared at the mess. "You OK?" she said.

"Yeah, I'm OK."

"I'm sorry honey, but we're closed. Jerry's gone and I was just about to leave."

"No coffee?" he mumbled.

"Yeah, maybe I can stir up some dregs. You sit here while I finish up. But you gotta' be fast. I'm tired and I gotta' get up early tomorrow."

He nodded, his face down, touching the counter.

"Where'd you get that shiner?"

"At the bar down the street," he whispered. "You know it?"

She laughed. "Honey, in this town, there's one bar, one diner, and not much else. What you doing here anyway?"

He looked up. "What d'ya mean?"

"I mean what you doing in this town?"

"Don't know. Just traveling through. On the bus, ya' know. I liked the looks of the place, so I got off."

"You really got no taste or you stupid. Nobody comes here, baby. Everybody leaves."

"Guess I made a mistake."

"Looks like it wasn't the only mistake you made. That looks bad."

"I've had worse."

She sized him up, slim hips, piercing eyes, pretty good looking but young, very young. "You don't look old enough for knowing worse."

"Yeah, well."

"So you came in here 'cause there ain't no place to stay."

"Yeah. I saw the light and thought maybe you'd be one of those all-night places."

"Well we're not."

"Yeah, I can see that. So maybe I can crash, sleep on the floor or something?"

She laughed. "Sure. You just make yourself right at home. Pull some chairs together, make a bed. Maybe fry yourself up a steak and potatoes. And tomorrow morning, Jerry comes in and I lose the only damned job in a hundred miles."

"Yeah, I get it. Guess I'll find myself an alley."

"So how'd you get the shiner?'

"I chatted up this chick, quite a good looker, ya know. Nice smile, short skirt, really nice legs. Ya' know what I mean? And she came up to me and I thought I had a sure thing, a place to stay, maybe some fun. And we were having a good time, laughing and drinking and she touched my arm, and I touched her face and then this guy comes up and we have words and I end up on the floor."

"His girl, huh?"

"Nah. His wife."

"I guess you are stupid. You go after strange women you don't know nothin' about, and you get yourself a problem. But I don't blame her. You look good enough to eat. We're a lonely bunch here, especially the women. The only real people we get to talk to are on the telly. And they don't talk back. But, I gotta tell you, you watch who you touch."

"Yeah, well, we all have problems." He rose to leave, waving his hand.

"Hey, wait a sec. Look, I've got a couch."

"Yeah?"

"Yeah, why not? But no funny stuff. I'll take care of that shiner. Maybe we'll have a drink or two. But no funny stuff."

"Yeah, I know."

"I know you know, baby."

"Don't call me, baby!"

"Then what should I call you."

"Just Craig. 'Cause that's my name."

13.

Joan

———————

FOR SORROW, THERE IS NO REMEDY AS SHE WELL KNEW. So when Joan urged her to come to the city, *You need to get out of there. You need to start again. Forty is young. Time to move on. Start a new life.* Eleanor agreed. No prodding needed, no deep roots in the suburban town. She had been there but not there, present like a stray cat, friendly and receptive but never joining up.

Seven years her junior, a sibling born out of desperation in a crumbling home, Joan was adored by everyone, protected and shielded amidst shouts and recriminations, the child too young to understand or respond. They were never close, Eleanor and Joan. While Joan was still a toddler, Eleanor worked the store and endured the pain of alcohol and disappointments, financial and paternal, the pain that shaped the soul.

Joan was a nurse. Not just any nurse but a nurse of the rich and famous, helping "society" doctors handle the most "delicate" cases, alcoholism, ODs, fat issues, and unmentionables. The stuff of supermarket tabloids. Joan was loved as nurses frequently are, jovial and caring, not threatening to the insecure set for she was round and chunky and certainly not attractive. So suitable to care for hubby's or wifey's "illness." Like her elder sibling, she knew how to remove the bottle and the pills and humor the addict.

Good ol' Joan, everyone called her, funny, always helping, the perfect nurse. Always a good guy. A little loud perhaps but with strong arms from lifting, turning and pulling ailing bodies. Joan loved a good joke, the type of woman who could not stand silence, talkative about this and that, weather, sports, or the TV heart throb. Good ol' happy Joan, so unlike Eleanor.

Eleanor moved into Joan's small apartment, a tasteful rental a few blocks from the "institute" where the wealthy dried out. A small place meant for a single woman with a living room, a sole bedroom, a tiny kitchen and a bath. Simple and modest with sunlight. Eleanor on the couch, Joan in her bedroom, they became sisters as they never had been before. The reading lamp, the convoluted copper contraction made by their father was placed on a table, the only remnant of Eleanor's former life. Beside it she read deep into the night.

14.

Pastor Wainwright

———————————————————

WHILE JOAN WORKED, ELEANOR EXPLORED AND SEARCHED. Was she trying to make sense of her life, the one now gone and the new existence in the city? Or was she in a daze? Was she cracking up, as her old neighbors thought? Now, a pattern emerged. She rose early and drifted, a few blocks here and there, on sidewalks jammed with prams and peddlers, students and hotdog stands, beggars and aged, drunkards and cops. She stared at passing faces and was taken aback when the faces returned the look. She nodded or mumbled a brief greeting.

When she tired, she stopped for breakfast. The pattern took hold: each morning a new direction, a new neighborhood, and a new breakfast, one day, eggs and salsa and tortilla, the next, a feta omelet, or croissants and café con leche or bacon and eggs, or oatmeal, or grits, or a bagel, or a bagel with cream cheese and lox. or just a quick coffee.

Breakfast became the most important meal of the day. Just as they used to say.

"Why don't you come to Church with me," Joan asked

"I'm not religious," Eleanor said. "I don't see the point," Eleanor resisted.

"You need to make friends. It's lonely in the city."

"Do I really need friends?"

"Don't be silly. Come with me. What can it hurt?"

Pastor James Wainwright welcomed the sisters. Tall and austere, some might call him severe, he offered tea and cookies and led them to his study. Joan spoke of Eleanor's travails as if she wasn't there. Eleanor remained quiet, wondering at her sister's frankness.

The Pastor spoke as if giving a sermon: *This town is filled with transients, migrants from a hundred countries, from the boroughs, from Long Island, even from New Jersey. They're all looking for a better life, excitement, or a new beginning. They work for a while, some find basic jobs, others marry, and still others move on. The city is where you come to forget, get lost, and then to start anew. That's the pattern. You come and you do your thing. You are anonymous. Evils left behind. New beginnings.*

We've been around for 150 years, this church, and it has been a foundation for this city. Our parishioners have been members for many generations. Once in a while, migrants come and join, like Joan here, and they become a part of the strength of this city. I know I'm sounding like a pastor, but I hope you will consider coming by. If you're anything like Joan, I think we all will benefit."

Eleanor nodded, smiled and thanked the Pastor. "I appreciate your kindness," she said. "I'm still not sure if I'm going to stay. In fact, I'm not sure of anything."

"Of course," he responded. "An open offer."

The sisters played the city, the parks, museums, and river walks. Over time, Eleanor was restored, but Joan kept pushing. "You gotta keep busy." Against Eleanor's protests, she made small dinners with single men, divorcees, widowers, or bachelors. "The woods are filled with them," Joan said. "They'll flatter and show you the city. They're rich. They think they rule the world. They're so self-confident. Enjoy it."

The dinners always went the same. Joan, talking and laughing, the men, happy to be invited, loving the chatter, with two single women. But if their talk was with Joan, their thoughts were of Eleanor, blonde and petite, neatly dressed, quiet, sad and seductive in her way, in contrast to Joan. *Do you believe they're sisters? Incredible.*

Exhaustion. Too many walks, too many dinners. Joan kept pushing (*come on! Let's get going, Snap out of it.*) and, after a while, Eleanor rankled. "I think

I want to be alone," she said quietly.

"Nonsense. You gotta jump in, get going, you can't hide away, Sis. Come on. I know a great bar with nice looking guys."

And then, as if the fates had not done enough, they delivered one more blow.

15.

Joan

———•————————————————•———

"COME, LET'S HAVE LUNCH," Joan urged her.

"No, not today, I'm not up to it. I think I'd rather be alone."

"Bumblescupin, I'm coming to get you."

"No, really. Please don't."

"Yes, I insist, I'm coming."

They strolled the crowded streets, Joan chatting away. Eleanor remained silent. "Cat got your tongue? Come on, Sis. Tell me. What are we gonna' do tomorrow?"

It happened so fast. Nobody really saw it, a speeding delivery truck, screeching brakes, a screaming crowd. "You were going too fast," witnesses yelled at the driver who stared in shock, saying nothing, just sitting and sobbing.

Her body lay crumbled by the curb, Eleanor standing over her sister, shaking her head, and moaning. The ambulance came. Joan died en route.

16.

Craig

————————•————————

S HE RAN HER FINGERS DOWN THE BOY'S CHEST. "You really are a bad boy."

"I'll leave any time. You just say the word."

"No, that's not what I mean," the waitress said. "Why do you go stealing like that? I mean, I give you whatever you want, I mean, within reason."

"Yeah, well, I saw that beer and I was thirsty and I wasn't gonna go to back to the diner and say "Betty, peeleasse, give me some bucks for my thirst. I mean I've got pride."

"Everybody knows you now. They all talkin' about you. They don't think I hear but I hear. Years of practice, ya' know?"

"So you're embarrassed. So maybe I'll move on. Take the next bus."

"No, baby," she pleaded. "I don't mean that."

"I don't like you calling me that."

"What?"

"Baby. My name's Craig. Don't you get it?"

She laughed. "I'm not that much older than you. Just a little more 'perience."

"Yeah, I can see that."

"What's that mean?"

"Nuthin. You just, well, you just showing me things I never felt before."

"So I'm your teacher?"

"Maybe it's time to move on."

"No, baby, don't say that."

"I told you I don't like you callin' me that."

"OK, Baby." She laughed. "Oh, I'm sorry, truly sorry, my honey-child."

"You asking for it, I'm telling you."

"Then give it to me."

17.

Eleanor Tibbett

⸻

Joan's will was settled. A single woman with few large expenses had amassed a sizeable estate, all left to her sister. And then there was the condo. The lawyer prepared the contract transferring the apartment to Eleanor. She read it closely as she always did. She called the lawyer and asked for a change. The name on the lease, "Eleanor White," was wrong. No, the name on the deed should read Eleanor Tibbett, her maiden name. Eleanor White was gone, buried with the unhappy past.

18.

Alić

PASTOR WAINWRIGHT TELEPHONED. No answer. He left a message. Two days later, he tried again. Then, the voicemail machine was filled. He went to the apartment. A large burly doorman greeted him.

"I've come to inquire about Eleanor Tibbett, I am her Pastor."

"Yes," the doorman said with a thick accent.

"She is not answering her phone, and I am concerned."

"Yes?" the doorman repeated.

The Pastor shook his head. "I don't think you understand, I wonder if you could ring her apartment."

"I am sorry. She left instructions not to be disturbed."

"I am her Pastor."

"I understand what you are saying. She does not wish visitors."

"OK, may I leave her a note?"

"Of course."

"And would you make sure she gets it?"

"There will be no problem." His accent was strong, Eastern-European, but his speech, clear. A strong smell about him which the Pastor ascribed to hard work.

Wainwright studied the large man. A scar ran from his left ear down his neck, a deep slice, a face shouting trouble. "What is your name, sir?"

"My name is Alić Ohran, but you may call me Alex. Everybody does."

Wainwright jotted a note and handed it to him. "Thank you Alex. It is important I hear from her. We are all concerned."

"You have no worry. She will get it."

19.

Alex

"M"RS. TIBBETT," SAID THE DOORMAN. "You had a visitor. He was quite insistent."

"Who was that, Alex?"

"A Pastor. He left a note."

"Yes, I know him"

"Mrs. Tibbett, I don't wish to be forward but with Miss Joan gone, you seem to be by yourself. Alone."

"Perhaps, I am."

"If you think anyone is trying to harm you or you don't want them around, you just tell Alex."

She smiled. "Oh, that's so nice. But he is not a bad man. He means well, the Pastor."

"I've been watching you, leaving early the way you do, wandering off all alone. Any trouble, you call me."

"Don't worry, I'm a big girl."

"Even big girls get hurt. Anybody can get hurt in this town. Any time. I know," his face turned from care to a stiff anger. Then she saw the deep scar, bifurcating his face. As he frowned, the scar expanded into hate.

"Thank you, Alex. I consider you my friend."

"And I consider you my friend."

20.

Breakfast

———————•———————

HER SLEEP GREW LESS AND HER WALKS LONGER, extending into poorer
and more alien neighborhoods, through a mix of skin colors and a
babel of languages. She stared and absorbed, exploring alleys and tunnels paved
with empty bottles, discarded cartons and broken glass, parks overgrown with
weeds, streets jammed with carts and prams and wheelchairs and scooters. On
and on, absorbing her new world, buses swerving in and out avoiding people
crossing in mid-block, taxis fighting for riders, blaring horns and barking dogs.

Every morning into a different eatery offering breakfast. Putrid smells of
greased grills, burnt fat and fried flour grabbed her senses, luring her into diners
and cafes. She surprised luncheonettes in midafternoon insisting on breakfast
in her quiet but emphatic way. The server, Korean, Indian, Swahili, Haitian
or Azherbani, shook his head, but still she insisted, her power unmistakable.
"Senora, it is 3, we don't serve breakfast at 3" "Try," she responded. "I'm sure
you'll do a good job."

In a trance or zealous or with an obsession to overcome grief, she devoured
pale white Ethiopian fava bean mush, blackened Haitian fish over grits, eggs
mashed with garlic and onions and cilantro, burnt pork and curry, Italian

uova Modenese, poached eggs with hash spinach and tomato, African fufu, Taiwanese Congee, Chinese onion pancakes, deep fried Andalusian churros, stinking Japanese nattochick peas, rotten Korean kimchi cabbage, and mild Vietnamese pho.

She was not a wanderer like those shaggy folk who stroll here and there in search of what? Nutrition? Survival? Meaning? No, dressed primly and walking stoutly, she scrounged for a new life, one filled with the flavors and spices so foreign to her past. She avoided Broadway tourist ghettos, Madison Avenue shops, Soho galleries, and Village hip bars. Instead, she found life in the joints, for that is what they were, that fed the city's seed stock, busboys and cleaning women, delivery kids and bank clerks, secretaries and dental hygienists, truckers and builders, and all those searching for "the dream." She might have been in San Juan or Bangkok, Nairobi or Kiev. She was in Babel.

She was hassled for money and approached by men. But the worst for her were long and threatening stares, eyes questioning what does this white woman want, what was she doing exploring the rainbow scrub beyond her own little ghetto? Why did they stare? Why did they threaten? She was just a woman not meaning any harm, but still they attacked with their eyes, with slight glances and sexual leers.

As she ate in tiny food sanctuaries, they turned, these strange faces, to watch her take a tiny nibble of the alien dishes and then consume the whole meal, for she was brought up to be polite, to not offend, and to clean her plate.

How did she view them, with their unintelligible jabber, men making deals, women laughing, mothers yelling at children with foreign words? What did she think of their lives, troubles, joys and sorrows? At home, on our own block, we know our neighbors. We stop to chat or nod with a brief hello. We ask about him or her, admire the children and pet the dog. We imagine our neighbors' lives, inaccurately to be sure but with context. Here, in the urban forest, no one divines the lives of others. Artists and writers may try, but they create fantasy.

Did she wonder? Was she curious? But, then again, was she ever? Were these aliens just another "book" to be read, new chapters and characters spurring visions that the written word creates? Or, did these foreign lands protect her? No need for pedestrian conversation, no commitment, and no false pretense.

And was this one more strategy, one more defense to keep out the world, isolating her, one more chapter in an empty vapid existence, a life limited to bookish fantasies rather than life experiences that fertilize our souls?

21.

Irish

———————————•———————————

I T WAS LATE AND SHE STILL HAD NOT EATEN. A new section of town at the very top of the city, with strange streets, shops, and faces. Was she going mad at long last? She came upon an Irish pub. Signs touted beer and bangers. Old men on stools sipped beer. The red-headed barmaid laughed boisterously at her demand for breakfast. No, she said, this was the time for potato skins and suds. Shepherds' pie? Maybe a burger? No, Eleanor insisted strongly. "I've come for breakfast. I'm sure you can handle that."

The waitress shrugged and called the cook. Minutes later, a giant emerged, his balloon stomach covered by a grease-soiled apron, his face marred by whiskey. The cook looked at her, so well dressed, and erupted in a huge guffaw. He grabbed her shoulders mightily, pushed her to the kitchen and plunked her on a chair. "You want breakfast, well then you've got ta' tell me why?" And she told him. She was new to the city and the only thing she could think of to do in the city was breakfast. He laughed again. He poured her a jigger of Tyrconnell, swigged one himself, put on a Chieftains cassette and threw a bunch of rashers onto the skillet followed by bacon, bangers and sausages. Eggs, tomatoes and beans followed.

"You ever been to Ireland?" he asked.

"No"

"You must go. You like breakfast? You find there's no place like Ireland for breakfast."

"I don't know," she responded. "Have you ever had blueberry pancakes or waffles? That's how we do it back home."

"Blueberry pancakes. That's not breakfast. That's fuggin' Haagan Daz."

"It's an American breakfast."

"Well then sweetee, I'll give you everything a real Irishman has." He was smitten. He tossed the eggs and moved the bacon and sausages around the grill. He threw a gob of potatoes next to them.

She devoured the feast.

"I understand why you like breakfast," he said.

"Yes?"

"The fuggin' English. They eat breakfast too, but when they eat it, it's gotta be proper. The Irish, we're more basic. I mean we eat the same food, the Limeys and us, but we do it better with lust."

"Really?" she said. "But if you eat the same food, why do you call them like that?"

"Like what?"

"You know."

"You mean, 'fuggin' English." He poured another whiskey for himself.

"Yes."

"'Cause of our history. They owe us. Big time."

"I wonder if I could have another cup of coffee," Eleanor said.

"More whiskey?"

"Just coffee"

"More breakfast?"

"Just coffee."

"OK," he downed another jigger. "For hundreds of years, dem' Brits stole our land and wealth. Drove us into the ground, they did. Then, in '45, the blight wiped out the potatoes. We starved." His voice began to tremble and raise. "My family lost half, children and adults alike, they died from lack of food. Imagine that! Children, dying of food. And what did the English do?

Nothing. Nothing at all. So we left and came here. We love our homeland but we had to survive. Don't you understand? That was the fuggin' choice, die or move. Isn't that right?"

"You tell her Irish," voices from the barroom stools. "That's right, you've got it right."

"Quiet down," the waitress yelled.

He ignored her. "So we come over and build your railroads, dying along the way, we fought your fuggin' civil war, we didn't want to but we did it none the less. Jesus, Mary and Joseph, we became your soldiers, police, your firemen, your politicians. Right?"

"That's right, Irish," the old men echoed.

"We elect an Irish President and what do they do? They kill him, the bastards. Then his brother. Right?

"That's right, Irish."

And now," he shouted, his large body looming over Eleanor, "we give you breakfast at sundown. And that, in a nutshell, is our fuggin' history."

"Enough," the waitress pushed forward. She grabbed the bottle. "You've had enough with this poor lady and all your stories.

"Well it's true," he yelled. "We ain't from the old sod no more. Our country is this city. No land. No air. Our ancestors lie rotting in the ground. And we wouldn't be here except for them."

"You go," the waitress said to Eleanor.

"How much I owe you?"

"Never you mind. It's on the house. You've paid already."

22.

Accidents

———————————

"So I DON'T WANT TO MAKE A BIG DEAL OF THIS, OK?" Sam Devlin sat back and stared at the black detective.

"What?"

"We got a call from New York, the police."

"Yeah, we must have made the big-time."

"It was about your friend Eleanor."

"Really," Cindy Williams eyes lit up. "Who did she kill in the Apple?"

"I told you. Not a big deal, OK?"

"Sure, Chief, lay it on."

"Seems there was an accident. She and her sister were walking down the street."

"And the sister died," Williams said.

"Yeah."

"Yeah?" She laughed and stumbled into her chair, catching her breath. "I don't believe it."

"It was an accident."

"Sure."

"A truck going too fast. She stepped off the curb."

"She stepped off the curb, my ass. This woman is killing faster than Charlie Manson."

"They called it an accident."

"Yeah, I know. Until the next one. Did you tell them about what went on here?"

"Weren't interested. A traffic accident, they said. The call was routine, covering all bases."

"White killers," Williams muttered.

"Or bad luck. Some people just have it."

"Yeah, like skin color."

"Don't go there."

"Sorry Chief. But I know killers. I smell them. And she's one. Let's add 'em up. Her hubby, that kid who they said ran away, without a trace. Yeah, he's dead and buried. Guaranteed. And now the sister. Any more family left we should call on?"

"Eleanor's gone, Cindy. Gone. She's not our problem anymore. As for me, there's a parade next week that needs policing, I got to figure out manpower. You free?"

23.

Cindy Williams

———————●————————————●———————

EACH DAY, SKINNY CINDY WILLIAMS followed the same route from school as Auntie ordered: Dexter to Clairmount to Rosa Parks Boulevard to the church, walking past frame houses, crumbling porches rusting junk cars, and the old Motown place, once the center of African-American music before Gordy moved out to LA, and now a run-down relic.

She was tall for twelve, filling out, and guys were noticing, yelling cat calls, hitting on her, touching her shoulder. "You just ignore them and move on" Auntie May said. "They are evil. Up to no good, doin' the work of the devil and all that. You just stay away and mind your own business." Which she did until one day, an old red Chevy convertible drove past, two guys in front, staring at her. The car headed down the street made a quick U-turn and returned. She started running, looking for shelter, in vain.

Later, after it was over, after the emergency room, the rude examinations, the interviews and the crying, the "I told you not to talk to those devils," she went to church to pray. "I can't watch over you all the time. I've gotta work," Auntie May said. "I just don't know what to do."

Two years later, Cindy Williams, now tall, erect and beautiful, left high school and headed to work at the supermarket. The butcher was old, at least 30, tall and beefy, strong arms bulged out from his tee shirt. "How ya' doing, honey?" he asked, blocking her way.

"You just leave me alone," she said flatly.

"I've been watching you, ya' know? The way you walk and swing that thing. I don't mean no harm."

"Then you'll just better leave me alone."

"Oh, come on, how 'bout a little kiss, just one kiss. It won't hurt. Maybe I'll buy you an ice cream or something."

He pulled her to him, forcing his tongue into her mouth. She grew taut, fighting in vain and then fell limp, allowing his lips to crush hers. He fondled her breasts. "I thought so," he mumbled. "You really hot. We go to my place?"

He grabbed her arm and pulled. She turned away. He grabbed her hair.

The mace struck his eyes full force. He screamed. Then he felt a thin oily line run down his cheek. He heard the strike of the match. And that was all he remembered.

"I told you not to touch me."

"You really are something," her Aunt said at the station house. "I don't know what I'm gonna do with you."

"I tell you what you should do," the Sergeant said. "Get this child out of town. This guy comes back, he's gonna kill her."

"Just let him try," Cindy Williams said. "I know what to do to those devils. My Auntie told me. Just let him try."

"Listen, young lady, you think you can take on everyone who does bad? That's what we're here for."

Cindy looked at the cop, shaking her head and smiled and turned away. "Yeah, whatever. Just let him come and try."

24.

Craig

———————————————————

"THIS YOUNG LAD OF YOURS, CRAIG? That's his name? He's becoming a problem," the Texas cop said.

The waitress served up the eggs. "You said whole wheat?"

"I always say whole wheat, Betty."

"What did he do now?"

"Shoplifting again. I mean doesn't he know that everyone's watching? What is he, stupid?"

"Maybe, just a bit, I don't know."

"Just barely of age, too. You really pick them. He must be great in the sack." She ignored him. "You've got him now?"

"Yeah, we'll hold him until you get free here. But I gotta' tell you. One more time, and we'll press charges. He either behaves or gets out of town. Otherwise, it's jail time."

25.

Alex

· ———————————— ·

ARLY MORNING, SHE DESCENDED TO THE LOBBY. "Good morning Alex."

"Good morning, Madam. All goes well."

"Absolutely fine." Eleanor Tibbett waved and headed to the corner, dim
flickering street lamps lighted her way. It was earlier than usual, with little
traffic and empty sidewalks. A quiet, sleeping city. A figure emerged from the
shadows and grabbed her bag. Instinctively, she pulled back. He threw her to
the ground and put his hand on her throat. "Don't fuck with me or I'll fuck
you over good."

"What?" Her eyes blurred.

Just as fast, his body fell away. No, it was pulled away. She heard kicks and
screams and anguish and saw Alex pummeling the mugger, like a cat with dead
mouse. "Stop," she cried. "You'll kill him."

"You a dead man," Alex said to the bloody figure.

She sat up. "Stop. Please stop."

"Why? He is deep shit. Dirt. We get rid of him."

"No, just stop, please. Please."

After the police came, she returned to the building. "You gotta be careful," Alex said. "You don't know this city."

'I know," Eleanor said. "I just never thought. I mean, it's never happened before."

"This city filled with good people and a few, how do you say, rotten apples? You strong and independent but not that strong, if you know what I'm saying."

"I'll be more careful."

"You look in front, behind and around you. All the time. And you have any problems, you call Alex."

"Yes Alex."

"Alex your friend. You don't forget."

"Yes Alex." She noticed his smell, a deep, pungent smell. Probably from the fight, she figured.

26.

Cheppi

·————————————·

A POOR DAY FOR WANDERING. Snow and sleet in the face, wind blowing trash, slush on the corners, skidding cars and falling bodies. Faces masked against the elements. A truck speeds through a red light, ignoring yells and splattering salt and dirt and ice and cold wet mush.

Eleanor was tired and worn. What is she doing? What is she searching for? This town seems to have no direction, she thought, no center. She wandered from English to Spanish. Banks became pawn shops, bodegas in the place of supermarkets, beauty parlors and laundromats instead of trendy restaurants. Western Union shops proclaim: "A World of Betters: We Send Your Money Anywhere in the World."

Chilled and seeking refuge, she ducked into a crowded luncheonette and pushed to the rear, away from the cold. A large, peroxide blonde guarded the cash register upfront. A crucified Jesus dangled above her. Spanish filled the room. Men sat astride stools drinking coffee, *El Diario* spread before them. Burnt grease mixed with cigarette smoke filled the air. The cook worked the grill.

"May I see a menu?" Eleanor asked him.

"No menu," he said with a slight accent. "What you want?"

"Breakfast. Eggs, I guess."

"Breakfast? You want chorizo? Sausage? Some papas fritas?

"Chorizo would be nice. No papas."

"I'll give you some frijoles. You must have frijoles. Platanos?"

"What?"

"Platanos. They're like bananas. I give you a couple. If you like, you eat them."

"Sounds like a deal. But a cup of coffee would be nice."

"Of course. You came in to get warm. Esperanza," he yelled to the blonde, "dale un café. Tiene frio."

"Si," Esperanza responded, "Y tu quieres calentarle. No?"

He whistled as he worked the grill, a rough face with a slight attractive smile, not young, Eleanor noted, but strong with broad shoulders. The blonde spied her looking at him.

"You are a pretty woman," the cook said. "I don't think you been here before."

"No. First time."

"You don't live around here?"

"No, I live downtown a bit."

"You a lawyer?"

"No, why do you ask?"

"Only Anglo lawyers come to Quisqueya Heights, or cops. And you no cop. Too skinny. Too pretty."

"What is Quisqueya Heights?"

"This is. I am King of Quisqueya Heights where we Dominicans live."

"Really," she smiled.

"Cuidado, Cheppi," the blonde yelled from the front.

"What is she saying?" Eleanor asked.

"Oh nothing. She is always jealous. Doesn't trust women sitting by themselves in front of the best cook in this city, especially pretty women."

He placed the plate in front of her. Slowly she picked at the eggs.

He smiled. "They OK?"

"Yes, thank you."

"Try the platanos."

She sliced the fried fruit, darkened with burnt sugar and grease.

"Yes, it's quite good."

"Glad you like it. You come for dinner. If you like my breakfast, you'll love my dinner. What is your name?"

"My name? Eleanor?"

"Eleanor, like Eleanor Rigby."

"Yes."

"I like the Beatles. You like the Beatles?"

"Yes, I suppose so."

"My name is Cheppi." He held out his hand. She hesitated and shook.

"Cheppi!" The blonde yelled from the front.

"See," he laughed. "I told you that was my name. They also call me the Mayor 'cause I know everything that goes on here and everyone."

"Really?"

"Sure, everyone comes to Cheppi to eat and talk. You ever need anything, you come by."

She smiled.

"I am serious."

"I'm sure you are. I'll remember."

"You like my breakfast?"

"It's quite good."

"No, it isn't."

"What?"

"It is wonderful, the essence of la vida latina, warm, salty, spicy and, how do you say it, it fills the senses. It satisfies. You know the secret?"

"No," her fork reaching her mouth.

"Actually three secrets. First is Cheppi. Me. You've got to have me."

"I see," she laughed.

"The second is grease. You go downtown you don't get no grease. But we, we Dominicans, we specialize in grease. Not just any grease but Dominican grease."

"Special grease?"

"Yes, of course. Secret recipe. You walk past my place there is a smell no one can avoid. It seduces pretty girls like you. Nothing like that downtown. The City, it don't want us to get all the guapitas. So the law says no fats, what the City calls polyunsaturated."

"Does it?"

"Yep, it's the law. The hue puta Mayor wants to save our souls by starving us. Nobody else uses it because it gets you into trouble. Like Heroin or Crack."

"Surely, not that bad."

"They close you down. I take a big risk giving you this secret. But I think I can trust you."

"And you break the law?"

"What do you think? I am a law-abiding citizen."

"So, your grease?"

"OK. So I am no an angel. Sometimes I cheat. You never cheat?"

She shook her head.

"Just kidding, Eleanor Rigby, just kidding."

"So what's the third ingredient?"

"I'm glad you asked, 'cause that's the real secret."

"Which is?"

"Ajo."

'Ajo?"

"Garlic. You need the right garlic and then just the right amount. I mean, you go to one of your fancy places with white linens and fancy silver, and they make you breakfast. Tastes like cardboard. You know why?"

"Garlic?"

"That's right. They don't know garlic. They need the right type of garlic, too. Not your everyday garlic. Some people like elephant garlic but that's 'cause they're lazy and cheap. Easy to peel and cut. No flavor. Me, I'm partial to hardneck garlic."

Eleanor kept eating, nodding her head respectfully.

"Hardneck garlic has good taste and if you can get the stalk, and that ain't easy if you know what I mean, it's wonderful. A few slices of the stalk mixed in with the ajo and" he kissed his fingers, "paradise."

"I didn't know that."

"Yep, and garlic, garlic is good for you. Very good for the goma. Especially after a night out on the town."

"Goma?"

"Yeah, goma. The thing down here in your stomach that aches the next morning. Garlic clears it all up."

"I see."

"Cures all sorts of ailments, it does. I get sick, the first thing I do is eat a few cloves of garlic."

She laughed. "I bet that keeps people away from you."

"Yep, but I almost never get sick. Know why?"

"Garlic?"

"That's the ticket. You a fast learner. Now there's another thing that makes Cheppi's breakfast the best."

The blonde came back and handed her the check. "Tome," she said, staring at Eleanor. "Paga al frente," she pointed to the cash register in the front.

Cheppi shook his head. "She so rude. It is cold outside. You sit here as long as you want, you hear? I'll leave the other ingredient for another time. You come back?"

"I might, yes."

"And if you like I will tell you about my barrio, this neighborhood. You know George Washington was here."

Eleanor laughed. "I don't think I have time to go back that far."

"Any time, Eleanor Rigby. You come back and I'll show you around."

27.

The Break

————•————

IT WAS NOT THAT SHE WAS OBLIVIOUS TO FLIRTING, she was inured, a heart petrified on a hardware store stool. Still, Cheppi left a taste, a slight tingle, and a chink in her armor. He was not unattractive, a friendly look, not lascivious in the least and more sympathetic than suggestive. He played, she thought, he played with food and he played with her, so unlike the middle-aged suitors from the church. So unlike Joey, she thought.

She left the restaurant, paused as if to head home and turned to wander on. She strolled, glancing at small, untidy shops, guys half asleep behind empty counters, past liquor stores and candle shops, a music studio, and a secretarial school. In the snow and sleet, she trudged past children laughing, couples holding hands, and young and aged struggling through the slush.

This was not Lincoln Gardens, the quiet and placid place back home. Here, cars bounced from pothole to pothole, trucks and buses cut and in out, blowing their horns. Here, pure noise, sirens instead of silence. No, this was not like home.

A trumpet blared in the distance above the urban din. She wandered mindlessly to a trestle and the screeching sound of wheels. Sleet beat against her face.

She lost direction. Wayward newspaper sheets blew about. Corner garbage cans spilled into the street.

"Hey, chica," a large brown man yelled out, "Venga con nosotros." A small group of men huddled around a fire in a trashcan, drinking whiskey. "Come on baby, come on." A man reached out to grab her arm and laughed as she skittered away. She ran for cover under a torn awning, announcing H-TEL. A large black woman opened the door. "Come inside honey, warm up."

She ran on, shivering against the cold, crossing against traffic. A car slammed on its brakes, skidding away. A train passed noisily overhead. She tripped, caught herself, slipped on ice and turned to head for home, exhausted. And then, thoughtlessly, she stepped off a curb. A taxi honked and swerved, splashing ice onto her face and clothes. The driver screamed in heavily accented English, "Why the fuck don't you watch where you're going, you asshole? Don't you see the goddamn light?"

Slurry blurred her vision. Shivering to the bone, she said nothing, smeared her hands on her coat and rubbed her eyes on her sleeve. She gave out a slight, imperceptible and mournful cry, and then deep throbbing sobs. These were not tears of hurt. No, these were tears of anger, of rage suppressed, of being out of control, and of being lost. She struggled to recover, like a good midwestern woman. She shook her head, clenched her teeth, straightened her back, and walked on.

At home, she showered, threw on a bathrobe, made a cup of coffee and sat and stared.

If this were fiction, we would see a new superhero emerge, a woman bent on fighting for good to cure the world's ills and destroy its villains. But this is not fiction. And Eleanor was real.

What was real was that they were all gone, her family and her old life. She was alone, isolated in an alien city. On that icy corner, the self-assured stoic and solid woman cracked like a dam before a tsunami. A surge of fierce anger swelled and broke.

Her half-life was over. It was time. Time to move on.

Part Three

28.

Rebirth

———•————————————•———

THE FRUITS OF TRAGEDY HAD MADE HER RICH, an irony she understood. Her careful savings, Joey's insurance, the pension, the sale of the car dealership and of her home created a small fortune. Her soldier son's death benefits and Joan's not insubstantial estate added to the prosperity. Now, in her widowhood and solitude, her fury and passion, and alone in her bathrobe and recovering from her walk, she sipped coffee and considered the wealth that she had never dreamt of.

Eleanor knew money, the price of nails and widgets, tools and wires, hammers, drills and all the stuff packed into hardware stores. She understood profit and loss, the cost of money, the price of cars, the leases, insurances, and taxes. Supply and demand. And she learned through her life and her readings duplicity, both commercial and personal life's vicissitudes. The Wars and Peace. The Prides and Prejudices.

And as she considered her wealth, her angry face stared at the city below and something changed, radically if not perceptively. The old Eleanor, the girl on the stool and the woman in the car showroom, died. The cocoon of midwestern nicety and passivity was destroyed by urban lava. The equilibrium which she had struggled to maintain, despite herself, dissolved.

Yet, there was no outward evidence of the new Eleanor. The sweet smile and outward politesse remained. Still, on that wintry day a cold chill froze her heart. The chill of loss, betrayal and solitude and the slap of urban mush created an uncertain and vague morality in a savage heart.

A new woman emerged, not perhaps a hero the way we understand heroism, but a woman with an undertaking, maybe even a vendetta, a quest to salve an angry soul by whatever means.

29.

Obsession

———————————————

"**G**OT A PRESENT FOR YOU, CINDY."
The African-American cop cocked her head. "A present, for little old me. Is it a raise?"

"Nah, the State wouldn't allow that, would they? Something better."

"Better?"

"Yeah. Got a call from some place in Texas. They found Craig White."

"Who?"

"You know, Craig White, Joey and Eleanor's lost son, the one you thought she killed."

"So he's not dead?"

"Nah, he's just causing trouble, again."

"Again?"

"Yeah. A bad apple. You don't know the headaches he gave me back in the day. Stolen cars, drunken fights, kid stuff verging on felony. It was really not right. They were such a nice family. Didn't deserve it, they didn't."

"So he's alive. I was sure she did him in."

"Yeah, I know. You gotta watch that paranoia."

"Maybe there was a reason he left all of a sudden."

"There you go again."

"No, I'm not being crazy. Look, first this kid leaves and goes missing and what do they do, nothing? And then their other kid signs up for the war and gets himself killed. Something's gotta be bad there."

"Bad, maybe, but not criminal. Every family has secrets, let me tell you. In this town, if those motel walls could speak…"

"Yeah. Don't tell me about it. White people playing at being bad. I walk into a market, I see guys staring at my ass, elbowing each other, a wink here and there. But that isn't what went on with this Eleanor White. Nah, she bad in another way. I dig the name, White."

"I think I smell a perfume."

"What you talking about."

"Yeah, I know it when I smell it."

"I don't got on perfume."

"Yes you do. I smell it, like the first day of spring. And the name is, the name is, it's coming to me, yeah, that's it, you wearing obsession, Cindy. Obsession."

30.

The Leak

———————————————

SPRING CAME EARLY, APRIL rains in March. Melting snow clogged sewers and splattered walkers. In Eleanor's apartment, water dripped into the living room, a leak in her window, it seemed. Eleanor called downstairs.

Alex arrived, carrying his tool chest. Eleanor mopped. He surveyed. The room filled with his dank odor. She wondered if he ever washed. "This happens a lot in these old buildings," he said with a rough accent. "Ice under the sill breaks the wood. The place needs new windows but the owners, they cheap."

"Can you fix it?"

"For you, no problem." He rummaged among the tools, found a small, plastic knife and puttied the window sill, his large hands gently moving back and forth across the rubber. He checked the other windows. "Where is your television?"

"No. No television."

"How can you not have television? What do you do at nights?"

"I read."

"You must have a television. All Americans have television. Big television. Cable too! You don't have cable?"

"Nope."

"You, a very strange lady. I have television. Two hundred stations. I even watch Bosnian station. Actually, I have three televisions, one for kitchen, another for living room and one in bedroom?"

"Really?" She retreated from his sweaty stench.

"Of course. I need to watch my team, keep up on politics, you know. And pets, where are your pets?"

"No, I've never taken to animals."

"You should have a pet. You people have pets. Lots of tenants have dogs and when they don't have dogs, they have cats and when they don't have cats, they have birds. Or fish. Americans have pets. You should get a dog. Take him for a walk. Meet people in the park."

"No, I don't think so. They seem a bother." He pulled at the window frame which rattled dangerously. "Bad work. Never coated. These people, they are very cheap. And where is your computer?"

Eleanor laughed. "No computer."

He shook his head. "You need a computer to write."

"The mail will do. Are you married, Alex?" She changed the subject.

"No, I'm not married."

"I'm sorry. If you don't mind me asking, why not?"

He looked to the wall. "No. I am just single."

"But surely there are women . . ."

"There were women. Once."

"I'm sorry. I don't understand."

"They died. In the war."

"War?"

"Our war for independence. Our women were killed and those not killed, they are like me."

She looked at him and fell quiet. He continued about his work.

"My son died in a war too," she said quietly.

He continued quietly, adjusting window sashes. He looked out the window. "Where is your husband?"

"He is dead too."

"Your son died? Your husband died? Do you have other children?"

"Yes, one other. But he's gone."

"Where is he? How come he doesn't live with you?"

"A long story. He just upped and vanished. Gone off to the world."

"This, very strange. In my country, children never leave their parents. There are so many threats and enemies. The parents they defend the children then the children defend their parents."

She said nothing.

He turned to her, putting down his tools. "Back in my country, we have many troubles, many deaths. Bad times. But we always say you must continue to live, no matter what. We had wars and diseases. Nazis and Communists. Dictators and hoodlums. Our towns, they were burned to the ground., our women were violated and our children butchered to death. Too much blood. Too much death. It's in our souls, our beings, and we never forget."

"In my mosque we pray for our lost families. Our friends. We cry. Every week. But you know what I think? I think that is the past. We have to keep going. Living is hard, especially after all this. You know that and I know that. But we have to move on, don't we? If we hang onto corpses, we get dragged to hell."

She said nothing.

He looked at her for a moment "What is it that your Bible says? If you look back, you turn to salt. And that would be a waste."

"I suppose so."

"Maybe a little dog?" He stowed his tools.

"No," she shook her head. "I don't want a dog."

"You cannot be alone or live alone without television or internet or cable or dog. I am not an educated man, but I think you should call your Pastor."

"The Pastor? Oh my, I forgot. You did tell me he came by, didn't you? I get into my head too much, I guess."

"Excuse me, I don't wish to be, you know…"

"That's all right, Alex. I understand." She wanted him to leave, to leave her alone.

"You should call that Pastor, I think. You promise me you call him."

"Yes, I promise."

"Missus, you look around the streets in this city, you see many crazy people. They wear funny clothes and walk about muttering. They wander up and down the streets like refugees. You see them all over, in the subways, the parks, on the corners, asking for money. You don't want to be like them."

"I will call him. I promise."

31.

The Church

————————————

THEY MET OVER COFFEE, the Pastor in khakis and an open shirt. He spoke quietly and she strained to hear. They exchanged pleasantries, memories of Joan, how she was getting on, and how come she hadn't returned his calls. He asked about Bobby. Why had he joined the military? She shook her head slowly and looked into space. "Oh, you know, to save the world."

"I would like you to help me, if you would," the Pastor said. "Our Church Board meets every Monday night. Unfortunately, it is mostly men, businessmen, very busy men, but they provide the financial support. We need new blood and, frankly, I'm bored of their stocks and bonds. It's endless. I'd like you to sit in and if you like and if it seems to work, join the Board."

"I'm not sure I'm qualified," she said. "And I am new here."

"Yes, well that's what we need. And you do have a view of the world quite unlike any of ours, coming from where you come from."

"I don't know."

"Listen Eleanor, you're a smart woman. I can see that. I owe it to Joan to be your friend. She was a great woman and we miss her. But aside from that, it's kind of hard to make friends around here. Especially a pretty and intelligent single woman. Come and try. What have you got to lose?"

32.

The Board

—————————•

STRANGE HOW THESE THINGS COME ABOUT. A woman alone, a victim of tragedy after tragedy with an obsessive, perhaps neurotic, need for long walks and daily breakfasts, solitude and isolation, a woman stirred to action by a Bosnian refugee, himself a victim of unbearable tragedy, that proves the point that psychologists have proclaimed for a century that any action is better than none at all and that action will create more action.

And now the cleric, a man she barely knows, lures her to his church and then to sit on the Church board to meet the city's business elite, lawyers, corporate types, doctors, each more than willing to assist the attractive widow to understand the church's finances and undertakings over lunch or perhaps dinner.

The Church was the oasis where the city's elite came to pray and if per chance a business deal arose, all the better. Its board oversaw it all, headed by its Chairman, Daniel Trepin, Jr., the world-renown real estate mogul. Short and balding with a sagging face, he strutted about like so many egos in this town, garbed in Italian suits and French shirts. His second on the Board, Dave Galloway of Galloway, Simpson, Childs and Cuomo, was everything Trepin was not. Tall, a straight, handsome jaw and self-possessed, one of those lawyers who the wealthy look to. He was also Trepin's lead counsel. Then, Marion Lewis, a squinty-eyed banker in double-breasted suit and pasted-down hair, the man who provided Trepin with the capital to finance the empire. The widow Clara Fitzsimmons, benefactor of so many of the city's charities, the museum, the opera and the church. She welcomed Eleanor with open arms and a "at least I'll have someone to talk to here."

Was Eleanor pretty? No. Attractive? Maybe. Prim with short blonde hair, a face as white as snow, what they call small features, certainly not gorgeous. It was her shy, quiet qualities that attracted men, or what they perceived as shyness. Men might gawk at a gorgeous 25-year-old 6-foot model in a tight skirt and high heels. Brief fantasies come and vanish like a flash. But a diminutive and attractive 40-year-old woman smiles a slight smile, a smile learned decades before on a store stool, who listens intently to conversations, stares into their eyes and nods in an understanding and sympathetic manner, that woman is cared for, invited out, and offered advice. They dream of her for weeks. And so, Eleanor came to the Church Board and entered the world of Montrachet and truffled pate, vintage Barolo and Kobe beef, Sevres porcelain, tuxedos, furs and diamonds.

No furs and diamonds for her, no "reciprocations" for the flattery, for her shield remained intact. When offered the Bentley for a ride home, she accepted gracefully as if it were her nature. She arrived alone, Alex at the door greeting her with a brief, "Good Evening, Missus, I hope you had a good night." She responded with "It was quite nice, Alex. Thank you."

Did she know her power, how men came to help, guide, or protect? Hard to tell for the shield blocked scrutiny. Did she know herself? Surely, as time passed, this power was useful in building an empire. Her empire? Did she know that was her goal? Her ambition?

33.

Clara Fitzimmons

———————•———————

O NE DAY, AFTER A BOARD MEETING, Clara Fitzsimmons invited her for tea. The apartment was on Fifth Avenue across from the park, a few blocks south of the Met Museum. Eleanor looked about in awe. "We bought this rug in Iran before that terrible revolution," she said, "and here, here is a picture of my late dear husband with Nelson Rockefeller. The Rockefellers were such nice people considering how powerful they were. And here, here's Allen and John Dulles after they left Washington. And here's Nasser, he was a nice man, made sure that we had such a wonderful tour of the pyramids and quite courteous."

The maid offered tea with a dish of sugar cookies. "I just love this Wedgwood, it is so beautiful, don't you think?"

"It is very nice, I don't think I've ever…"

"Of course not, dear. Of course not." She waved her hand. "From where you're from. I hear you're a widow too."

"Yes."

"It is a terrible ordeal, isn't it? Everything reminds me of my Henry, the times we had, the travels and adventures, the parties, and our courtship, but you know over time you get over it, you move on. But you must give it time."

"I know. It is hard."

Fitzsimmons interrupted. "You can't let it get you down. You must keep your head up and push forward. My mother was also a widow, you know. For many years, yes, yes, had nothing but her memories, and oh what memories she had. But she never let herself get down. She kept her head up and persevered until the end."

Eleanor smiled graciously.

"I came from the Midwest like you, Grosse Point, came East to school and that is how I met Henry. He wasn't the most attractive catch, that's for sure, but he had his talents, you know." She winked. "You don't know how many girls I know who have come to find their man. I'm surprised there are any women left out there! But I'm rambling."

Eleanor gazed at the Degas dancer over the fireplace. "My pride and joy," Fitzsimmons said. "We bought it at auction in Paris during our honeymoon. Really couldn't afford it back in those days, but Daddy helped out. I used to dance although now you would never know it."

"You still have a youthful figure," Eleanor said.

"You are so kind. So kind. But I do go on and on. What I wanted to tell you, the Church is a great sanctuary," Fitzsimmons said. "There are so many good works we can do, supporting the Board and the community. I lead the women's club and help out in the homeless kitchen. I also run the annual bazaar. I hope you'll come and help too."

"Thanks, I'll try," she lied.

"You know Dan Trepin is a great man. He has done so much to help us out whenever we need anything. And don't believe everything you read about him. They make up lies and write anything to sell their dirty rags. I know for a fact that half the women he is supposed to have been with, well it just isn't true. But he is a man, isn't he?"

"I suppose so."

"And he has so much pressure. You can't believe the pressure he's under. I believe in forgive and forget, don't you?"

"Yes."

"Now, my dear Henry, he never would do such things. Anyway, I wouldn't let him. But you've never had that problem either, I suppose."

"No," Eleanor said flatly.

"No, of course not. We're good American stock. We aren't like some people."

"I think I should be going."

"You're leaving already? Oh my, I guess I said too much. But we will get together again, soon, I hope."

"Yes, of course."

"And don't forget what I said about Dan. He can be a good friend. See you at Church."

34.

Cindy Williams

———————•———————

"**D**ON'T MIND THE LOOKS. We don't see many black faces around here," the waitress said, across the counter. 'Specially one as pretty and dressed like you. You from Dallas?

"No, from up north, doing a little investigation."

"You a Fed?"

"No, just a Detective."

"You're a long way from home, honey."

"Just trying to track down a killer."

The waitress turned away. "Who you looking for?"

"I'm trying to find a kid by the name of Craig White. You know him?"

"No, don't rightly think so."

"This is quite a small town. I would think everyone knows everyone."

"Well, maybe he came through. Maybe he left."

"Ya' see we got some information that he was arrested here a few weeks back. From the database, you know? So I know he's been around. But if you can't help, I'll just go ask your local constabulary.

The waitress paused. "Well, maybe I know him and maybe I don't."

"Look, honey, I'm not after Craig as the killer. I just think he can give me some information. 'Matter of fact. He was no place close to the killing. I just need background."

"Background?"

"Yeah, on the person I suspect."

"So you don't think he's the killer?"

"I promise you he's not the killer. I'm not after him. I just need info, that's all."

"Well, maybe I know him."

"So where can I find him?"

"He's in the town jail, locked up. They got him for breakin' and entering."

Cindy Williams strolled to the jail. "We used to be a much larger force," the cop at the front said. "but that was years ago, He huffed as he spoke. "I've been on the force now for over 20 years, and this is the first time we've had anyone like this kid."

"He's a bad one?"

"No, not bad, like some people are really bad. He just goes after trouble. We don't want to send him away, he being a friend of Betty's, and he ain't done nothing that merits the big house."

"Who's Betty?"

"Betty, she's the waitress at the diner. Everyone knows Betty, a hot little number."

"Oh yes, I met Betty," she smiled. "So you don't know what to do with this boy?"

"Yeah, I guess that's right."

"Well maybe I can help out, that is if you can help me out."

"I'd appreciate anything you can do."

Craig sat in a bare room behind an old wooden desk. When he saw her, he broke out laughing. "You the parole officer? I'm in luck today."

"You behave, Craig," the cop said, smacking his head. "I'm not gonna cuff you 'cause, well, you know."

"Yeah, I know," Craig said. "Where am I gonna run to?"

"That's right."

"That's right" the young man mocked. He turned towards the black woman. "So, to what do I owe the honor? Am I a civil rights case?"

"Yeah, you're a civil rights case, violating everyone's civil rights from what I hear."

"That's pretty funny."

"So I hear you getting it on with the waitress?" He didn't respond. "Is it serious, because I don't want to waste my time. If it's serious and you don't want a 'Get Out of Jail Free'" card, I'll just move on.

"Well, it ain't that serious if the price is right. And you're a pretty woman, a little old for me, but."

"'Cause the reason I ask is if you give me the right answers, then you and me, we're gonna take a long ride home."

"Home. I come from *your* town?"

"Listen, kid, I'm not about to start arguing over words so why don't you keep quiet and see if you can convince me that you deserve to get out of here. I mean you just don't seem the type to settle down with the town's waitress."

"So what are you asking?"

"First, I gotta give you some bad news."

"Just what I need, bad news."

"Your brother was killed in action."

"Bobby joined up?" he laughed. "What an idiot."

"He died fighting for his country."

"Yeah, whatever. Bobby was my brother but not my brother. We never got along. He was straight-arrow. So he's gone and got himself killed. Well, I'll be."

"And, your father died."

His body jumped, his head cocked to the side. "Yeah, no kiddin?"

"No kidding," she said flatly

"How? No, nevermind. Whatever. I don't want to know."

"I'm investigating his death."

"He was murdered?"

"No, the verdict was suicide."

"Suicide? Dad? That don't make sense."

"Yeah, well, that's what I thought, too. So I decided to dig, and I found you under the sagebrush."

"Dad, a suicide? Don't make sense," he repeated. "I mean he was always so straight, so balanced. Nothing I ever did got him angry. Maybe once or twice," he shrugged, "that time I hit that girl 'cause she was makin' fun of me, but Dad kill himself?

"That's what they say."

"But you don't believe it."

"Do you?"

"No. He'd never do it."

"So I'd like you to tell me a few things about your mother."

He laughed again. "Mom? You suspect her?"

"I didn't say that."

"Jeez. I leave home and everything collapses." He shook his head and laughed. "I didn't know I was so important."

"What do you mean?"

"I mean like when I. No, wait a minute," his face turned serious. "You asking me to rat out my own mother?"

"No, I'm asking you to help me solve your father's death. That is, unless you don't care to."

"And if I don't help, you keep me here in this shit-hole."

"Yeah, well, you made your life, and after your 60 days are up, there will be Betty waiting for you and taking you in and mothering you. Things could be worse."

"You're a tough bitch, aren't you?"

"Let's just say you don't fuck with a tough bitch."

"So I send over my mother who you think killed my father and . . ."

"I didn't say that."

"Nah, but you're not asking about the neighbors or some golfing buddy, you're asking about my mother."

"All I want to know is what sort of person is she?"

"She? She's a mother. She made sure everything was right and proper and clean. We had food. We got to school. She took care of us the way she took care of the accounts. How she handled Dad. That's what mothers do."

"Were your parents warm, I mean?"

"You mean did they love each other? How do I know? They were tight, if you know what I mean. They were together more than most, what with the car store."

"She ever get angry, fly off the handle?"

"Ma? Nah. She wanted something done, she said it flatly and if we yelled and cursed, she would ask us to lower our voices, that's what she always said, 'you just lower your voices,' she said. Never fought back."

Cindy Williams wrote notes in the red notebook.

"You gettin' everything down right there?"

"Yeah, everything."

"You can't remember, huh?"

"Ya know, Craig," Williams said, I didn't have a mother and a father and a lawn and cars and all that stuff. My Auntie May raised me, and she taught me three things, to be good, to watch out for the devil, and to take down everything 'cause you can't remember everything and someday you'll need to remember."

"Yeah, well. I hope you got it all down."

"Not much here. I don't think you're getting out of jail. Too bad, I've traveled a long way and I thought you'd might drive back with me, get some burgers and fries, and hit the road."

He looked out at the bare street below watching two men leaning against a post, smoking and talking. A dog crossed the street. He turned. "There was one thing."

"One thing?"

"Yeah, but I don't think it means much."

"You let me be the judge."

"Ranger."

"Ranger? Whose Ranger?"

"Ranger's a dog, or was a dog, a stray, ya' know. One day I was walkin' home from school and this dog came over and sniffed my hand. Didn't have a collar or nothing."

"So you took him home?"

"Yep and Mom didn't like it at all. No sir. Not at all. Said dogs did nothing except eat and go to the bathroom, that's what she said. Mom never liked pets."

"How come you were walking home alone?"

"I always walked home alone. Didn't have many friends to speak of. I liked being alone anyway."

"So Ranger was your pet and you loved him. He was your friend."

"Yeah, Ranger was a good friend." He shook his head. "For a little while."

"A little while?"

"We fought over him, Ma and me, whether to take him to the pound and we knew what that meant and that dog loved me. Problem was it brought in fleas and we had to fumigate everything but that was no big deal. Ranger used to sleep with me and when Mom came in in the morning, she'd throw him down on the floor, like a dirty, ol' rag. And then one day, I came home and Ranger wasn't there. And we looked and looked, put up signs around town and I wanted to go look again and then Bobby took me aside and told me he was gonna to do me a favor and show me where Ranger was but I had to swear not to tell no one so I swore and so we went out into the woods about a half mile from where we lived, the woods being some scruffy lots where these bums used to hang out before they were cleared out and sure enough, under some leaves, there was fresh earth. Over Ranger. Mom had taken that dog out and shot him. Had Bobby dig the grave, she did."

"She shot him?"

"Yep."

"She didn't say anything?"

"I never said anything. Didn't want to get Bobby in trouble, though I should of, that asshole."

"What did your father say?"

"Him, he never said anything. He let Mom handle this stuff, the school work, the gettin' out of trouble. He was too busy with the cars."

"So your Mom never knew that you knew."

"Nope, I don't believe so. I kept my mouth shut. That Bobby, what an asshole. He was the good kid, the kid they said was gonna' do great things, so fuckin' clean although he was fuckin' girls left and right and they didn't know about it."

"They?"

"Mom and Dad. So he's dead, huh?"

"Yep."

"Whataya know?"

35.

Daniel Trepin, Jr.

———————————

TOP FLOOR. TREPIN TOWERS. Executive suite. Large glassed sweeping panorama of the harbor. The sign on the door: "Trepin Associates."

"WELCOME HOME, HERO," cried the headline on the framed *Daily News* tabloid on the desk. The face of Lieutenant Daniel Trepin, tired, gaunt and serious, stared at Daniel Trepin, Jr.

Trepin looked at his father, the war hero, picked his nose and glanced down at the plans for the Trepin Goa Casino. Short and paunchy despite regular workouts, he stared at the paper, like a child bored with school work. He ran his hands across his balding head.

"Sally," he spoke into the intercom, "why the fuck do I have to look at these? Haven't the Injuns signed off?"

"They want your sign-off Mr. Trepin," the voice said. "They also want to make sure you like the signage."

"The signage," he mumbled. TREPIN CASINO GOA: A NEW ADVENTURE, the banner read. "How come there are elephants on the sign? Why not have my picture?"

"Hindu Gods, Mr. Trepin," the voice said. "For good luck."

"We don't want good luck. Don't those fuckers know that if our guests have good luck, we lose money?"

"I think our partners are insisting."

"I hate elephants. They're big and clumsy. This foreign shit is not fun. Why didn't we just stay at home?" He looked at the plans again. "Did Salisbury approve?"

"Yes, they were copied."

"All right, if the Brits are OK and the Injuns insist. They want elephants? Fuck 'em, let 'em have their elephants/"

"Gods, Mr. Trepin."

"Yeah, yeah, Gods."

For years now, Wall Street beat a path to his doors, seeking to finance his strategic moves. Pensions, college endowments, hedge funds, and the world's banks financed his co-ops and office buildings, movie productions, and now the Arab and Asian casinos.

Daniel Trepin Jr., ruled the world, his name opened doors to the world's wealth. Failures as well, of course, a gaggle of scandals, flings with Hollywood starlets, marriages to women half his age and twice his height and then three angry divorces. Wherever he went, the paparazzi followed, trying to catch that one embarrassing photo of arm candy, young girls just over the legal age. How long could he keep this up, he wondered.

Why did he keep going, keep pushing? His kids were grown, off on their own with enough money for a tribe of Trepins. The divorces were all settled, neat and clean. Why more investments, more opportunities, and more turf to conquer? No one at home, chicks jumping at him wherever he went. A man filled with success. A God sitting above the corporate world and the glistening blue harbor below. A man unfulfilled. He felt his paunch. "I do work out," he mumbled to his pectoral father but nothing helps."

"Sure you do," he thought he heard the photo say. "But you need to work harder. Harder."

"Did you say something," the voice on the intercom said.

"No, just talking to myself."

"If you are free?" the voice said.

He sighed, a cruise ship sailed into the harbor below, a mass of windows floating like a building on its side. "Trepin Cruise lines," he muttered. "That's an idea."

"Did you say something, sir?" the intercom said.

"No, just muttering. What's up?"

"That Eleanor Tibbett," the intercom said. "She turned down the dinner invite."

"Who?"

"Eleanor Tibbett, you know, the one Pastor Wainwright asked you to see? He said she was attractive, that you'd like her."

"So set another date."

"She prefers breakfast."

"I don't do breakfast, you know that Sally. I'm trying to lose weight."

"How about brunch," the voice said.

"Brunch, shit, I suppose so. Playing hard to get, are we?"

"I suppose."

"Well, let it be brunch."

He looked back at the picture of his father. "You never had this problem."

"Sir?" the speaker said.

"Nothing. Ignore me." He flipped off the intercom.

"Everything was simple for you. You joined the army, came home a hero and they gave you the fucking keys to the city. I got to go to fucking India to make money, deal with A-rabs, work with limey architects. And now deal with elephants. I can't believe it."

He rose and looked out the window, sunlight blinding his view. "Now, I'm fucking talking to myself."

36.

Foundation–1946

———————————————————

1946 AND THE WAR WAS OVER. For months, destroyers and battleships crammed the harbor, fleets filled with returning soldiers. At first, the celebrations were overwhelming, fireboats spraying water jets, evening fireworks, and marching bands on the docks. A military invasion overwhelmed the city, soldiers in the streets, and parties all night. A time for peace.

The scene was always the same: mothers and fathers crammed the docks, a roar as the gangplanks descended, and out marched the young men, faces forward and serious. Then, "Company. Platoon. Dismissed! And cheers."

No celebrations for Lt. Daniel Trepin. Peace was now a year old. A dark limo waited on the dock. His parents waved as Trepin descended the gangplank. They were dressed formally, as at a society ball or perhaps a wedding.

Flash bulbs popped and reporters mobbed the embracing family. "What's all this?" he asked.

"Why, it's the return of the hero," his father said quietly. "Smile and wave to the cameras, will you?"

"Hero?"

"Absolutely, the man who held off the Huns in the Ardennes. It's been in all the newspapers."

"I don't understand."

"Just wave, will you? I'll explain in the car."

"This is ridiculous," he muttered, turned and smiled wanly at the cameras.

"Hey Dan, how does it feel to be home?" a reporter shouted.

His mother nudged his side and covered her mouth. "Happy to be home with family and friends in the land of the free. At peace."

"What?" he said to her.

"Happy to be home with family and friends in the land of the free. At peace." She muttered again. "Just say it."

"I'm really happy to be home with my family and have time to relax," he said. "Thanks to all of you for coming out."

"You have an interview with Winchell tomorrow morning," his father said. "He's anxious to hear about your exploits."

"Winchell? Exploits? What are you talking about?"

"You're a hero, dear," his mother said. "You've been the talk of all the papers."

"I don't understand," he said. "What have you two been up to?"

"Great things," his father said, looking out at the passing docks. "Great things."

"Your letters dear," his mother said. "We just had to let some people see them. And I don't know how it happened but they showed up in the *News* and *Journal-American*. Those stories of how you stopped the Germans at Lanzerath in ice and snow, risking life and limb. You were so brave, and we, so proud."

"What are you talking about? I didn't stop the Germans, the 89th did. I was just a looey with a company of men."

"Oh, don't be modest," she said.

"I am not being modest!" his voice grew tense. "They'll know I am a fake hero. A fraud."

"A fake hero?" the elder Trepin said. "That's ridiculous. If your pals think you're a fake hero, they'll get over it."

"*I* can't forget it. We fought together. You have no idea. We lost so many."

"I know, I know. But the war's finished, done. You have to think of the future. What are you going to do with your life?"

"I owe them. I've betrayed them."

"You haven't betrayed anyone. Is it your fault that the papers have written you up the way they did?

"I owe them. I can't do this."

"Daniel, let's talk about this later, OK?" his father said, quietly. "You're tired. I just want you to look at this." He pointed out the window.

"What?" Daniel said, irritably.

"These docks, this harbor, just look at it. This is your future. Our future. The sky's the limit."

The next day, they walked to the neighborhood Church, the staid 19th century building wedged among the most fashionable apartments in town. "You can do this," the older man said. "You *must* do this, for your mother and me, for the city, and for the guys you fought with. You'll see. After we get done with this, they'll all have jobs."

"If they'll talk to me."

"Time heals. If you don't know that from war, you will. Time forgets too. In a few years the war will be gone, a faint, distant memory in history books. Nobody will remember who did what. Only the dead remember. Just listen to the good reverend, don't ask too many questions. We'll answer them later."

They entered the Church. "Thanks for coming," the cleric said, extending his hand. He wore a business suit and had the manner of a banker. "Let me speak to your son alone," he said, taking Daniel by the arm and leading him into his study.

"We're all proud of you, Lt. Trepin, and I'm sure your parents are proud of you too."

"Thank you, father. I'm not sure I deserve all this praise."

The prelate put up his hand. "No modesty, son, no modesty. I know, all our boys are heroes. Makes no difference. You all went over, risked your lives and defended our country. We owe all of you a great debt of gratitude."

"Yes, I can agree with that."

"You've given the best years of your life. Now it's time to repay that debt, building on what you and your chums accomplished. It's a new age, our country is going places we've never dreamed. The war is over and the depression is finished. New businesses are opening every day and new jobs are there to take advantage of."

"The time is now," he continued. "There will be leaders and there will be those who follow, those who will make lots of money and those who will just live peaceful and settled lives."

The prelate put his arm around the soldier's shoulder. "Your father and I have been talking, well more than talking, and we've set out what you guys call a battle plan. It involves many people, important people and it has to be kept extremely secret."

"Sir?" Trepin looked befuddled.

"I know. This is a church. We handle the concerns of the soul, not Mammon. But this church has been around a long time, the center of this town's life. You look at these brick walls, solid, mahogany pews, the marble pulpit and the glorious windows and what you see is a refuge, a place of worship, a place where men of money can come and pray, get married and meet quietly. This building is the bedrock, the moral base of the city, the place where leaders meet to guide this country and the world."

Trepin said nothing. "So while you were over there, putting your body on the line, your father has been working. The banks are on board as well as the Mayor. We've also got Sulzberger and Hearst involved, so no problems with the news guys."

"On board for what?" Trepin asked. "I'm sorry sir, I'm not really following."

"What we need from you is to run a business. A quiet, unassuming enterprise. We've got you a small office at 65 Broadway. The phones are up. We're printing stationery."

"Business? What business?"

The cleric guided Trepin to his desk and unfurled a map of the harbor. "Your father and you are going to set up a new company, Trepin and Son, or something like that. A family business, you know, small and unobtrusive. And quietly we want you to buy up all these warehouses up and down the river, some in Manhattan and Brooklyn, by the docks, you know. Some in the Bronx."

"Just listen," the father had advised the soldier. "Don't ask too many questions. We'll answer them later."

"The banks will provide the financing. That's all settled. The land will serve as collateral. We've got the lawyers ready to go. But we have to work quickly and quietly. Anything leaks out, the deal collapses. You, the hero, will approach the landlords, they're mostly small businesses, chandlers, boot smiths, metal guys, and electricians. Some own warehouses. You offer to buy their places. Offer them a better place out in Brooklyn or the Bronx. Or Jersey. Help them move. Make it easy for them."

"They'll want to know why, won't they?"

"You just say that after the war you want to start a business for your pals, the veterans of the Fighting 89th. Call on their patriotic duty. Tell them how hard it was over there in the trenches and all that."

Trepin chuckled. "Not many trenches."

"You know what I'm getting at."

"What if they don't wish to sell?"

"You don't worry about that. They'll sell."

"And if they don't."

"Well God will punish them, won't he?"

Trepin stared, then the cleric winked. "Just kidding. We'll cross that bridge when we get there."

"And what are we going to do with all those buildings?"

The cleric looked at him for a moment. "Would you like a drink?"

"No. Too early."

"Come my son, you're a soldier. Don't tell me you don't drink? Straight? Ice? Water?"

"Ice, I guess. Not too much"

He poured two whiskeys, one straight, one with ice. "Cheers!"

"Cheers," he said quietly.

"You've got to keep all this quiet," he repeated. "It gets out, lots of people will be unhappy. Top secret or whatever you boys call it."

"I got it, sir."

"Have you been up on Broadway lately? Uptown?"

"Not really, haven't had much of a chance."

"You should go up there. Take a look. You know what you'll see? Guys tearing up tracks. Paving the streets."

"Tracks?"

"Yep, the trolley tracks. You know why?"

"Because we have the subway, I guess."

"That's one reason."

"And I guess once Moses built those bridges out to the island, everyone wanted a car."

"Good lad, now you're getting there. We're destroying the rails because the future is cars, cars and more cars."

"Rights of way," Trepin said. "You're buying those buildings for rights of way."

"Good lad. Your Dad always said you were as fast as Ty Cobb. How are we going to get everyone to Jersey, Long Island and up north to the Catskills? Not by train, that's for sure.

You soldiers are going to have families, and you're going to buy cars and cars need roads."

"How do you know?"

"Where the roads will go?" The cleric winked. "It's a gamble to be sure, but we have God on our side along with the banks, the newspapers, the pols and the car companies. Let's just call it an educated guess."

"So we buy the rights of way, and then what?"

"Well, then the city will have to condemn the land and pay us. Full market value."

"Us?"

"Your company. And you pay the banks, the lawyers and all the rest, and I'm sure you won't forget your religious obligations."

Trepin looked at the map.

"You think it over," the Minister said. "Talk to your Dad. Everyone wins. Everyone. And once you're established, you'll be a presence in this town. Banks will throw money at you. You'll be invited to all the right parties. You'll have all the money you need to marry the right girl, go sailing on the sound, play golf, run for office, even hire some of your old buddies from the army.

"And then if this works, then the rest of the country will follow and build what the Germans call Autobahns right across America. Imagine all the rights of way, the possibilities, and the opportunities! We will lead America, guide its way, design its routes, build the roads and bridges and provide the support for a god-fearing America.

"And why are *you* doing this?"

"Listen, my son, this church is the bedrock. I keep repeating myself. It does God's work on earth. It ensures that America stays straight in its mission. You've destroyed evil in Europe, you and all you soldiers, but the fight never ends, and we have to make sure that we control that fight.

37.

Church Business

————————•————————

ELEANOR TIBBETT TOOK HER NEW RESPONSIBILITY SERIOUSLY, as she always had. As a member of the church board, she reviewed its finances, the inflows and estimated expenses. She tried to understand the investments, bond funds, annuities, real estate holdings and the like. She had never seen so many zeros, the value of prime real estate, government bonds and blue-chip stocks. This was no car dealership in the middle of America, this was a religious institution in the center of the center of the world.

She called back her college finance courses. Why, she wondered, was so much of the endowment invested in real estate? What was the relative risk of lending to commercial office buildings versus residential holdings? Why was so much centered in the city and not spread throughout the country? "You shouldn't worry too much about this, dear," Clara Fitzsimmons counseled. "We should serve the tea and leave the rest to Dan. He knows best."

Eleanor ignored her advice, politely to be sure. For if this was to be her life, she would need to understand.

They met at the Plaza, a compromise between her breakfast and Trepin's need for lunch and a drink. Trepin strolled in donning dark glasses and a Stetson hat.

All eyes turned his way. The maitre d' ushered him to a dark corner booth. "I've got to avoid crowds, paparazzi, any notice," he said to her. "You won't believe what people will do to get my attention."

Over Eggs Benedict, she wondered why the Church's real estate holdings were downtown, knowing that the best investment strategy was to diversify.

Drenched with eau de cologne, Trepin moved closer to her. "You make a good point, Eleanor," he said, touching her hand. "But what we have here is an old, staid institution. Way before we freed the slaves, this Church was putting in its foundations. Its investments go back forever, they pay a pretty good rate of return, and I gotta tell you, me being in the business, I'm not about to rock the ark, if you get what I mean."

She moved away. "But surely there are other areas in the city?"

"Yeah, but this town has its own little fiefdoms and they each make deals in their own little ghettos. Albanians, Syrians, Russians, Yids, the Blacks, and the Irish. They're all bastards and will screw their mother for a deal. I go to the wrong place, and I run up against some goombah, or a guy who used to work for the KGB, or Black Muslims. They defend their territory like it's back in the old country. They resent outsiders and protect it in not very nice ways. And they know when to buy, who to call, and the price. They know what to avoid, whose arm to twist, whose knees to cap, ya' know, how to get things done. In this business, it's hard to make money unless you're in with the in-crowd."

"But you're in Real Estate. And you've got buildings all over the place."

"Yeah, but the business I'm in is finding prime stuff, underused properties. We keep our eye on downtown, maybe get some zoning changes, put together packages, tear down some shit and put up large projects. This ain't Peoria, Eleanor, and I don't work alone. I work with banks, insurance companies, the Mayor, his allies, and some union pension guys. We put together financing, take hold of property, make sure everyone gets skin in the game, and make sure nobody elbows in."

"But buying buildings is safe?"

"Yeah, if it's done right and if you don't expect to make big money fast. You don't mind if I smoke, do you?" He pulled out a cigar. "I don't work alone. I form partnerships, corporations. All these buildings with my name on them, they're not mine. I take a few points up front, manage 'em, take a share of the profits, but you've got to be careful and spread your risks.

"Why buildings?"

"Hedge against inflation and all that crap. Look, honey, you've got a good head on your shoulders, I can see that. And I'm happy you're going through the church books. I think the last person to do that was Franklin Roosevelt, before he got sick. But I gotta tell you, I think this Church is in great shape, got more money than the Pope himself. The parishioners have a great deal going. They just pray and collect rents. And, by the way, it's all tax free, being a religion and all that. I even considered setting up my own church, ya' know, like Scientology, 'cause I hate those taxes, but it didn't work."

38.

Carmela Chan

———————————•———————————•

THE ELEMENTS WERE SET, the wealth from her sad life, an obsessive need to use it for something, anything, and the connection to the city's elite. Breakfasts, breakfast and more breakfasts. A widow's web, translucent, scarcely visible, spinning out. But the magic ingredient to Eleanor Tibbett and her empire, the amalgam to bring it all together, that was not yet present.

Perhaps it was the Caribbean taste that lingered in her mouth, the grease and garlic, that pulled her back, or the draw of the clamorous, vibrant neighborhood, or the desire to sample Cheppi's banter and smile, so unlike the downtown suits. Or, perhaps the mystery of it all, so different from her humdrum life. Or, just a search for adventure.

As she approached the restaurant, she passed a real estate store, one of those places that hang placards advertising apartment rentals. Carmela Chan, realtor, the sign proclaimed.

Eleanor read the listings in the window.

Studio in doorman building.

Three bedrooms riv-vu, perfect for young marrieds.

Third floor apartment floor-through in renovated brownstone.

She walked in and a head peaked out. "May I help you?"

"Oh, I'm just looking, curious."

"Killed the cat, they say" the woman said. "Why don't you come into my lair?"

"Don't want to waste your time."

"Nothing going on. Come on in. Have a cup of coffee," she smiled "I'm Carmela Chan."

She was dark and Asian, maybe forty, Eleanor guessed. The office was spare, with a wooden desk, a tiny bookshelf and a circular table in the middle.

"Don't be afraid. Here, have a seat. You interested in renting an apartment? We're here to help." She spoke with a Spanish accent.

"I don't know. Not sure. I'm pretty new in the city and don't know exactly what I want."

"Don't worry, we'll match you up. In this neighborhood, something for everyone. Coffee?"

And that is how it began. Chan went through the usual ritual, filling out the forms, single woman and not sure what she wanted. Money appeared to be no object. An apartment? Buy? Rent? Condo?

"The neighborhood is growing fast. Lots of artists and young couples, professionals. That's always a good sign. Multicultural, too. We've Dominican and PRs, a splattering of Chinese and Koreans and a small Haitian community. Some old Italian families are still around."

Eleanor thought for a moment. "Let me think about it. Actually, I was heading next door."

"To Cheppi's? You know Cheppi? Good food. He's good-looking too, no?"

"Oh I don't know," Eleanor said. "You know him?"

"Sure, I eat there. Cheppi knows this neighborhood. Been here forever. Knows everyone. You go to Cheppi's, ask him about me. then you come back. We'll take a walk. Just watch out for Cheppi's hands, you hear?"

39.

Cheppi's

———————•———————

THE BLONDE STOPPED TALKING and shot darts at her.

"Ah, Eleanor Rigby, you've returned," Cheppi said, smiling. "What a wonderful surprise."

"I thought I'd sample your breakfast again."

"Breakfast! Of course. Whatever you want. It gives me great pleasure to see you. Great pleasure."

The blonde wandered over. "May I take your order," she asked.

"No, No, Esperanza, I'll take care of Eleanor Rigby. I think she likes my breakfasts. Come, let's go to the back."

"No se hace tonto, Cheppi," the blonde said.

"What did she say?" Eleanor asked.

"Don't you worry. She is very possessive. You are my customer, not hers."

Cheppi leaned on the counter as she ate. "You like my huevos. They're the best in town."

"Are they?"

"That's because of my secret ingredients."

"I know your secret ingredients. You already told me."

"Oh yes. I forget sometimes."

"Too many women?" Eleanor asked.

"No, I am not like that. Do you think I tell me secrets to anyone? You, you are special. I can see that."

"I will keep your secrets, you can trust me."

He looked at her. "You have a beautiful shape for someone who eats so much."

She sipped her coffee and looked up. "Tell me, is this a safe neighborhood?"

"Safe? As safe as any. We have our crimes, but you must take the right precautions. Why you ask?"

"No, nothing."

"You have any trouble with anyone, you come straight to Cheppi."

"No, no, it's not that. It's just I'm thinking of renting a place here. And I'm a single woman."

Cheppi smiled briefly and nodded his head. "You want to find a place, I'll help you. I know lots of people."

"I spoke with Mrs. Chan, next door. We're going to take a tour."

"Carmela? That's right. Buena persona. She won't steer you wrong. But before you do anything, you come back to Cheppi. You need a place that is safe, with good neighbors? You always have to be careful. Wrong block, you have gangs. Wrong street, drugs. Bad lighting. Muggings."

"Maybe I'm making a mistake."

"Mistake? No mistake. Everywhere is the same. This is a fine barrio. Good church-going people. Working people. It's just there are bad apples everywhere. I know who they are and where they are. You listen to Cheppi. Everyone comes to Cheppi. They talk. They complain. They ask for help.

Esperanza wandered down the counter and stared at Cheppi. "Es de la Salud?"

He shook his head scornfully. "She think you're from the Health Department, an Inspector.

"I'm not," Eleanor said.

"Donde esta Simon?" the waitress asked.

"Esta abajo. No se preocupe." He turned to Eleanor. "She's worried about Simon, Simon Bolivar."

"Who?"

"Our gatito. She lives downstairs. The City doesn't want us to keep cats.

But we do anyway."

"Why?"

"Simon, he keeps the mice and ratones away. Simon Bolivar is a real killer. You should meet him some day. The city, they don't want cats but they don't want rats. Why don't they make up their minds? So we keep Simon."

"You're a little bit untrustworthy, aren't you?" Eleanor said.

"He's more than untrustworthy," the waitress said, "he's an hijo de puta, he's an asshole."

"Vayate," Cheppi pushed her away. "Me, I am not untrustworthy. On the contrary. You my friend, you can trust me. We'll find you a nice place in a safe street, well-lighted, lots of traffic. You go first with Carmela then you come back to me. I don't want to get in her way, being neighbors and everything. But you come to me. Cheppi has lots of friends."

Part Four

40.

Real Estate

———————•———————•———————

Eleanor and Carmela Chan toured the neighborhood, visiting apartment after apartment, passing crowded dwellings with crying children and guys sitting idly on stoops, smoking, chugging beer or eyeing women. Perhaps the neighborhood wasn't right for her, Eleanor thought.

Cheppi wandered into Carmela's office. "Eleanor Rigby, I've been looking for you. Carmela tells me you've become, how do you say it, frustrated."

She smiled. "I imagine so. I'm thinking that there's nothing here for me."

"I told you to come to Cheppi, didn't I? Cheppi has friends and my friends have friends. Here, it doesn't hurt to have too many friends."

Carmela looked at him. "What are you getting at?"

"There's a set of buildings overlooking the river, 8 units, on Riverside Drive. One on the top floor is coming vacant. I think we can persuade the neighbor to vacate as well. The building has its own alley for parking. Nice place, river view and all that. Lots of light.

"Chinga, Cheppi," Carmela said. "I know that building, it's rent controlled. You'd never get anyone out of there."

"Maybe yes, maybe no. Why don't we go have a look?"

They strolled to the building. A disheveled man leaned against the tall, dirty brick structure, a bottle in his hand. The building had hints of happier times, with carved 1920's curlicue moldings and old Spanish tiles. Laundry dangled from windows. Trash covered the front sidewalk. The elevator trembled as it struggled to carry them to the top floor.

The cry of a child. A barking dog.

They walked down a dim hallway, a bare exposed light bulb dangling above. Cheppi pushed and shoved at the apartment door. It gave way, crashing into the wall. "Chinga, they haven't been here in a long time," he said, rushing to open the windows. Paint chips hung from the walls like butterfly wings.

"Cheppi," Carmela Chan said, "I don't think this will do for Ms. Tibbett. This place is too far gone."

Eleanor looked through a grimy picture window out onto the river. A tanker drifted slowly downstream, a tug at its side, a faint drone of cars on the highway below. "Why too far gone?" she asked.

"These are poor people, Chan said. "Not your type. I don't think you'd get along."

Eleanor paced the hall, peering into rooms. A faint smell of rotting garbage came from the kitchen. "Where is the tenant?"

"AWOL."

"What?"

"Absent without Lease," Cheppi said. "These apartments go for nothing. They're regulated by the city so you can't get the people out. They hang onto them for years, sometimes saving them for their children, paying little rent."

"That's allowed?"

"Everything's allowed, chica, if you can get away with it. I think we can persuade the guy with the lease to sign it over. What you think Carmela?"

"I don't know, Cheppi."

"But I do. We can handle it. The smell, that's going to be a problem, but not the guy."

"You sure?" Eleanor said. "I don't want any problems."

Cheppi put his hand on her shoulder. "You leave it to me."

"You said something about asking a neighbor to leave?"

"I think it can be arranged."

"Is this a rental or a sale?"

"Must be a rental," Chan said. "Rent control."

"The owner won't sell?" Eleanor asked, continuing to look around.

"We can always make inquiries," Cheppi said. "What are you thinking?"

"Back home, we always bought. We never rented. That's the way it was. You know, the American dream."

"Yes," Cheppi said. "But Carmela is right. This building is all rental."

Eleanor looked out the window again. "I'm wondering what it would take to buy the whole building."

"What the fuck?" Cheppi exclaimed. "Oh, excuse me. You just sort of surprised me."

"I'm sorry. I don't know if I can afford it, but this place seems to have so many possibilities, what with the river and all."

Chan and Cheppi stared at each other. "You could buy it," the agent said. "But you'd still be stuck with all these tenants. They pay low rents. It's the law."

"Let's work on this," Cheppi said. "I think I see what Eleanor Rigby is saying. Let's see if we can make something happen. She'll have a home and everyone will be happy."

"I don't think you want to go in that direction," Chan said.

"Why's that? Eleanor said.

"Lots of lawyers. Plenty of trouble. There's the city to deal with, regulations, licenses and the people in the *barrio* might get upset."

"Shhh, Carmela. Let's look into it. We can handle the gente in the barrio," Cheppi said.

They left the apartment. An elderly woman shouted "Que hace aqui?"

"Nada," Cheppi responded.

"Policia?"

"No, senora, mirando."

"El Welfare?"

"No senora, nada de eso. No se preocupe. Don't worry."

41.

Power

—————•—————

T HERE MUST HAVE COME A TIME, now that we look back, that Eleanor
Tibbett recognized that she could cause men to open doors, go out of
their way and do that which they would never do for their business partners,
wives, or mistresses. Her smile led men to repair windows, offer rides home,
and fix breakfasts.

Manipulative? No more or less than anyone else, certainly less than your average car salesman or stockbroker. She was gracious, attractive, and modest. Her
power was subtle. Men *wanted* to help. They introduced her to the city's elite
and then, like teenage boys crying for attention from the prom queen, offered
to help on business deals, paving the way for her success. They got pleasure,
perhaps fantastical, but pleasure, nonetheless.

A conscious strategy? Not at first, for this was her innate personality from
an earlier life. Still, we now know that she decided to seize her destiny. Did it
happen with the knock on the door, the shot in the bedroom, at some small
breakfast joint sitting at a counter, asking for a croissant, tortilla or another cup
of coffee, or from the slight touch on the arm of a foolish suitor?

A meeting of the church board. The annual budget was approved and renovations to the sacristy were discussed. A sub-committee was formed to examine whether to allow concerts on the premises. Trepin wandered over to Eleanor. "Buy you a drink?"

"I don't drink much."

"Come, I'll take you to a nice place. Then I'll call a carriage to take you home, Cinderella." His hand led her on.

The hotel elevator rose to a dark bar overlooking the city. Couples snuggled on small banquettes. "My building," he remarked.

"I imagined as much."

She said nothing.

"I only deal in class with a capital C. Top shelf." Trepin wore a solid, business suit. His face bore the marks of an aging man, a fading hairline and a slight stoop in his walk. "Everything going OK for you?"

"Yes, I think so."

"If there's anything I can do, I'd be more than happy. I'm a single man."

"So I hear."

"Don't listen to rumors, babe."

They ordered drinks, she a chardonnay, he a malt whiskey, 30-year aged.

She was not flirting, at least from her side. She was acting like any nice girl from the Midwest, despite the older man's hints and winks, the smell of cigar on his breath, and his overbearing self-confidence. Did she know what she was doing?

"I need your advice, if you don't mind," she said.

"Yes?"

"I'm thinking of buying a building uptown overlooking the river. They are, how do you say it, 'rent-controlled.' But the people are quite old."

"Don't touch it."

"There's this guy I know. He says he can make them offers to move, get them nicer places. Then we can renovate.'

"Who is this guy?"

"Some guy I met. He seems to know the neighborhood. And there's a real estate agent I'm using. Nice woman."

"Some guy you met. Some nice woman." Trepin scoffed. "In this town you don't do business with some guy you meet on the street and some nice woman.

Sharks all over the place."

"I know. That's why I came to you. This thing you told me a while ago, about forming of a corporation, I thought you might help."

"And the money?"

"I've got a nest egg, I'd be willing to put some in. You said something about banks? Investors?" She smiled at him. They clinked glasses.

"Forget it, save your cash. If you want to go into real estate, give me the dough, I'll put it into a bunch of places, spread out your investment. Diversify, that's the only safe thing to do."

"Yes, of course and maybe I'll do that later, but this building has, you know, turned me on. You must have had experiences like this?"

"Yeah, well, maybe when I was your age, but now it's bricks and mortar, condemnation and high-rises. But yeah, I know, you're sold on this place. I don't know how many people get taken by their fantasies.

"Maybe I'm being foolish, but I want to give it a try, if it's possible, Dan. If it's possible"

"Anything's possible given the right connections. But I gotta say, babe, I can't get involved. I deal only with big stuff."

"But you could point me in the right direction? Would you?"

"I tell you what I'll do. Let's call Dave Galloway, my lawyer. He owes me. Let him go over the paperwork. Then I've got some guys who check out my projects. I'll lend them to you. It might be fun."

"Yes," she smiled, "Exactly my thought."

"So, can we have dinner sometime?"

"Of course," she said, she tilted her head. "You don't know how much this means to me, Dan. I really appreciate it."

The Bentley dropped her home. She walked to the doorman. "Good evening, Alex,"

"Madam, another successful night."

"Oh yes, it was very good."

"I'm very happy for you."

She was tipsy. "Alex, you know about buildings, plumbing, electricity, that sort of things."

"Yes, Mam, that's what I do in my spare time. Don't tell anyone but my second job it is in the Bronx, plumbing, electricity. I am what you call a handyman."

"Two jobs?"

"You've got to work hard to live in this city."

"I'm looking at a building. Can I hire you to check it out?"

"You don't have to pay me. I do it as a favor. For you."

In her apartment, she poured a glass of wine and looked out on the city below. She stifled a chuckle and then giggled, just briefly and then broke out into uncontrollable laughter, loud and long. She threw herself into bed.

The new life had begun.

42.

Craig

———————•————————————•———————

S O, THIS WOMAN COMES INTO MY CELL. *I mean, she's the strangest woman I've ever met. Tall, nice breasts and black as can be. Can you believe it? She's a cop, a sexy cop, and she makes me an offer I can't refuse, and I'm thinkin' this is my day. But she wants me to fink out my mom. Now I may be a bad apple or whatever they call me, but I'm not about to give up my mother. Not that there's so much to say about her. I did tell her about the dog, but I had to say something to get out of that dump. And I don't mean the lockup. Jails are fine, 'specially in small towns where there's no one else around. The jailer is so lonely he talks to you non-stop. He slips me a pizza and a coke every once in a while. But I'm thinking it's time to skip town, ya' know, move on from that waitress who was OK, being nice and warm but she was getting too close for comfort. I don't like people to get close. I'd rather be by myself.*

So this Miss Williams, she gets me out. And I'm thinking the town is saying, "good riddance." They don't want me in their lockup, and they don't want me on their streets. Probably didn't like me fucking the town waitress, either. She tells me, the black woman does, to go say good-bye to Betty, and she waits by the car, and I go to see Betty and get my things and tell her I'm goin' away for a few days, and she just smiles, like she knows I'm lying, and she doesn't ask me to call or write, she just says, "you take care of yourself, Craig Boy, I think that lady will treat you right if you behave." And I don't know what that means at all.

We drive a long way, Miss Williams and me in this old Malibu, comfortable enough but how long can you stay in a Chevy without getting antsy? First night, we stopped in this place somewhere in the South, a cheap one, like a Motel 6 'cept it has no name, and I ask her if we are gonna share a bed, and she says, "what d'you think?" and I say well I can dream and she smacks me across the face real hard like it hurt for three days and says "you get the devil out of you right now, boy. You ain't messin' with some cheapie waitress." So we get separate rooms. I wait awhile and then head to the bar across the street, looks like a place to have a drink, relax, maybe get lucky. The music is that country shit. Some really fat guys are sittin' in the corner, drinkin' away and looking at me, and a couple of bikers are playing pool. So I'm having a beer with a whiskey chaser when my hair is pulled and I turn around and there she is and says in a quiet voice, "let's be gettin' home. What I tell you about the devil?"

Now the bikers see her and start comin' over, and she ignores them, and I just sit there, wonderin' what's gonna happen, and she grabs my arm real hard, I mean this chick doesn't know her strength. But as we head to the door, the bikers are standin' there and they ask her where she's goin? and she says, "Where I'm going is none of your business so please stand aside" but they just shimmied and shammied and said, don't be hostile, come have a drink and I'm thinkin' holy shit we're in for it now but she said, "I asked you nice, please let us through," and they still didn't move and just looked at her hostile-like, so she says, "you with the devil? 'Cause if you with the devil, I gotta know," and they break out laughin' and look around at the fat guys who are comin' over to watch, and they didn't see her pull out the can. She maced 'em like they were cockroaches in a bathroom. Like, she didn't just hit their eyes once. They put up their hands and yelled and she kept sprayin and then looked around at the fatties who pulled back. So we went back to our rooms and I said, "Holy shit, you really gave it to them," and all she said was, "don't use bad language, it ain't becomin'." I went back to my room and just stared at the ceilin'.

The next day we're driving and she looks real tired and I ask her if she didn't get much sleep, and she tells me to mind my own business. Then I ask her about the scar on her face and she says, "you don't ever listen, do you?" Then we stop at a

McDonalds. She bought a big Mac and a chocolate shake. I love those shakes. We sit there, she, sippin' her coffee and she asks me about how come I left home, and I'm beginning to like her, I mean, she's tough and she goes wherever she wants and boy is she pretty. Too bad she's so old, must be 30. Too bad she don't like young men, like Betty. So I say I wasn't quite sure why I left 'cept there was nothing in that town for me. Guys were bullying me, girls were laughing at me, and Bobby, my brother, everyone was looking at him as the big man, the guy who was gonna' make it. Well he sure did make it. I mean even Bobby, whenever I got caught drunk or fighting, he would just shake his head pitying like as if I was just no good. I didn't do good in school. I didn't go to class that much, and I got stoned a lot. Lot of kids were gettin' stoned though they were smarter than me, I guess. I wasn't getting laid, and there just wasn't anything or anyone, so I left.

So she asks, how did I get along with Mom and Dad and I say I felt bad I left the way I did, they being my parents, but I knew they didn't care. Seemed like they were always just tolerating me. Sure, they took me to counselors and tutors and even a shrink like I was sick or something. Then they started talking about sending me to a private school and I just thought, fuck that, I've had enough of school I might as well go and stop causing 'em trouble and Cindy, that's Miss Williams which is what I call her now, she thinks they cared although she really never knew them and she asks me how come I didn't write or call and I didn't say anything again and then she touches my hand, gently, and says she understands although I can't figure out how.

That night, we head to a nice place, Italian food, and I eat lots of pasta and she smiles as I wolf it down. People are looking at us. I don't know if it's the way I ate or that I'm with this beautiful babe, or that she's twice my age, or ya know, I'm white, she's black, and we're still in the South, I think around Atlanta, and she says she's sorry she slapped me when she did, that it wasn't right, but the devil takes hold of everyone every once in a while and you always have to be on watch, and I say that's OK, I've had worse, and I tell her about the guy in that town who beat me up for chattin' up his wife. And she laughs and says she hopes that's the worst thing that's ever happened to me since I left home. I don't say nothing 'cause what happens, happens, and no reason to share anything. Then she asks me if I thought my parents loved me. And I say I didn't really know. Did my mother have celebrations for me, like birthday parties, and I think for a while and I remember maybe when I was ten or eleven they had a party for me, but that was the last time. After all, Mom was hardly there. Sure, she made sure we had breakfast and dinner and drove us around but most of the time she was at the car shop, at some women's thing, or just sitting in the corner reading. They didn't do much celebrating, having to sell cars and everything, and she smiles and tells me that her Auntie made sure she had a birthday dinner with her favorite food every year even when she was grown until she died. I ask her what happened to her parents and she says they're long since gone and forgotten and I ask her if they're still alive and she says she didn't rightly know or care. Your parents are your parents and sometimes they forget, but her real mother was her Auntie who is now in heaven.

On the way north, we stop in Washington and look around at the President's house and it's the first time for either of us, and we both thought the city really pretty. We go to the Air and Space museum and I say I want to be a pilot and she says I can be whatever I want to be, like the TV ad, and I shake my head and say no, I just don't have it in me. Then she slaps my face, lightly, not like the last time, and tells me that I can make my own future and can do whatever I want. I just got to get the devil out of my system.

That night we eat really good pizza and she asks me about Ranger and if what I said was true back in the jail, and I say sure it was true, why would I lie and she says maybe I made it up to get out of jail, but I say no, it was true, and she asks me where the dog's buried and I tell her in the little woods off the golf course, and then did I know where my parents kept the gun and I start to say something and stop and shake my head and she apologizes and says that I shared enough with her and how she really enjoyed our trip together. I smile and I think, why didn't I ever have a mother like this?

43.

Ranger

———————•———————

A s Eleanor showered, she hummed one of those background tunes you hear in stores or elevators, like the "Shadow of Your Smile" or "Natural Woman." She stepped out and toweled herself off. She looked at her body, still slender, her breasts, still firm. She smiled.

The buzzer rang. "Miss Tibbett, there's a woman down here to see you. She says she knows you from your old town."

"From my old town? I don't think so, Alex."

"Tell her I'm a black woman. She'll know," the voice behind him said.

"You've got to be kidding me?"

"What's that?" the doorman said.

Eleanor sighed. "Show her up, show her up."

She opened the door and Cindy Williams strolled in and looked about. "Nice digs."

"Miss Williams?"

"Good to see you Mrs. White."

"I'm Tibbett, now."

"Tibbett?"

"My maiden name."

"So you killed off your name?"

Eleanor shook her head. "You still on my case? This is unbelievable. You either come to say what you want to say or get out."

"Mrs. Tibbett, or is it Miss Tibbett, I come all this way and you don't offer me a seat, maybe a cup of coffee?"

"I'm really sorry Miss Williams, but I have things to do, appointments to keep. You understand?"

"So you disappeared and started a new life?"

"Miss Williams, I don't want to be rude. . ."

"Yes, I know. You would never want to be rude."

"If there is anything.......".

"It's about your son."

"My son?"

Cindy Williams stared at her, playing with her. "Yes."

Eleanor looked confused. You talking about Bobby or Craig?"

"Craig."

"Craig?"

"Yes, Craig. Your son. I found him."

Eleanor paused and looked out the window. "I guess you should have a seat."

"Happy to," the Detective said. "You offering coffee?"

"Of course. How do you take it?"

"Black. I always take it black."

They sat quietly. "Must be a shock, Mrs. Tibbett."

"Yes, of course. How is he?"

"Fine or as fine as a drifting, homeless soul can be."

"And, where is he?"

"He's here. I got him in a hotel. He's probably watching a porno movie right now."

"Where'd you find him?"

"He got himself into trouble in Texas and they couldn't find you, you having run off and everything, and so I went down to get him out of jail. See, I'm not that bad."

What he'd do?"

"Nothing to cause any real heartache. Just a thing they do. "

"They?"

"People without family, suffering souls, or people afflicted by the devil."

"Is he all right?"

"Yes, I think so," Williams said. "Funny though, you haven't asked to see him. To help him out."

"No, I was getting to that."

"Maybe you were afraid he might have told me something you didn't want me to know."

"No. What would he tell you?"

"We had a long drive up from Texas. He's a good boy, your Craig, a bit confused but with a little loving and maybe church going, he'll turn out all right."

"Yes, well, you didn't go through what we went through."

"Yes. Kids are tough. They're like animals sometimes, wild and uncontrollable. Is that what happened with Ranger?"

"Ranger?"

"Yes, Ranger, the dog."

Eleanor looked at her. "I don't know any Ranger."

"Craig didn't bring home a stray dog?"

"Craig? No, of course not. He hated dogs. Hated all animals. What did he tell you?"

"He didn't bring home a stray and you didn't shoot and bury him?"

"Miss Williams either you have an incredible imagination or that boy has sold you a bill of goods. What'd ya give him for that story? I hope it wasn't too much."

"You tellin' me he lied?"

Eleanor smiled. "Lie? That boy never knew how to tell the truth. A dog never existed. It's a figment, something out of some book Craig read."

The detective said nothing. "So, let's see," Eleanor continued. "You went all the way to Texas. You bring him all the way here 'cause you think I shot a dog that never existed and then killed my husband everyone says is a suicide. You crazy?"

"Yeah, I know. People call me nuts 'cause I don't like the works of the devil. Still, I can sense evil, ya' know?"

"You are nuts."

"I can sense evil when one day someone tells me they've never used the gun 'cept for target practice and then I find out they shot a dog, not nicely, but as a vengeful act. I mean, I know some dogs have to be put down, I surely know that, but this Ranger, he seemed like a nice dog, loved your son, didn't he?"

Eleanor shook her head. "I can't believe it. You come here with false accusations. You've got some nerve."

"Maybe, but Craig did say a few things about you that fit."

"What's that?"

The detective stood to leave. "Never mind." She sipped. "You make good coffee, Eleanor. I bet you buy the high price gourmet stuff."

"So, are you going to let me see Craig?"

"Yeah, I was coming to that. He and I thought that you two should see each other without me."

"I think that's a great idea."

"I mean, he didn't know about his brother or his father."

"No, I would guess not. He never got hold of us."

"Or his Aunt Joan."

Eleanor tapped on the table. "So, you going to bring him to me?"

"No, I think it best you meet someplace neutral. He likes pizza. You mind eating a slice?"

44.

Pastor Wainwright

———————•———————

Pastor Wainwright sat beside Eleanor in a pew. "So there was no problem?"

"No, it was not easy but I think I did the right thing."

"I'm glad you called. That's why we're here to help, in good times and bad. We've had bad kids before and we know how to deal with them. Sounds like your Craig was not so bad, just a bit confused, needs some shaping up. I mean, we've had kids who have killed, raped, OD'd, you just won't believe what happens even in the best of families."

"Well. I'm very thankful."

"I always believe in tough love. We're the nation's bedrock and if our children cannot act in a civil way, where are we? Anyway, tell me, how did it go?"

"When I told him about his father and brother, he just smiled and said he knew, that woman told him."

"That woman?"

"The woman who found him and brought him to me. And then he said he thought I looked well and that I must be enjoying life, sarcastically I think."

"So he still is in revolt," the Pastor said.

"And then I said how sorry I was how things had turned out and that I was going to try to make things right, but he had to help me. I told him that I was willing to support him, but he had to promise to return to school, and he said he could do that and then I said I had a school for him in Connecticut, and he looked surprised and he thought that maybe he could go to school in New York and I agreed, but first he had to make sure he had grown up and I said this school was in a pretty spot, had horses and cattle, and he could spend his time thinking. And he laughed and said he had spent the last few years thinking but said he could do that. The school's like a jail, he said, with horses. And I was stern like you told me to be and said it was not a jail but an institution that if he did well, he could start all over and we could forget the past. Otherwise, he could walk out the door and I would never see him again."

"How did he take it?"

"He asked for another Coke, thought some, and said OK. And then I said there was one other part of the deal, that he could never see that woman again."

"That woman?"

"Yes that woman who brought him up from Texas. I don't know what was going on between the two of them, but it clearly was not healthy."

"Yes, that was the right thing to do."

"And he thought some more and asked what we were going to do until he went to school and I pointed to the black car sitting outside and I said he'd be leaving right away and that really shook him up and I asked him to write me, not to leave me wondering like he had before and he said he would and I asked him to promise and he did. And I walked him to the car."

She began to cry. "You've done the right thing, Eleanor."

"Oh, I hope so."

45.

Cindy Williams

"**T**HAT WOMAN IS HERE TO SEE YOU AGAIN, Miss Tibbett," Alex said on the intercom.

"The black woman," Cindy Williams said from behind.

"Give her the note I left, would you?"

"Oh yes,"

"Then send her away. And if she comes back, I'm not at home."

Williams opened the letter. It read:

Miss Williams, thank you so much for reuniting me with my son. You don't know how much it means to me. He has had a rough time of it. I hope you understand that Craig needs time to reflect and so we have made sure that he is in a good school, ready to resume his learning. I appreciate all you have done. I have no more need for your services. I enclose a check to cover any expenses you might have incurred.

Williams laughed. She looked at the $5,000 check. "The devil's money," and tore it up. "No chance of me going upstairs?" she said to the doorman.

"No, she left specific instructions not to be disturbed."

On a cool spring day in New England, a young man strutted from a black limo to a large Victorian house standing in the middle of a well-tended, green pasture. He looked about and spotted horses in the distance, watering at a pond. Wind whistled through the valley rustling the pines. A man stood at the door, put a hand on his shoulder and guided him in. The sign on the door said "Andover School for Boys."

46.

Alex

THE NEXT MORNING ELEANOR TOOK ALEX TO SEE THE BUILDING. They stopped at Cheppi's. You should have seen the looks. Esperanza, the blonde, sees Alex and looks at Cheppi, Cheppi sees Alex and looks at Eleanor, Esperanza looks at Eleanor, Cheppi looks at Eleanor. She smiles. "Hi, this is Alex, he works in my building downtown." The two men shake hands, Alex generously. Both men speak with accents, one Hispanic, the other Bosnian.

"What is that smell?" Cheppi asked.

Eleanor stared at him. "I don't notice it."

"You don't notice it? Smells like rotten potatoes."

"It is my smell," Alex said. "I have a problem, but it is not important."

"If you say so. So, what is it you do?" Cheppi asked skeptically.

"Me, I do a little of everything, plumbing, electricity. I am what you Americans call a Jack-of-All-Trades."

"Jack-of-all-trades?" Cheppi repeated. "He does everything, does he? Who is he?"

Eleanor said "I told you. He's sort of a friend. He helped me out when I had hard times. He's a good man, Cheppi. I'm taking him to check the building?"

"The building? Why do you do that? I told you I take care of everything."

"I know, Cheppi. I'm putting a lot of money into this. I need to have a second opinion. You don't mind, do you?" She smiled.

"I don't know."

"I am a cautious person. I am new to all this, you know that, and you know I trust you completely. I think we're developing a wonderful partnership." She touched his arm. "Please?"

Cheppi looked at the grill. "Yeah, OK. I suppose so. So, you want breakfast?"

"He makes great meals," she said to Alex. "I told you. He's wonderful. The usual for me."

"Just coffee for me," Alex ordered.

"Yes sir," Cheppi said, turning away. Esperanza sauntered over, "Yo te digo," she said quietly. "I told you she fuck you."

"Callate, mujer. Go feed Simon, will you? This is business"

"Si, puta business."

47.

Renovations

———————————

"NICE BUILDING," ALEX SAID LOOKING AT THE OUTSIDE. "Great view. But, how do you say it? This building is really old. It's got a lot of stuff that'll need to be done. They've redone the electricity?"

"Nothing," Cheppi said. "1920 crumbling copper wire. No paint in years. The slum lord wants the tenants out, but they're not leaving so he just let it rot. It's a mess."

They walked down the darkened halls. "Lots of leaks," Alex said, pointing at water marks on the ceiling. His odor filled the building.

"Yep, leaks all the time."

Alex turned to Eleanor. "Why you want this place? This not your style. You belong downtown."

"That's sweet, Alex."

"We don't need this guy, I told you," Cheppi said.

"Come on," Eleanor said. "I've got to know what I'm getting into."

"It stinks in here. I think I'll wait outside."

"Alex, look at this wood," she said.

"Needs work."

"It all needs work. Did you see the brick? We clean that off and it will really be something. We open up the walls, make floor-through apartments, take out the old windows, put in, how do you call them, large windows?'

"Bay."

"Yes, that's right. Bay windows. What a view! What do you think?"

"Lots of money."

"I know. It's a gamble, but I think it might work. It would be exciting for us."

"Us?"

"Sure. I'll need your help. When you're free, of course. We'll negotiate some salary."

"I don't want salary. I will help for free."

48.

Rent Control

———————————•———————————

THERE ARE THOSE WHO MIGHT WONDER how Cheppi got the tenants out. After all, the law is on their side, this being rent-control and all that. Residents have life-time rights to stay at good, low, affordable rents. It says so. In the law.

In the naked city there are laws and laws. Cheppi knew the drill. With a little cash up front, he offered tenants places uptown, buildings that had been empty for some time, and had trouble attracting renters. Sure, they had issues, broken elevators, leaking pipes, and druggies hanging out on the corner, but all that would be fixed, he promised. He put some paint in the lobby and hired a couple of security guards. At least for a few months. He'd throw in some cash as an incentive, 10G each, he told them. "Take the deal now or it's going away, and yeah, didn't I mention three months' free rent."

If there was any hesitation or resistance, a small fire outside an apartment. Then, a couple of drug dealers began to hang out in the lobby, talking nice-like to the kids. A break-in down the hall, an electricity outage, no heat? In thirty days, the building was empty. "Clean," as they say.

Did Eleanor know? Maybe yes, maybe no. After all, it was Cheppi's idea to have the tenants removed. "They're being given free rent, a free move, some cash," he said. "They'll be happy." Cheppi would do anything to please her.

Was she naïve? Would she have cared? A business woman, for that is what she had been, and a woman whose life had been one of successive tragedies, had a vision. How hard was she? How hard had life made her?

She called Trepin. "You have an interesting fellow there," Trepin said. "If I did what he did, I'd be out of business."

49.

Dominoes

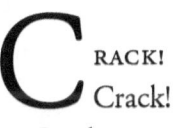

CRACK!
Crack!
Crack!

Four old men sat around a card table, slapping black and white dominoes, one after another. Each slap like a rifle crack echoed down the street. In rapid-fire puertoquieno, they slapped and talked, slapped and talked. They watched the elms in the park and the slow drifting river. Pretty girls walked by and they flirted.

Hour after hour they played, each Crack announcing their presence in the world until no pieces were left. And then the game began again, the tiles were jumbled and redistributed.

If you asked the *barrio,* they'd say these old men had been there forever, morning to night, laughing and yelling, swilling beer, arguing politics, , recalling golden days, girls they had laid, los Mets, and the promise that sometime in the future, they would return to la Isla.

They watched as the building across the street was laid bare, mumbling "Malo" "Que problema!" "Quien sabe que pasara."

"It is progreso." Crack!

"Que progreso? Getting rid of los pobres?" Crack!

"You can't stop it."

 "Mierda. This is not right."

"It is progreso, I tell you."

"Nada a ser. Nothing to be done. You goin' to keep playin' maricon, or what?"

"There is always something to be done. This is our place. Our barrio." Crack!

"Our *barrio?* Don't fuck with me. We may have been born here and we're certainly gonna die here, but it ain't our *barrio.* Crack!

"Seems like it." Crack!

"Just cause we've been sitting here watching chicas all our lives, don't mean it's our place. Tu no sabes from where you come?"

"Chinga, this is our tierra. We live here. They can't take it from us."

"Yep, I bet the Indios said that too. Do you think the Indios played dominos?"

"Maybe they did."

"I doubt it. Whose turn is it?"

Crack! "Yeah, los Indios too dumb to play."

And what about the Dutch." Crack!

"What Dutch?" Crack!

"You estupido or something?" Crack!

"No Dutch here," Crack!

"Yeah they were here. Then the English, then quien sabe cuantos blancos, Irish, Germans, Judios." Crack!

"And now los dominicanos" Crack!

"Yeah, but they our raza." Crack!

"Seems to me some time ago you called our raza vagos, lazy good-for-nothings."

"That still don't give 'em the right to push us out." Crack!

"You call La Raza when it suits you, chingado."

"So this is not our land?"

"Our Savior allowed us to come and play here. But it's not forever, amigo. It's temporary. Just like everything else. I gotta go pee"

"So you give up? You go to our Savior and that's that."

"This is fucking up the game. I'm going to pee."

50.

Salud, Pesos et Amor

—————————•—————————

"N O TRESPASSING" SIGNS WERE PASTED ON THE FRONT DOOR, and ground floor windows were boarded up. The building was laid bare in a month. The *barrio* could only wonder. Que pasa? Rumors spread of ghosts or disease or pushers or spies. Never, never in anyone's memory had anything like this occurred here.

The building's sale was concluded without problems. In a downtown office, lawyers chatted and gossiped. Eleanor and Cheppi sat in the back while the lawyer for the seller exchanged papers with the lawyer for the buyer and the lawyer for the title company and the lawyer for the banker and another lawyer who just oversaw it all, sat quietly. They signed and signed. Checks were exchanged and then keys. One hour and that was that. Handshakes around the table and congratulations to the new owner, little kisses on Eleanor's cheek and quiet, "good lucks." Attaché cases snapped closed with sharp cracks and the meeting was over.

"I've never seen so many fucking suits," Cheppi said.

"Me neither," said Eleanor.

"Come," said Cheppi.

"Where we going?" Eleanor responded.

They taxied to El Escorial. Dark brown, medieval walls. Discreet, quiet corners. Don Quixote and Spanish palaces on the walls. A Flamenco guitar played quietly in the background.

"I will order, yes?"

"Yes, please," she said.

"We'll have gambas al ajillo, shrimp in garlic sauce. Some ceviche, clams in lime juice. Some wine, that OK?"

"Sounds wonderful."

"You know what they say about shellfish," Cheppi said

"What?"

"No, I better not."

"Go ahead." She touched his hand and quickly pulled it back."

"It's good for sex."

She looked straight at him, neither smiling nor frowning, but hiding the shock. "That's interesting," she said flatly.

"I want to tell you about me," Cheppi said. "I hope I won't bore you."

"No, please, go ahead. I'd like to know."

"You tell me if I bore you."

"Please."

"I was in my late teens. We were living in La Dominicana, what you call the Dominican Republic. In the Caribbean."

"I know."

"Yes, of course, you are educated. Many people do not. Anyway, we live in a beautiful, little fishing town called Samana. On a bay. My grandfather, he was a fisherman and he taught me how to fish. We loved the sea. It was a good life. The men worked hard and we didn't have much, but we were happy. We had our families and our friends."

"And your mother? And father?"

"My father, I don't know. I was raised by my mother and grandparents. That never bothered me. My grandfather was a good man, and he was a father to me. He was not that old. A strong man. Full of vigor."

"We were happy then. We had our families and our dignity. We lived in small houses near the water. It was so beautiful, with palm trees, beaches, and warm breezes. Que paradiso!"

"Sounds wonderful."

"So one day, out of the blue, El Alcalde, the Mayor, calls us for a big meeting. And he announces that we have to leave our homes because the government was going to build hotels. Just like that. He said it was for the national good. That it would create jobs. That we would have nice modern apartment houses with good plumbing, better sanitary conditions, you know? And we would all have jobs. He said everyone would be happy, that the World Bank was giving us the money to do this. That the country would be rich."

"That's terrible. Didn't you object? Didn't you call your Congressman?"

"Congressman, hue puta. In those days, you raised your hand, you lose your hand. So this old fat General, brother-in-law of the President, his name is Vargas, comes and gives us a day to pack our things and move into tents. Then, armored cars rolled in, followed by bulldozers, big fucking machines,"

"You should have seen it. The machines tore down a forest of palm trees, pulling them up by their roots as if there was nothing holding them. They flattened the land into sand and dust."

He stared straight ahead. An eye twitched. "So we don't like this. We Dominicans don't like to be pushed around? Vargas, he had a rep for torture and making people disappear, but this was too much. They were taking our homes! So me and my friends, we were teenagers, we went to the army encampment where we were supposed to live in tents until they built our new hue puta apartment houses. It was an ugly place. The trees were gone. All sand. Tents. Portable toilets. Mosquitos all about.

He stopped and drank some wine.

"What did you do?"

"These soldiers, most of 'em were campesinos, so they were pretty useless, far from their families and all that, so they drank and drank, and when they slept nothing bothered them. So we doused all the tents with petrol and yelled at the top of our lungs 'Fuego! Fuego!' You know, fire, fire."

"You should have seen it, Eleanor." He laughed. "Those maricons, they didn't like it one bit. We really put it to them."

"Anyone hurt?"

"Nah, a few scratches. A couple of people got burned running back in to get their stuff but no matter. We didn't kill anybody but boy oh boy was that a fire! You could see it for miles."

"Those maricons were not happy. The next day, fat Vargas marched into town with a platoon of soldiers. He called everyone into the streets and said that if anything else happened, he would personally line up and shoot every man. And if he'd figure out who set the fire, they would go away for a long time. Then, he declared that all men over the age of 16 were to work building the hotels. No pay until all damages were paid up, you know. He said that all men should report the next morning. Any man who didn't would be shot. And that's what happened, worked them like slaves."

"Them? What about you?"

"My grandpapi was a smart man. He knew I was involved, smelled it on my clothes. They all knew, all my friends' folks. But he also knew that people would turn against me, getting them to work without pay. He said to us that we had no choice. So that night, we sneaked to the port where his boat was, got on and chugged our way to the USA."

He had tears in his eyes. Eleanor took his hand. "So he saved your life?"

"Yes, and we came here. I never saw him again."

"I'm so sorry," she said.

"Why? Not your fault. You bring me happiness."

They ate quietly. "Now we go to celebrate," he said.

"I thought this was the celebration."

"No, this was dinner."

"So where are we going?"

Where else? Your new digs."

"What? There's nothing there."

"We can fix that."

They taxied to the empty building.

Across the street, the domino players stopped and looked. "Quienes son?"

"Muy estrano. Very strange."

"Drogas, I think."

"No se hace estupido. Amorosos. Lovers"

"I don't know, these times are getting very strange. Just the other day I saw two women making out in the park."

"Let's play."

"Yes, let's play." Crack!

Cheppi and Eleanor entered the dark building. Cheppi turned on a flashlight. Scrambling noises.

"What?" Eleanor said. She moved closer towards Cheppi.

"Ratones, Rats. Don't worry, they are more afraid of us."

Hand in hand they climbed the dark stairs to the top floor. "I wish they hadn't turned off the electricity," she said.

"Don't worry. We have all the light we need." The sun shone through the window reflecting wine glasses and two candles on the table beneath.

"What is this?" Eleanor said.

"A surprise," Cheppi said. He lighted the candles and pulled out a bottle of Dom Perignon from a cooler. "Una fiesta, para la nueva propietaria."

"Oh Cheppi, how sweet."

He popped the cork. "Come," he said, "to see your river." He led her to the window and the scene below, the street, the domino players, the park and the river gliding by,

"Salud, Pesos et Amor," he said. Their glasses touched. Their eyes met. They sipped.

"What does that mean?"

"Health, money and love." He poured more. Their glasses touched again. Their eyes met. He pushed her glass aside. Their lips touched, first gently and then violently. Their bodies merged. He took her hand and led her into the bedroom to a canopy bed, filled with pillows.

"What?" she laughed.

"For my Goddess," he said.

He picked her up and placed her on the bed, gently.

They kissed and kissed, their hands moved, entwined, their legs crossed, and their bodies merged.

He entered her. First a moan, then a scream, then a loud scream, like a maiden, her first time. "You all right?" he whispered.

"Shh, shh. Don't say anything. I am very all right." She trembled.

"Tranquillo," he said quietly. "Tranquillo."

She plunged her face into the pillow. Tears flowed in anguished joy. She sobbed, on and on.

"Eleanor?" he said.

Sobs like waves crashing on the shore over and over. In the distance the sound of Cracks, like thunder, announcing change.

51.

Passion

————————•————————

PASSION. HOW DOES IT CHANGE OUR LIVES? Youthful passion sets us on fire, leads us in directions we never thought possible, good or bad, marriage, children, disastrous relationships, or lifelong love.

Middle-aged passion is a different story, isn't it? A tale of, "I never thought this would happen to me? What, me? A mature woman? What have I become?" Or, rather, "what have I been missing?" In Eleanor's case, the revelation in that bare apartment was one more step in regeneration.

Like an adolescent, her values were tossed, jumbled and reassembled. The anger from the past was still there surely, buried deep, even if a new soul emerged into the urban life of wheeling and dealing and meetings and deals and soirees and manipulations and yes, basic, raw sex.

In the early morning, he moved and whispered, "I have to go."

She held him tightly.

"I have to go to work. Open the place."

"Don't," she said. Can't someone else?"

"No. This is my place. I have to be there. I'm sorry."

"What about Esperanza?" she whispered.

"She can't run the place by herself."

"That's not what I mean."

He looked at her and touched her face. "Don't worry about Esperanza. She is not a problem."

Eleanor said nothing. How could she? Passion. Sin. Love in a vacant building. Her body renewed, fulfilled and content.

After he left, she rose and looked out upon the slow, drifting river below. A tug guided a flat oil tanker upriver. Flotsam bobbed up and down. Was it garbage, driftwood, or an animal? Did she sink into slumber? Was she dreaming?

Her eyes opened, and she shook her head in that reverie we all suffer. "How did I come to this? Is this really happening? What's going on?" She downed the last champagne, and went to the bathroom to wash. No water.

Slowly, in the dark, she made her way down the stairs and out to the morning light. She crossed to the park.

The domino players stopped. "Buenos dias, Senora," one said.

"Hello," she responded.

"Duerme bien?"

"Excuse me."

"Did you sleep well?"

"Oh yes. Very well. Thank you."

She moved on. One player mumbled "Puta." Whore.

"No me jodas, hombre," another responded, "es una diosa, una goddess."

"Como sabes."

"Una vez. Yo tenia una diosa." I had a goddess once. And it was wonderful.

"Maricon, the only diosa you ever fucked was your perro."

"Nope, not true. Before I came here. Back in the islands, there were diosas."

The old men laughed. "Chinga, let's play."

52.

Renovation

———————•————————————•———————

THE BUILDING WAS A MESS, broken pipes, leaking windows, vermin, dank odors from rot and mold, cracked formica and scarred walls. Hell on the Hudson. But Eleanor saw the value of an old brick structure overlooking the river. It was instinct, pure and simple.

Dan Trepin brought in Harry Kemp of Salisbury Architects, the famed English group with a rep in the emerging global real estate market, money flowing from Russia, Arabia, Asia and Latin America, west to east and east to west. It was Salisbury who worked with the Indians on the Trepin Goa Casino.

He surveyed the site. He walked along the rear alley, past overturned trash cans, strewn flat tires and beer empties. A rat crossed his path. He ignored it. He climbed to the roof and saw the park in front and the river in the distance. He looked out at the surrounding neighborhood. He checked the exterior bricks and the interior structure. He was there for less than an hour.

Trepin and Eleanor sat opposite Kemp. He spoke in a tight British accent. "Dan," he smiled. "You testing me?"

"Nope, I want your honest opinion and want Mrs. Tibbett to hear it all."

"I'm not going to write a report. I'll make it simple. Buy the block. Tear it all down. Put up a thirty-story co-op, like you do downtown."

"That's not going to happen. The location sucks. And we'd never get approval."

"What more can I say? You have a nice building, mam, maybe 100 years ago but, I mean, if you want, redo the interior, fix it up, but you don't need us, you just need a contractor, painter, electrician and plumber."

"That's what I told the lady," Trepin said. "But thanks for the help. I appreciate it." Trepin began to rise.

"You said something interesting," Eleanor said. They looked at her.

"Something interesting?" the Englishman said.

"Yes, about buying the block."

Kemp looked at Trepin. They broke out laughing. "Shit, I think I need a drink," Trepin said.

"In the old days," Eleanor said, "back in the small towns and cities in the Midwest, there were always alleyways where cars were parked and things stored. There was even a garden. It was a place neighbors congregated. The block was a neighborhood."

"Yeah," Trepin mumbled. "The old days were the old days."

She said. "No, listen. Four apartment houses on the block, all with river views, alleyway in the back and garages, all connected. Has possibilities, don't you think?"

"Eleanor," Trepin said, "I think we've reached the end of the line. One building was easy. A one-off."

"She's right," Kemp said.

"What the fuck?" Trepin stared at him.

"The woman's absolutely right. One building, isn't worth it and it would stand alone. If we can get hold of the whole block, the apartments, the garages and the alleys, we can redo the lot, pretty cheap, gut the shells, put in floor-throughs, give people parking and storage, maybe put up a gym with a pool and gate the whole place."

"Gate?" Eleanor asked.

"Yep, "the Englishman said. "A gated community. Solves the problem of security. Make a high-end residence. A view of the river. Drive in. Drive out."

"I don't think so," she said.

"If it works," the Englishman said, "it will transform the neighborhood.

Everybody will win."

Trepin drank his whiskey. "Is this why I bring you here? What the fuck. You dreaming?"

"Just throwing ideas around," the Englishman said winking at Eleanor. "What's the argument against it?"

"I don't get involved in crap real estate. That's the argument against it."

"You don't have to be involved, Dan," Eleanor said. "You did say that getting a mortgage was a piece of cake."

"Yeah, for one building." His voice rose. "One fucking building. A couple of million. Bubkis. But the price just went up five or six-fold. You putting in a fucking gym and a gate. Who are you, Donald Trump?"

"Can you draw up some plans easily," she asked Kemp.

"Wait a second," Trepin said. "I ain't here? Did you hear what I just said?"

"Please Dan, let's try," she said. "We draw up plans. I'll pay. We talk to the banks. Just think, clean, safe buildings, jewels to serve as a model for the neighborhood, as a foundation for new growth."

Trepin looked up at the ceiling. "Where the fuck did this woman come from? What did I do? Jeessus. Listen babe, you're getting way ahead of yourself."

"You know," Kemp said, "our Russian friends keep looking for quiet places to stow their cash without making too much noise. Could work."

"Shit! Trepin stood up and paced the room. "Shit. Shit. Shit."

"They've been pushing, and we do owe them for that St Petersburg job."

"If you don't want. . ." Eleanor said.

"If you don't want, if you don't want," Trepin mocked her. "Shit. Shit. What the fuck have I done to deserve this?"

"Kemp and I will work on this," she said. "We'll try to keep you out of this."

"Out of this? I'm in up to my fucking neck. I've got half of City Hall working for you." He paced back and forth and stared out at the harbor. He turned, "OK. Just a trial balloon. Rough sketches. Nothing expensive."

"I understand, Dan," she said.

"I'll check with our friends in the Building Department. But babe, you owe me dinner. No, bullshit, you owe me more than dinner, you owe me a night on the town.

53.

Percentages

———————————•———————————

WE KNOW THE HISTORY OF THE ROBBER BARONS, the railroad
tycoons, and the real estate moguls. It all seems so happenstance,
so lucky. A Scottish immigrant comes to America as a penniless kid and builds
a steel empire and becomes the richest man in America. A Seattle banker's son
gets hold of some patents, makes the right deal, and builds the world's largest
software company. It doesn't "just happen," but there are always the fates and
the timing.

Looking back, we don't wonder at her success. Eleanor could have opened a
tea shop, and it would have done well. But it was the convergence of the orbs,
the bankers, lawyers, architects, and the diner owner. What is it that Andrew
Carnegie said? Every act you have ever performed since the day you were born
was performed because you wanted something.

Trepin was no fool. He may not have liked playing with "junk" apartment
houses, but the idea of developing a hidden neighborhood, even "uptown," had
its benefits. In real estate, if you're not developing, you lose your edge and the
banks go elsewhere. Cheap land and no competition turned him on. Kemp
drew the preliminary plans showing beautifully renovated buildings overlooking

the city on a tree lined boulevard and in a secure spot. Not on Park or Fifth or Madison where the *uber* live. Not in Soho for the X-generation. A place for the adventuresome set with money. Young marrieds. Artists. Those with a dream and little cash. For Trepin, this was an opening close to home, not in India or Russia but just uptown. And Trepin had a nose for opportunities.

Eleanor was the key. She had the contact in the neighborhood, and she would be the one to run the deal, Trepin understood. But, looking back, you've got to wonder why he gave her so much of the "pie." The contracts drawn by his own attorneys gave Trepin upfront fees and 25% of the corporation, the church got 10%, and Eleanor 51% with the rest spread between Russian financiers and friends in City Hall. Was he fearful of a backlash, of the Trepin name causing some radical Latino group to bring down the project?

Or was he smitten with the woman? Like a daughter? Or rather, like a lover? Men of a certain age do crazy things for love, and Trepin was a man alone, sitting high above the city in his luxury suite looking in one direction at his father and the other at the empty sky. You know the saying: "you don't know why people do what they do. They just do."

"So you want to do real estate, honey," Trepin said. "You gonna have to learn fast. I'm bringing in Galloway, my lawyer."

"Whatever you say, Dan."

"This is going to be your company. You get majority interest. I take my money in points, interest and, if it happens, some management fees."

"That's very generous."

"Just business, babe. Just business. You got skin in the game, you play hard and I want all your skin in this game. I want Dave Galloway on the Board. He's my lawyer and he'll handle all the nuts and bolts. We're gonna have to pay him."

"Whatever you say," she repeated.

"I'll handle the Russkis. I don't want you near them. And the banks, that will be my business."

"Sure."

"My people will do the work, the architects, the contractors, the buildings. All that shit."

"OK," she said. "But I've got a guy who I want on the building end of it."

"You got a guy?"

"Yeah, he does a little renovation here and there. But he works with those old buildings. And I trust him."

"Honey, we've been doing this for a long time."

"I know, I'd just like to have my guy watching things. As you say, 'skin in the game.' If you don't mind, Dan."

He laughed. "OK. OK. You get your guy. But your uptown pals come out of your end. You want to give them commissions, bonuses, salaries, that's your call. And you're in charge."

"That's a big responsibility."

"You're in charge and I trust you, I think."

"Sure."

"So I got this place, in the Hamptons. I think you'd like it."

She looked askance.

"I don't mean anything by it. It's where I do business. Away from the noise. We'll have the first board meeting out there. You OK with that?"

She paused. "Just me?"

Trepin laughed. "Babe, if I wanted just you, I wouldn't be bringing out a dozen old men."

"I guess."

"OK, now let's get to business. I want you to talk to the Spanish guy you know, what's his name?"

"Cheppi."

"Yeah, let's get him working on those other buildings."

54.

The Deal

———•———————•———

THEY MET AT THE ESCORIAL, Cheppi spotting her in the corner.

"Ah, a lovers' meeting," he said, embracing her. Then, he saw the man in the corner. Tie and Jacket. "Guess the cat's out of the bag," he said, laughing.

"This is Dave Galloway, my attorney," she said.

"Your attorney," he mocked. "So la chica brings in a suit?"

Galloway rose to shake his hand. "Pleased to meet you."

Cheppi stared at her like a deer in headlights. "And so?"

She said, "honey, we've been doing some thinking."

"We?"

"The people downtown. We've had some ideas."

"We?" he repeated, irritably.

"I think you'll like where we're heading."

"Oh really. You Anglos know what we spics like?"

"Before we go on," Galloway said, "what is being said here is strictly confidential. If you stay, you can't reveal this to anyone. That is why I am here."

He stared angrily at Eleanor "Well then, maybe I'll just go and you can stay with your new boyfriend. Confidentiality! What's this bullshit? I thought the deal was ours?"

"Cheppi, don't," Eleanor pleaded. "Just hear me out. Please."

He hesitated, then waved for a drink.

"We're thinking of buying the whole block."

"The whole block?"

"Yes. And if that's successful, move on to other places in the area."

"You gonna bring in the tanks and guns and cops and drive us out?"

"No," Eleanor said. "Nothing like that. We're going to find other places for the people and we're going to redo the whole block. If that works, we'll move on."

"Where have I heard this before?"

"If I can say something," Galloway said. "This is going to happen. It is either going to be us or someone else. You know that."

"Do I?"

"Look at the city," Galloway said. "Gentrification all over. People are finding new and different places to live. Look at Harlem. A few years ago, no whites would set foot there. Now, they're raising their kids in the streets. This neighborhood just seems right. You've already got artists and musicians all over the neighborhood. They're the first wave. And they have no money. We want to bring in the money, increase the value."

Cheppi looked at Eleanor. "We buy one little building, and now we gonna white out the 'hood?"

"No Cheppi," Eleanor said. "This just makes sense. We take over the block of buildings, redo them, sell them as condos and bring in new, young and . . ."

"White."

"White or yellow or brown, makes no difference."

"And you're asking me to lead the charge."

Galloway leaned forward and pointed his finger. "You'll profit, all the merchants will make money and if we do this right, even the current tenants will be given better places to live."

"Fucking white knights, you are." He stared at Eleanor.

"We've spoken to Carmela Chan," Galloway said. "She's on board."

"That Chink would sell her mother for a commission."

"That's what capitalism is all about," Galloway said, staring.

"Where'd you find this maricon," Cheppi looked at Eleanor.

"OK. OK," Galloway said, rising. "I've said my piece. You got your confidentiality warning. I've done my job. I'll move on."

"You do that," Cheppi said. "You do that."

"Cheppi," Eleanor asked, why are you being like this?"

"Just like the old days."

"No!"

"This is like the old days back home in the DR. You have a beautiful home and *barrio* and friends and neighbors and they bring in the guns to throw you out."

"It's not like that. We're being responsible. No guns."

"No guns? How'd you think we'll get rid of those people in those buildings? With candy? We don't use guns but they've got no choice."

She nodded. "OK, OK, but this is for both of us."

"Fuck you."

"Please. I'm not trying to trick you. It's the way of the world and as Dave said, it's going to happen."

Cheppi took a drink and stood up. "I'll be back." He marched outside, lit a cigarette and paced up and down, past the pawn shop and dollar store to the corner bank. An old woman stumbled down the block, carrying groceries. "Hey, mama, te ayudo?" He put out his hand.

She pulled back in fear "No me molesta."

"Jus' tryin' to help."

"Yeah, where were you when I was robbed last week by those kids? And last month. You keep away. I can take care of myself."

"Lo siento, mama. I am really sorry. Jus tryin' to help."

"You do what you do and me, I do what I do."

"Yeah, OK. OK."

He returned to the table and sat beside her. "You have to trust me," Eleanor said.

"Why? You take advantage of a dumb Latino and then you run downtown to your own kind and make your deals.'

"No, that's not true. They aren't my kind any more than . . ."

"Then I'm not your kind."

She sobbed. "I'm all by myself in this town. These people helped me. You helped me. You may have saved me. I don't know. Before I met you I was so adrift, so lost."

He laughed. "So now you found. . ."

"It's like a wind pushing me forward and I'm just doing what," she hesitated and sobbed, "what just seems to be falling into my hands. My life, you, these people, the building, I don't know why I'm doing it, I'm just doing it."

"Yeah, you doing it, not we doing it."

She grew angry. "Wait a minute. You've got your life, your restaurant, your wife and who knows what else."

"My wife?"

"That woman in the diner."

"Esperanza? She not my wife."

"No?"

"I'm not married."

"You're not married?"

"That's what I said."

"I thought."

"I know what you thought. Esperanza, she thinks she owns me, but she doesn't. Yeah, we've been together a few years but,"

"A few years?"

"Yeah, a bunch of years."

"So she's your girlfriend?"

Cheppi paused and drank. He hit her hand. "Wait a minute, we talking about you or me?"

She struck back "We're talking about us. What else is this about?"

He pulled her tight. They kissed, violently at first and then slowly, a peck on one cheek and then another.

"When you talk about you people going off and making decisions," Cheppi said, "I just thought you meant you, not us."

"We can do this together. This will work. You can leave your diner and . . ."

"I don't want to leave my diner. That is my life."

"OK. OK. But we can really do something positive. Change the neighborhood. Make it safer. Bring some money into it."

"Whiter."

"Yes, whiter, but not exclusively."

"Yeah, we'll see."

"Cheppi, I'm white. I'm not allowed?"

"You don't understand and you'll never understand. We Latinos have to protect our own. We've been fucked over so many times."

"The way Latino slum lords protect their own?"

"They're hijos de putas, whores."

"So Latino slumlords are OK," she said, but me, I'm white and want to spruce up the buildings and I'm the enemy."

'We have to protect what is ours. That's for sure."

"And don't you think you can protect your own with more money?"

He nodded. "Perhaps."

"This is what we thought. You tell me what you think. We take over the block and renovate it. Make it clean as a whistle. Sell the units as condos and then move on to other places. What do you think?"

"And who is going to pay for this?"

"That's what downtown is for. The suits, as you say."

He thought for a moment. 'And where do I fit in?"

"You'll run my side of the company. You'll get paid and get a commission. Carmela is being brought in to find and assess other properties. That's if you're OK with that."

"Yeah, yeah, she's OK."

She kissed him on the cheek. "What are the words you use? Eeeo de pootah?"

"Hijo de puta. Son of a whore. Son of a bitch."

"So you're a hijo de puta?"

"I've been called worse."

55.

The Hamptons

———•————————————————•———

S O THE LIMO COMES AND TAKES US *to a launch pad and this little old guy is waiting for us and he takes Mrs. Tibbett by the hand and leads her to the copter. He makes sure he sits next to her, pushing me aside. The copter takes off and angles over the river, throwing me to the door like I'm a piece of loose luggage. I'm hanging on for life. The old guy grabs Mrs. Tibbett to stop her from falling into me. And I'm here for protection or that is what she says, so I look at her, but she doesn't seem to mind the old guy grabbing her. He opens the window and it is god-awful cold but he has to do it to get rid of my odor and what is that smell he asks the pilot, but the guy says nothing and keeps flying. We cross over the city, the people below shrink but then we descend fast and the old guy points down to buildings. "That one is mine, that hotel, that penthouse, those co-ops," and he goes on and on as if he owns the whole town. He points at some housing projects and laughs about "that piece of shit," whatever that means, and then says he wants to buy land below the United Nations. The United Nations? Who is this guy?*

We fly to the ocean and I look way out at the deep blue, with little white specks here and there, fishing boats and tugs and sailboats and I've never been in a copter but the scene is so beautiful tears come to my eyes which I hide 'cause I don't want anyone to see and then we fly for maybe a half hour or so and we set down right next to a beach. There's a bright red Ferrari waiting and so I head to it, but some big fellow, a tough guy in pressed blue shorts and a white shirt, takes my elbow and pushes me to a Lexus. The old guy leads Mrs. Tibbett to the Ferrari, and they disappear like a bat out of hell. We follow them to the largest house I've ever seen, must have 30 or 40 rooms, and the place is filled with people talking loudly, beautiful women in white, flowing gowns and men in tuxedos and all sorts of help taking our bags and showing us our rooms. Mrs. Tibbett asks me how I'm doing, and I tell her I don't really know and she says that she has the same feeling and ain't it weird but I really don't know what I'm doing in this place but she asks if I could come with her for, like protection, not serious protection but something called safety in numbers and I don't know what she means but I love Mrs. Tibbett and she needs all the help she can get being all alone, and that's what I do, help, I open doors, I fix pipes, hail taxis, I carry bags. So I agree.

She suggests I go take a shower and gives me eau de cologne and says I should sprinkle myself with it and I know what she's trying to do, but it isn't going to work. It never works. I've got this stink that is me and will never leave me until I die. My room is as clean and new and bright as anything I've ever seen, better than any hotel and the bed is so soft, I mean I could just lay there for hours and there's a view of that blue sea and a closet full of swimming trunks of all sizes and I'm think how thoughtful that is. I take a shower and scrub my skin as hard as I can and toss that perfume all over myself but nothing's going to help. I know. She knocks on my door and asks me to escort her downstairs where a piano is playing and people are milling about, laughing loudly, sipping champagne in narrow glasses. A waiter offers me a glass but I don't like that stuff, it gives me a headache, so I ask for a vodka and he says yes sir and asks me if Stolichnaya will do and I'm thinking anything will do and I say, yeah, but make it a double and he asks if I want a slice of lime or mint and I say whatever he thinks. So he bows and I'm thinking whatthefuck, why is he bowing to me? Then this pretty young thing, she could have been my sister 'cept my sister is dead, comes to me with a tray, "May I offer you some Swedish meatballs," and I'm really hungry so I pick up three or four and then she hands me a napkin and then another girl comes and smiles at me and offers shrimp with bacon wrapped all around it, and why would they put bacon on shrimp and then another girl comes with something else and I notice that lots of people are just waving them away but that's OK since I'm really hungry, and I can see the little girls with the trays like me because they keep looking in my direction and smile, and I clean their trays so they can go off for more.

Mrs. Tibbett takes me to the little guy. He says he is pleased to work with me although it doesn't seem like he means it. I mean, he keeps looking about rather than at me but he tells me to take good care of Mrs. Tibbett, that she tells him that I'm her bodyguard, and he says he's sure I'll do a good job but if I don't, he's got friends, and he laughs in this really loud and disgusting way and punches me in the arm, and I say I'll do my best sir thinking his friends couldn't touch me if they were like him. He says to me, "Alex, don't call me sir, just Dan. After all we're gonna work together on this project" and I don't know what he's talking about and Mrs. Tibbett whispers to me, "I'll tell you later. Really good news. I think you'll like it" and I'm thinking beautiful blonde women, shrimp, bacon, vodka with lime, piano music and deep blue water and what's not to like? But the talk is about politics and banks and gold and oil and stuff and I'm not too much for all that. I'm just happy to be here in this country and anything they do is OK by me. I down my drink and I find that guy who bowed to me and got another vodka and Mrs. Tibbett touches my elbow and asks if I would sit next to her at dinner but I say I think I've had too much to drink, that I'm really not hungry, and I think I'll go for a walk, and she says she understands.

So I grab another drink and go to my room and put on the trunks and head to the ocean. The water is chilly, much colder than the Adriatic but the waves are soft, slight and rolling, only once in a while surging up to slap me in the face to tell me they're there, and I shouldn't get too confident, and I swim like I used to in the Adriatic when we all went for vacation back before the troubles, and I keep swimming and my mind wanders, I don't know why but it does, and I'm back hiding in the barn, under the potatoes, waiting for the bad men to leave like my ma told me to do and me hearing the screams and shootings and yelling and just lying there holding a skinny knife for peeling potatoes and stuff, and I'm peeing and shitting all over myself and rats scurrying around sniffing at my sweat and roaches crawling on my skin and when I get the chance I grab a potato or two but I make sure I'm always hidden but it is so hot that I sweat and sweat and the odor is unbearable. I wait for things to calm down and try to remember everything my ma told me, like I wait a whole day until I hear from her or if I hear nothing to wait another day for silence and I hear those guys come into the barn and look around and grab some potatoes and they're laughing and sitting on the pile and the pile shifts and I see a couple of them with their Kalashnikovs dangling from their side and I'm holding that knife so if they find me at least I'll take one of 'em out but they leave and I'm trembling and peeing some more and I must have been there three days when finally there was quiet, real quiet as if the world had come to an end. So I crawled out, my body covered with beetles and ants and shit and grime and I smell my own stink. I see the burnt shell of my house and no one is around. I hear nothing. Absolutely nothing. No mother. No sister. No brothers. Nothing. So I go the stream and throw myself in and wash as best possible, but the stink is still there. I hear a lone jeep approaching. I creep up the river bank and see this guy pee into the dark burnt ash of what was my house and family and I may be young but I know how to butcher pigs so I slice him good, like killing a pig for Christmas. I grab his jeep and drive off to Slovenia.

It's always there, the fear, even now as I swim in the cool water and a wave comes and smacks me turning me over once or twice and I take a little water and cough, but it's no big deal. I can't believe I am where I am after all these years and everything that's gone on and I bless my God and this country and these people and Mrs. Tibbett but what am I doing here? What is going on? I should not be here. I should be dead. I shiver and I want those memories to disappear with the smell. The smell's a problem, I know, just like the fear, always there, but the memories, they keep coming back at the strangest times. I walk unsteadily onto the beach, the water kicking at my shins and see the big house with all its lights and there is Mrs. Tibbett standing high on the deck alone, looking so beautiful, like a goddess, and she waves to me and I wave back and fall onto the sand, exhausted.

56.

Tibbett Enterprises

•————————————————•

SHE RETURNED TO THE PARTY. A small band played light bossa nova while two couples danced before them. And then, a trumpet blared, the party quieted and Dan Trepin moved to the front.

"I want to thank you all for coming. It's a great party, isn't it?"

The group applauded. "You're the best, Dan," a slurred voice yelled.

"Yeah, well you're fired, how the fuck you like that?"

The crowd tittered.

"I just want to make a brief announcement and then all you souses can raid my cognac and Havanas. For those of you who have not had the treat, I want to introduce a dear, close friend, Mrs. Eleanor Tibbett." He waved to her to stand. She heard a muted chuckle from behind. "Mrs. Tibbett is my newest business associate. She is head of Tibbett Enterprises and will be focusing on developing new properties outside our areas of expertise."

"She has my complete trust. I want you to all understand that when Mrs. Tibbett speaks, she is speaking for me. Welcome, Eleanor." He came to her and led her to the center of the floor. A voice yelled "a toast." and the voices rang out "hear, hear."

"Why did you do this?" she whispered.

"Because it is necessary. If you are going to be respected, they need to know it."

"I am terribly embarrassed."

"You'll get over it."

"You should have told me."

"Babe, you gotta get used to this. I've got a lot of things to handle. Now, you're part of the team."

"You should have told me."

"Babe, look around you. You've got some of the richest people in the country toasting you. What more do you want?"

She looked at the small, aging man. He smiled at her lasciviously. "I, I don't know."

"This all could be yours, babe, you know that."

"You barely know me. And, I'm just not . . ."

"Shut up. Don't say anything. I may be old, a little nuts, rough around the edges and I may have made mistakes in my life, but I know what I want, and I always get what I want."

She pulled back violently. "I am not a piece of real estate."

"Eleanor., relax. I make offers all the time. They're turned down all the time. That's the way life is."

"You're sick."

"No. Not sick. Just trying to survive, like the rest of the world. You think all this makes me happy? I couldn't give a shit about this house, these people. I need you."

"No."

"No, what?"

"You don't need me. You see me as a challenge."

"That may be. But I'm an old guy. Who knows how long I'm gonna live? I need someone at my side."

"It's not me." She looked up and saw Alex enter the room. She waved.

"Yeah, it's you. You just don't know it yet."

"I gotta go."

"To your loverman over there?"

"" I'm not going to talk about this."

"Or your spic?'

"What?"

"That guy? That Latin guy you are schtupping."

She stormed towards the door.

She heard a woman say, "where does he find these girls?" Eleanor said loudly to no one in particular "This girl is found on top and if she hears one more shitty remark, she's going to make sure you vanish."

57.

Serge Raskolnikov

———————————————

S HE WENT TO HER ROOM AND WASHED HER FACE. She looked in the mirror. She had lost control. She was rude. Not her style. She searched her face looking at the woman she once was, collapsed onto the bed and closed her eyes.

We all hear stories of those who rise too fast and their consequential fall. Helicopters and champagne with the rich and famous, media attention, a hint of scandal, nepotism, sex, or corruption. Grist for the mill, is what they say. "She got her claws into him." "She married him for the money." And then the fall from grace, the rumors, the hints, the messy divorce, the division, the house, the artwork, the dog and then the aftermath, the poor woman abused or the victim taking revenge on the poor man. Boring how repetitive this all is. Was Eleanor another story of a rise and fall? That was the question back then. But now we know the answer, don't we? She is still here and Trepin is, well, where he is.

A knock on the door. Then a stronger knock.

"Please, I think I need some sleep," she yelled.

"It's me, Dave."

"Dave? I didn't realize you were here."

"Yeah," the lawyer said. "We were meeting while you were having fun."

"Fun, huh?"

"I know what you mean. But we need to have you downstairs. Some of the guys are leaving tonight. Due back in the city.

"And I wasn't informed?"

"Come. You won't be unhappy."

"Give me ten minutes. I'll be down."

She took a cold shower, redid her makeup, tapped her hand on the toilet and sighed.

"My oh my," Dan Trepin stood as she entered the den. "You shouldn't have changed for us."

She looked around at the men staring at her. A slight whiff of cigar smoke. Cognac snifters in hand. "Just had to tidy up," she said.

"I want to apologize," he said quietly.

"No. We're friends. Too much to drink and all that. Let's move on."

"I really overstepped."

"Shush. So now what's this I hear about my board meeting behind my back?"

"Not really your board, Eleanor. There are other deals in the Trepin Empire, believe it or not. Come, I want you to meet Serge Raskolnikov." A trim, middle-aged man rose. He kissed her hand.

"Raskolnikov?"

"I know, I know. It's not a crime to have the name, but I am sure being punished for it."

She laughed. He was attractive with styled blonde hair combed to the rear and a dark blue silk suit. Elegant, she thought.

"And you know the name Raskolnikov?"

"Of course," she said. "The greatest character in Russian literature."

"Not Count Bezukhov?

"Too weak. No, Raskolnikov appeals to me."

"Then you are a nihilist."

She laughed. "I don't know what I am right now."

"Serge represents some of our St. Petersburg friends," Dan said. "They are increasing their New York portfolio. We told him about your project. I hope you don't mind."

"I found it very interesting," he said with a slight accent. "We Russians love creativity but I must admit I didn't quite understand your qualifications. Now that I meet you, I see."

She waved her hand. "Forget the nonsense, Serge. May I call you Serge?"

"Of course."

"But I don't understand," she said. "I thought financing was all arranged."

"We were going over the portfolio and mentioned the Tibbett plan in passing," Dave said, and Serge insisted on discussing it. He's a good friend, has helped us on many of our projects. So when he asked, we talked, and he wanted to explore it further. Which is why I bothered you so late at night."

Eleanor looked skeptical.

"Let me explain," Dan Trepin said to the Russian. "And I gotta tell you this is like a Little Shop of Horrors: a little flower from outer space takes over the world. And me, I'm the guy with the name on the plaque, and I can't stop the fucking thing from growing."

"Oh, Dan," Serge said, "you always complain and somehow you always profit."

Trepin continued, "anyway, what with the Russian army here and the banks screaming to sink dough into anything (I gotta tell you, there's so much money out there, it be a crime to let this all pass), the guys here are saying that your project could serve as a base for expanding into the whole neighborhood. Strike while the plots are cheap if you get my drift.

"It seems to me," Serge said, "that it's the last open place on the island. Sounds like a perfect place to invest."

"I don't know," she said. "This is more than I can handle."

"Right," Dan said. "Don't worry. We'll help you. You use your people and resources, you explore the possibilities and come up with projects. We'll look 'em over and figure out if there's any there, there."

"I don't know, Dan," Eleanor said.

He held up his hand. "Nothing is being signed. Just throwing around ideas.

"Dan, can we talk in private?"

58.

The Game

———————————————

THEY WALKED DOWN THE BEACH, water lapping at their feet. A crescent moon reflected a slight hazy glow off the water.

"This is going too fast," she said.

"I know you're nervous." Trepin said, "but you have to trust me."

"Why?"

"You don't trust me?"

"All I know is that a couple of months ago I wanted to buy one building. Now my partners are Russians."

"No, not your partners."

"Well, I'm anxious."

"Babe, let me tell you how the game works. We finish up your little project. Sell the apartments to nice couples who get easy mortgages. We walk away with a pretty profit. Nice and clean. Separately, Carmela and you and that other guy look for other places, quiet like, so that no one gets an idea of what's going on. And we set up sub-corporations. You get a share, I get a share, and we give the Church a little bit. Serge gets some, and maybe some guys downtown in City Hall. Then we package it all up and present it to the banks and some of Serge's friends. Maybe some Chinese, if we need them. You don't do shit. This is all done by the lawyers."

"But what if the projects fail?"

"He put his arm around her shoulder. Fail? That could happen. That's the risk. Though not to us."

"I don't understand."

"Look babe, each project has a corporation. Each project has its separate mortgage. The banks hold the mortgages and pass the money to us. They then take each mortgage and carve it up and sell it to other people around the world. So if there's risk, it's minimal. And it doesn't touch us at all because we've got the dough already. They go bankrupt? That's their problem.

"So what's the rush? Why don't we wait to see if my buildings are successful?"

His voice became more irritable, the sound of a man with a woman he is courting who doesn't understand him. "Babe, it's like this ocean. I've been watching it forever as did my Dad before me. I know the ebb and flow. One day the waves are strong and you can't go near the sea. You don't plunge in. Other days they're as gentle as a baby's wading pond and you dive in, full force. And then sometimes, the water appears dangerous with waves crashing onto the shore, but if you know what you're doing you can dive under them, swim past the surf and head out beyond the breakers and make a bundle. That's the way the game works. Sink or swim. Right now, there's so much cash around, they're giving it away. We could build teepees and they'd finance it. Lots of high waves but low risk with no undertow. Tomorrow, the game may be up and we drown. You're just lucky to be with me at the right time.

"And my buildings," she said.

"This new deal doesn't touch them. I'll make sure of that. But if it takes off, your buildings will be worth all the more.

"I don't know."

"As you once said to me, we can do it without you. But you've got your people who have been extremely helpful. You're valuable."

"And I get a share?"

"Yep."

"And no risk?"

"Nope."

Trepin turned her to him. "I want you to know this is the way my father worked, buying and building, pushing the risk off to others. It made the company. It bought me this estate. Shit, I almost own the ocean. And you can get wet too."

59.

Cheppi

———————————•———————————

"**Y**OU WANTED ME TO TELL YOU, so I'm telling you."

Cheppi rose, agitated, shook his head and began to pace back and forth. "Eleanor, this is not good."

"It is working. It is working," she repeated. "You should be happy."

"Why am I not involved?"

"Cheppi, don't be too proud. You know who you are and your talents. Let the big boys handle it."

"So I'm a little boy? I'm not white?"

"Yeah, that's it. I'm a racist. I love you but you've got to get over this. It's growing very fast."

"Too fast."

"If we don't do it, someone else will. Once we decided to move to buy that block, the next step was to take advantage."

"This is feeling out of control, like a landslide or something. No, a mudslide."

"I'm sorry. Even I can't control it anymore. I try, but Trepin is just too powerful. Lawyers. Architects. I'm over my head, it seems, over our heads."

"We should just chuck it all," Cheppi said.

"We could, but that wouldn't stop anything. Dan is putting together syndicates"

"Syndicates? Sounds like the mob."

"You know, packages. Foreigners want to invest here where it's safe. They're screaming at Dan to invest for them. It's amazing how fast this is moving. "

Cheppi shook his head. "You're right, I am a little boy."

"Nothing to do with it. We each have our own strengths."

"Yeah, mine is making breakfasts at a grill."

"Cheppi, please. This is so exciting. Everybody wins."

"Yeah, yeah. I never heard of a game where everybody wins."

"And we, you and I, are going to have more money than we ever dreamed of."

He looked at her. "We?"

"Yes!"

"We getting married?"

"No!" she said emphatically. "That's not what I meant."

"Then what's this 'we'"?

She stopped for a moment. "OK, I see. I'll have Dave draw up a contract for you."

"So we fuck a few times and now I get a contract."

"What do you want, Cheppi?"

"I don't know. Maybe to marry you."

"No. I'm not doing that again."

"We just fucking around, then? Am I your Latin lover?"

"Would you stop the shit?" She paused. "Now listen to me, I've been in this town a year or so and I'm already talking like . . ."

"Still, you seem to be doing all right. You make deals, then other deals, we screw, I mean we screw really good, don't you think?"

"Yes, of course."

"And then you go off with your white people and you take over the neighborhood and where does that leave me?'

"With me and we'll do this together."

"But not married."

"No, no," she said, a tear in her eye. "Honey, this is so confusing. You mean so much to me, but I'm not getting married. That's not going to happen."

"Are we to live together?"

She smiled. "Let's work on that. I think I'd like that."

"You're very exciting, Eleanor Rigby, but you fuck with my brain."

"I don't mean to."

"You seem to be like a car out of control, driving all over the place, knocking everything down."

"We can be a great team," she said.

"Yes, I suppose so."

"But I have a question."

"Yes?"

"Esperanza."

60.

Esperanza

———————•————————————•————

I CAME TO NEW YORK WITH NOTHING. *A few dollars and a ton of hate. Back in those days the hood was filled with hoodlums and smack, not the way it is today but worse, much worse. The way to make it was either steal or push drugs. I didn't have no green card or nothing and I wasn't gonna be a delivery boy. I mean, I've always been proud and I wasn't gonna carry anyone's groceries. I was an angry kid, afraid, I guess, spoke no English, pretty alone. My cousin Miguel took me in but told me I could only stay for a while. Not his fault, you know. The apartment was jammed. Five kids, my auntie and a couple of other people who came and went but it was nice and comfortable and everyone in the building was like family, you know? Sort of like home.*

So Miguel kept saying to me I had to get a job or something, and I had to find a place real soon because it was real crowded and he couldn't afford to feed and keep me in clothing and all that and why didn't I go to St. Patty's down on the corner and ask the Priest. But I wasn't that much for churches and especially no mackerel-snappers. And after a while, the hoods on the corner started calling me a wetback, a vago, you know vagabundo who didn't do shit, and what the fuck was I doing on their street? So I got chased and beaten up a few times.

There was this guy who always sat on a stoop across the street, smoking and chugging beer and looking at what was going on, chatting up the passing chicks. He was no kid but pretty young. Eddy was his name. One day he calls out and waves me over to sit by him, and I think maybe he's a pervert or something. He offers me some weed, and we get into talking and he wants to know where I come from, my pueblo, my family and my story, ya' know. So I tell him about General Vargas and how the army destroyed Samana and he tells me that's the way the world is. and that it's obvious I'm a brave kid, "inteligente y tonto" that means "smart and stupid" that's what he used to call me, but he said that even though I was just a kid, I had to think of where I was and that if I didn't make some decisions real fast, I was gonna find myself in the shits, especially with the toughs on the corner, and I needed to figure out what I was gonna to do and, well, he tells me that he knows some people, and would I like to meet them. So I got into the trade, ya' know, running and pushing shit. Nobody knew me in the 'hood, especially not the cops, so I was real valuable, being a sweet, young kid, just walkin' along, minding my own business, slinging coke and weed and a little bit of smack. And the assholes on the corner, they left me alone, must have got the word.

I got a rep and I was, you know, walking tall, making good money and having a good old time. I did some grass and snorted a little coke, but just to be sociable. Nothing serious. I mean, you'd look around and you'd see what the shit would do to people. Good people were good people back in the Isla where the air was clear and you could walk down the road keeping your head high but after coming north and doing shit work or being kicked around a bit by whitey or the cops and losing their manhood, I saw what it did. And my Granpoppi would call me every week and say, "you sure you're not doing anything I wouldn't do?" and I would answer, "I'm just doing the things you told me not to do but you do" and we'd all laugh but he'd say he was counting on me. And I had to lie to him and told him I was doing some part-time jobs and going to school and all that.

So everything was going fine. I was making lots of money tax-free you know and stashing it in my fridge which was really iced up, but I did that on purpose to hide it. Everyone kept asking how come I never defrosted the fridge. Life was great until some junkie ratted me out and I was busted. It was my first and I was underage and all that, so I did six months in Juvie but once I got out, I was no longer the kid no one knew, like the cops watched my tail and that's when I met Esperanza.

I came back to the hood and started delivering groceries like I swore I would never do 'cause I hated lock-up and I was tough but not like those guys on the corner, and I was never going back in again if I could help it. Eddy would wave to me to come over and sit by him, but I ignored him except when I had to walk by him, and he would yell, "Hey, you becoming a sissy or something?" and I would say, "No, just getting on with my life."

So I got some part-time work from this diner delivering lunches or coffees, and there was Esperanza working the front, young and pretty, she was really pretty back then, really sexy, slim hips and legs to die for, and she could really dance. She spoke English good I guess she learned at school and she was real smart working at the front of this restaurant on Dyckman Street and the guys would hang out, smoking and flirting with her for hours, and she thought me really sexy which I was.

We really took to each other and so we started going out, but then someone told her I was a druggie and that's how I made my money, but I told her my history in Samana and that how I had no choice but to sling shit, and she said "everyone has a choice, you either good or you bad," and I gotta admit she changed my life. She got me a job helping the cook, a guy by the name of Juan Antonio, a really sweet fellow, but a bit of a drunk. You'd be a drunk too if you spent your entire life slinging burgers, and he took to me, calling me "chico," and he taught me everything about the grill. You know, he'd say to be a short order cook is to be close to God, cooking for the gente, flipping eggs, frying up papas, making toast. A cook is serving God by serving man, that's what he said, although he also said that there comes a time when even God gets tired. And as time went on, he was taking time out to go off for a smoke and a drink and maybe another drink and I was working more and after a while, it was my job slinging burgers.

This was a neighborhood place and everyone knew everyone and everyone knew that I had done drugs. but they didn't hold it against me none, you know, forgive and forget, especially seeing how Esperanza and me were a thing, so they sort of helped us out. It was her idea to open our own place. I had some money in the fridge and she had some money and the guy at the bank who came in every morning for his coffee and bagel and flirting with Esperanza was willing to give us a little credit, and it was amazing how easy it was. So we opened up a couple of blocks away and as Juan Antonio got more and more juiced, people came over to our place.

So we became partners, sort of, and lovers but we never got married, never got around to it. I'm a Dominican man, you know, and well, lots of us never bother to get married, and for a time she was OK with that. We lived together but I sort of had an independent streak and Esperanza really liked control, like the cash register, like where we were gonna live, and like who I could talk to in the restaurant or not. If they were young and pretty, she shot me a look and made me pay for it at night.

Esperanza is a good woman, church-goer and caring. She doesn't deserve me. Back when we were first starting out, and we were living hand to mouth, she was in charge of coming up with the cash to buy the goods. the papas and lechugas and tomatoes and meat. Got to the point the Coke deliveryman said no money, no cola, not that I blamed him 'cause he'd been stiffed so much he just had to make the rule.

We were just scrapping by. Each evening, we would gather up the left-overs and she cooked a soup out of it, boiled out the bacteria. And her soups are wonderful, achiote, cilantro, lots of papas or arroz, heavenly. And even though we were poor, some homeless guy would ask for something to eat and she'd be sitting up front at the register and look him over and didn't care if he was an alky or a druggie or just down on his luck and even if he stunk to high hell, she'd yell back to me and I'd make him a melted cheese sandwich and send him on his way.

She's a good woman, Esperanza is. I didn't treat her right, but you know, a man's gotta do what a man's gotta do. After a few years I started going out with the guys and she got pissed and I started playing around and there came a time when we decided to move apart, keep the business relationship, you know, but not live together.

61.

Race

"SO YOU NEVER GOT MARRIED," Eleanor said.

"Nope."

"Any other serious relationships?"

"No, I just had an independent streak."

"Had?"

"Until you. I gotta admit, you're really something?"

"For how long?"

"What?"

"For how long? Until you get bored and a pretty young thing walks by?"

"No, chica, this is different. We have something really happening here."

"I see."

"Look," Cheppi said, touching her arm. "You ask me to trust you with this whitey shit downtown. You gotta trust me as well."

"This is different," she said.

"Why?"

"Why?" she asked incredulously.

"Yeah, I know. Sex is sex. Business is business."

"That's right. You're still with Esperanza in the diner, aren't you?"

"OK. OK. Don't trust. Just give it a chance."

"There's something that's bothered me since we've, you know, come together."

"What's that?"

"Every time we have a fight you call me whitey or you say something is racist, sort of"

"Yeah, so?"

"I'm not racist."

"You white and anglo. You got more money than anyone. You come in here with your anglo friends and buy up everything. Look around at us, the Puerto Ricans, Dominicans, Mexicans, many of us Hispanos have been here for two or three generations. We read Spanish newspapers and we get paid shitty wages. We're different."

"I know that but that doesn't mean I'm racist. Where I come from we never hear Spanish spoken. Except in schools. I'm as much an outsider as you"

"Look, honey. I know. Whites want to be lovey-dovey with us, especially whites with dough."

"So you're saying we're not going to get closer."

"No, I'm not saying that. I'm saying that we have differences, that's all and all we've got to do is trust. And if I say "whitey" here and there, just don't take it so seriously."

"I've trusted before," she said.

He pulled her closer to him, her head touched his shoulder. "You never told me your story but whatever it is, I know this time is different."

"It certainly is different," she chuckled.

"This is the future. Not the past."

62.

The Cracks

———————

"YO NO LO CREO, I don't believe this shit." Crack!
"I told you huevon." Crack!

"These guys move fucking fast. How long has it been since that girl walked by us?"

"Two months. Three months." Crack!

"And now, everything is boarded up. The whole fucking block." Crack!

"Condemned." Crack!

"And the putas with suits all over the place. Big fucking SUVs" Crack!

"Looking around, measuring, drawing plans."

"Last time I saw so many suits was my poor mammy's funeral."

"Money, man. Money. Money talks. Bullshit walks."

"You think the fucking money's gonna renovate our park?" Crack!

"Get rid of all the graffiti." Crack!

"And the gar-bage" Crack!

"And us." Crack!

"They ain't gonna move us. No fucking way." Crack!

"Things are sure changing." Crack!

"They fuckin' with us, they are." Crack!

"Ain't it the truth." Crack!

"It ain't gonna be the same." Crack!

"Yeah, they takin' our place. That's just not right." Crack!

"Nope, not right. No way." Crack!

"I'm gonna go pee. You make sure those buildings are still standing when I'm back."

'Hurry up. Looks like it's gonna rain."

63.

Cindy Williams

———————————•———————————

S HE SAID SHE SPOTTED OUR GUY *at that office building near the Empire State Building, the one with the Bolano sculpture and all those investment bankers. He was outside, having a smoke. So she asked him about his badge, Security Guardians, and wondered if we were hiring and he sent her to me. When she came in, I could've dropped my pants. Gorgeous woman, tall, and skinny, everything you'd want 'though I don't know if it's good for the security business. I mean we're fatsos who stand around being invisible. A babe like this is gonna attract all sorts of attention, and not just from the brothers. I tried to keep my cool, had her fill out the paperwork, background shit and that stuff. Turns out she's a Motown girl, college grad, and was a cop somewhere in America. I had to ask her why she wanted to work for us. She said she was laid off and wanted to come to the Apple for some excitement, and she wanted me to know that she didn't know how long she'd be with us, but she needed a job. I was kinda' suspicious. I did all the background stuff and everything checked out. She's as pure as could be, honest, although I don't know if I dig having someone being squeaky clean. So I thought, what the hell, maybe I lucked out, with a girl like that. Business could pick up and maybe I'd get something on the side, even if I am fat.*

She worked for us for a couple of months, settled in good. No problems, nothing uppity even if she did do college, so I took her to a party with some of the guys in Brooklyn, didn't tell her I was married or nothing, and we walk in and the air is filled with pot so she says she'd prefer not to stay, and I tell her not to worry most of the guys were cops but she still said she'd prefer to go to a quiet bar. Now I'm getting excited so I take her to Duke's, you know the place overlooking the water.

And she asks me how I got into the business and I tell her about Desert Storm and the excitement and how, when I got back, I couldn't get a job 'cause they said I had Post-Traumatic Stress disorder just 'cause I lose my temper. Not that it's a cushy job, it's really boring standing around offices or providing back-up for the cops and there's no action except when we get rid of the homeless guys from lobbies or demonstrators in the wrong place, and then people call us pigs, which is why I got the stomach I got, standing around, taking abuse. I really do have to get back in shape sometime.

And I asked her if she gets high every once in a while. And she says no, that she's a churchgoer, and I said I know loads of girls who pray and toke. She didn't like that at all and said the devil works in strange ways. That's when I started to get nervous so I asked if she'd mind if I went out for a smoke, and she said fine in this stern manner. I looked in the mirror as I walked outside, and I saw a fat guy who was never gonna make it with this bitch. When I returned, I apologized about the weed and all that, and I hoped it wouldn't hurt our professional relationship and she said that's all right, maybe I could go to her church some Sunday and I agreed, knowing that there was no way I was gonna be Bibled up and anyway Sunday was the day with the wife and kid. Some opportunities just don't pan out, do they?

Then, a few days later, she comes in with a copy of The Post and she shows me this picture of Trepin walking into the 21 Club with a babe, not a young chick but a nice looking one, more mature. She asked me who the guy was, and I was amazed. Didn't she know Dan Trepin? Everybody knows him. He fucks every model on the runway, though I didn't exactly use those words. I said he probably pays them good money too. So he goes with hookers, she asks. I said no, not hookers, models who rich guys pay to hang out, take trips to Europe, and make them look macho. We do security for them at charity events, and he's always there with a babe but I didn't think the woman in the picture was a babe, maybe his daughter. And she said, angry-like, that's not his daughter. Turns out she knew that woman from the past. I'm amazed. How does a sister know a white chick hanging out with Trepin?

So I ask her. And she says something about a dog, how the woman once had a dog. Then she goes quiet like, like, in Church.

64.

Hudson View Terrace

———————————•———————————

O LD WORLD COMFORT WITH NEW WORLD LIVING *at Hudson View Terrace. A new standard in luxury.*

- *Stunning, private floor-through apartments with hardwood floors and brilliant river and city views.*
- *Kitchens with granite counter-tops and the most advanced appliances.*
- *Secure internet through Hudson Views proprietary fiber optic network.*
- *Round-the-clock concierge and valet staff.*
- *24-hour CCTV security.*
- *Secure, gated garage parking.*
- *A state-of-the-art fitness center with a non-chlorinated, oxidized Olympic size swimming pool;*

The HV club lounge with wide-screen TV and billiard tables.
This is not modern living, it's 21st century living for those who deserve it.
Prices begin at $4.5 million. Monthly maintenance starts at $7,500.
A Trepin Development

65.

Community

———————•———————

"**A**ND THE HOUSE OF Israel called the name of Manna: and it was like coriander seed, white; and the taste of it was like wafers made with honey."

She looked at him strangely.

"That's from the Bible," he said, stirring the spice onto the garlic, wine and butter in the heavy pot. He threw in mussels and noisily stirred the combination. "I love coriander; it is my favorite spice. I like garlic as well, but it's not really a spice is it? But coriander! The smell is wonderful, like a woman's breast."

"Cheppi!"

"Sorry, I get carried away. But there is a sweetness just like the little sweat between your breasts I love to lick." He bent to her. She pushed him away. "Good for the goma, it is, you know the stomach, helps with digestion. They also say it's good for memory. I've got a good memory, I remember just about everything. "

The kitchen gleamed with a stainless-steel stove wedged beside a Sub-Zero refrigerator with glass doors showing rum, vodka and a half dozen white wines. They sat at a teak counter picking at grilled shrimp and sipping wine. Tiny halogen lights dangled from the ceiling casting a slight, aquamarine glow.

"I didn't know you were religious."

"Back in the isla, we always had to go to church. Study the bible. Memorize passages and all that shit. The Minister was a mean old guy, didn't want us to drink or dance. He thought it was the way to hell, but we found our way." He picked up a shrimp and put it against her lips, moving it around her mouth and then slowly putting it on her tongue.

She laughed and slapped his hand, "But you don't believe?"

"Of course I do, chica. We all must believe. It keeps the *pueblo* together."

"Pueblo?"

"Yes, the people. We might fuck around and sin and do drugs, but everyone has a little Jesus hanging about their heads. He is part of our, of our, I don't know what to call it."

"Community? Oh come on."

"Yeah, that's it. Jesus is our community. Our existence. We grew up with Jesus and we'll die with Jesus. Can't ignore him, can we?"

"Community, huh," she said.

"Yeah, community. What of it? When I first came to this town, it was the community that took me in, and now when someone comes into my place, I'll help them if I can. That's what it's all about."

He took her hand in his. "Come on, let's go and fuck."

"Didn't we just do it?"

"Fuck?"

"Yeah."

"Say it."

"Say what?"

"Fuck." She shook her head. "You can't, can you?"

"Sure I can."

He pressed his mouth towards her. "Say it."

"No." She turned away.

He grabbed her from behind and kissed her neck. He moved his hands to her breasts.

"Jesus, huh?"

"That's right," he whispered.

"Community?"

"Don't change the subject." He squeezed playfully. "Say it."

66.

Vargas

———————•———————

THE MILITARY JEEP BOUNCED over an uneven and curving gravel road abutting a beach. Behind, a black Hummer scrambled to keep up. The old man in the back of the Hummer yelled to slow down. The driver ignored him. Orders were orders. Keep close to the protection. Never let it out of your sight.

The driver radioed the jeep but only heard static. The forward jeep pulled further and further ahead, brushing palm fronds as it sped. The old man yelled again and banged his hand on the driver's seat. "Slow down, I tell you. I am getting sick." The driver mumbled "que puta, we can't handle these roads. We're losing them." He yelled into the cellphone "Ayyy, donde van, despacio hombres, slow the fuck down" to no effect. No cell reception.

The Hummer rounded the bend past a thatched roof hut and a broken ox-cart. A gaunt, old man with a peasant's hat, torn shirt and a long-pointed spear stared at the speeding vehicles. Idle oxen, shorn of their yoke, grazed on the roadside beside an old wooden fence. Cattle grazed in the distance. A peaceful pastoral scene. The peasant's eyes met the old man's.

The noise was heard for miles around. The bomb raised the Hummer off its wheels and threw it onto the fence. It erupted in flames and exploded. An ox was thrown across the road, its body torn apart, the peasant hit the ground, the blood of the beast covered his clothes. The forward jeep returned. A driver dismounted and looked onto the destruction. "Estan muertos," he mumbled. He walked back and forth examining the debris. "Y yo," the ox cart driver yelled. "Me, what am I to do? You killed one of my beasts. What am I to do, the other ox is useless? What am I to do?"

"Sell it for meat, old man, and I didn't kill your beast."

"And who did?"

"Better not to ask, not to ask."

67.

Cindy Williams

—————————•—————————

"YOU REALLY ARE PERSISTENT, I told you, Miss Tibbett doesn't want to see you."

"I need to speak with her."

"Can't help you."

"Can I leave her a note?"

"You can but she won't get it."

"She won't get it?"

"She doesn't live here anymore."

"What?"

"She moved."

"Where? Do you have a forwarding address?"

"Nope."

"Nope? You have one and won't give it to me or nope you don't have one?"

"Just nope."

"You know she's evil."

"No, I don't know that. I think she's a wonderful person."

"So you know her well?"

"Nope."

"You sure are a man of few words." He didn't respond. "You know, a little bit of advice, you've got body odor. You should wash more often. I'll see you around."

68.

Gentrification

———————————————

THE NEIGHBORHOOD BECAME A BEEHIVE OF ACTIVITY. Demolition guys, plasterers, glaziers, plumbers, electricians, dump trucks, and delivery vans all over the place. Con Ed tore up the streets for new electricity. The city brought in new lighting. Private security cars filled with off-duty cops drove about. Remarkably, the Sanitation Department scoured the once-rubbished streets like they never had before. And local politicians proclaimed a new beginning for the community.

In less than a year, the prime properties were snatched up. Latinos remained to be sure but they were young and professional, hip and the "pioneers" to the new growing district, getting the news in Spanish language papers and given the first dibs on the cheap mortgages. The elderly were pushed to the boroughs or back to the islands with a fat check in their hands. Hudson Hills got the rep as the next place to live, to raise a young family with beautiful parks, river views, cafes, multicultural ethnic restaurants, and private kindergartens and schools. Close to work but not too close to work. Greenwich Village, Park Slope, SoHo and now Hudson Hills.

Behind the scenes, Trepin pushed as hard as possible. "Eleanor, we got to move faster. The dogs are sniffing and once they get the scent, prices go up and we're fucked."

Her initial bemusement at his screams became amusement and playful banter. "Oh, Dan, you're rich enough. Why not take a break?"

"I'm serious Eleanor, the snakes are weaving their way uptown."

"Don't you worry, honey," she responded. "We've got Carmela and Cheppi and most of all, you got me. Don't you forget me."

The more she played, the more he was smitten. "When are you going to leave that Spic lover and come play with me?"

"Dan, you know I don't like that language. Cheppi and I are really happy together and we, you and I, are good friends. We are good friends, aren't we?"

"Not fucking good enough."

"You don't like what I'm doing?"

"Stop teasing me, girl," he yelled into the phone. "I don't like that."

"I'm sorry, Dan."

"Just make sure we get these deals done."

"No worry, Babe. No worry."

Everyone seemed to win. If Eleanor was rich before, she was now super-rich. Cheppi earned his share, and Carmela Chan took her sales commissions. The new, young professionals got their new housing.

Everyone won. Dan Trepin, though, had a little secret. Not a real secret since all moguls knew the game. Others financed the buildings. The banks provided mortgages. If the new buildings failed, it was their problem. In the meantime, Trepin Management made long-term management contracts to provide service to each of the buildings. Consolidated Fuel, a Trepin subsidiary, had the monopoly for heating oil. Most important, Trepin kept ownership of the new shops on the ground floors renting them on long-term leases to Whole Foods, Starbucks, McDonalds, and the like.

Trepin had everything. Except Eleanor.

69.

Invisible

———————————

"I DON'T CARE IF WE GOTTA MOVE TO THE BRONX, you take the subway and come back. This game got to continue." Crack!

"You're just too, how do you say it, "demaciado tradicional." Crack!

"Tradicional? This is our tierra. Our park. We own it." Crack!

"You don't own shit, you old huevon." Crack!

"Look, all these tiny sniffing dogs, with bows on and all that shit. And the prams" Crack!

"But the young chicas are pretty, you got to admit." Crack!

Yeah, the chicas are nice. I prefer las morenas. They're caliente."

"And the rubias?"

"You changing the subject? Crack!

"You see some of those young Russian girls. They get out of their Mercedes." Crack!

"They don't see us, hombre. We're, how do say it? Invisible." Crack!

"Big blondes, what I could do with them." Crack!

"You dream on. They look at us like we're mierda." Crack!

"We are mierda. Old, fucking, Spanish mierda." Crack!

"I tell you. We gotta find another place. The old bodega. It closed down. We can't even get a cold beer. We gotta go up to the Bronx." Crack!

"I'm not moving. I'm never going to move. Cerveza or no cerveza. This is my tierra." Crack!

"Yeah, well, we'll see." Crack!

"I'm moving. I'm moving to take a piss."

"'Calidad de la vida,' they call it. Qualitee of life."

Which means "no habla espanol."

"Get used to it."

"I'm not goin' to the Bronx. No way. No fucking way."

70.

Trepin Garden School

———————•———————

PASTOR WAINWRIGHT STOOD ON THE PODIUM. On each side were the city's rich and famous, their faces hidden by large floral arrangements and giant snifters of cognac. The dinner was done, and the dishes removed. Dan Trepin sat beside Eleanor and Cheppi beside her. The Pastor spoke.

You all know that I don't lack a way with words (snickers), *and so I will take this opportunity to say a few* (sarcastic groans). *It was Plato who first told us about Orbs, those entities that move about the universe in what he called quintessence. I've often been fascinated by that view. After all, all the great philosophers agreed with him, Aristotle and, most important, Copernicus who described so well what we now know is our solar system.*

But I believe in another type of Orb, the societies in which we live, moving all about, glancing off each other, bouncing into each other, and only paying a slight regard for the other entity. But I think we make our own Orbs, our little living units that only pay lip service to the other bodies that comprise our social universe. Yes, I know, we talk of "the poor" or "the disadvantaged," but we really don't see or feel the other Orbs.

It takes special people to look out and see where we are in relation to others, how our congregations interact with others. How Orbs affect other Orbs. And Dan Trepin is that special kind of person. A man of this city, country, and of this world. A real patriot. And tonight we honor my good friend Dan for his massive contribution to our new school to be built across the street from our congregation, a school meant to bring together not only our own children, but special and talented children from other parts of the city, from less privileged families, from other Orbs.

The city has seen an enormous growth in population and the need for high quality education with well-paid teachers is obvious. As many of you know, we have been fortunate in having Dan's help in acquiring the three brownstones down the street from our Church. And tonight I have the honor to announce that after the renovations are complete, the sign over the portal will read the Trepin Garden School (applause).

The name honors not only my friend sitting here but also his father who gave so much to the community over the last half century. I knew Dan Trepin Sr. and there is no doubt in my mind that he would be so proud of his son. He is now in a different Orb, but I'm sure, she is with us tonight. (applause). *So let us all stand and give thanks to Dan for his generous contribution!* (Standing ovation).

Now, before I give Dan the floor, which he'll probably buy if we don't watch out (laughter), *I also want to add that a scholarship fund has been established in the name of our dear, departed, friend Joan Tibbett, with the initial contributions coming from Eleanor Tibbett and Dan.* (applause). *And Eleanor has graciously agreed to join the new school board and to serve as its President.*

Cheppi whispered in Eleanor's ear, "This is bullshit. I'm out of here."

"Please don't," she said. "Wait until Dan speaks."

"I'll see you at home." He downed his drink, stood unevenly and weaved his way through the chairs.

Clara Fitzsimmons, member of the Church board, was drunk. The speech was going too long and she was falling asleep. The Latino walked by her. She waved "Oh sir, oh sir, she motioned to him."

"Yes."

"Would you be so kind as to bring me another bottle of wine. We've seemed to have exhausted ours." She smiled politely.

"What?"

"Wine," she said, whispering. "You know, vino."

Cheppi stared for a moment. "Chinga tu madre," he said, and walked out the door.

"What did he say?" she turned to her table mates.

"You don't want to know, dear," someone said. "You don't want to know."

"What did I do wrong?"

"Nothing dear. You know he's with that Tibbett woman."

"He? Oh my God. I didn't realize. I thought . . ."

"Yes."

Fitzsimmons shook her head. "I should go apologize."

"Better not."

"Yes, I suppose not. But you know, ever since she came here, things have been turned topsy-turvy, don't you think?

"They have changed for sure."

"And not for the best, if you ask me. She has wound her little finger around Dan. Look at how he stares at her, his arm around her. It's truly indecent. And now she's on the Church board, running the school. I just think someone should speak to Pastor Wainwright."

A waiter approached with a bottle each of red and white wine. "Madam, I believe you wished...."

"Why yes," Fitzsimmons said. "Well thank you. How did you know?"

"Why a gentleman on his way out, he told me," the waiter smiled.

"Well, that was very nice of him"

"Yes, Madam. He is a real gentleman."

71.

Esperanza

——————●————————————●——————

As he passed El Escorial, he heard loud laughter and shouting. A fight? Hard to tell. He strolled in. Esperanza came to him and threw her arms around him.

"What now," Cheppi asked.

"El tirano esta muerto, al fin."

"Who?"

"Vargas, mi amorcito. They finally got este hijo de puta."

"What do you mean?"

"They blew him up on the beach road. Near the estate. That fucker. Finally."

Cheppi stood quietly and reached for the bottle and went to the bar. "Drinks for everyone." He looked at Esperanza. She returned his stare. He took her into his arms and squeezed. "Revenge. It's wonderful."

Esperanza hugged him. "Pass out the glasses," he shouted. "Vamos a fiestar. Dame una botella de ron."

"Oh Cheppi," she said. "We've waited so long."

"Yeah, and those cobardes in the gobierno, they protected him. He had so much shit on everyone." He slammed his fist down. "20 años. And our village is gone. And what have they done to him and his friends, nothing." He drank the rum from the bottle.

"But we are alive, mi vida."

"Yes, we are alive. And we are here and he is still there." He looked at her. She stroked his face. He took her in his arms for a long kiss. "Yes, yes," he said to the crowd. "To us. La victoria."

72.

Eleanor Tibbett

———————•———————

I T WAS LATE. SHE WAS WEARY. The limo driver called to the rear and then had to shake her. "You're home, madam," he said.

It had been a long night. Dan Trepin's speech, about his grandfather and father and his hopes for the city droned on and on. And then after, they adjourned to a rooftop bar. "You have to come," Trepin said. "They will all be disappointed."

Raskolnikov cornered her. "This is what we have to do, Eleanor, now you are one of us. I want to take you to Europe for a few weeks. Take a tour and maybe think about doing some deals together."

A bottle of Champagne was brought. "I don't know . . . "I'm really over my head as it is."

"Yes, but you have good friends to take care of you. Doesn't she, Dan," he shouted across the table.

Trepin was unhappy. The Russian had the favored seat next to Eleanor. He was showering her with attention. He was young, handsome and had all his hair. The lounge was noisy. All he could do was sit and watch.

"Just tell me you'll consider it," Raskolnikov said. "There's a world out there for you." He touched her shoulder. He was not unattractive but his confidence unnerved her. She pulled back instinctively.

"I offended you?" he said.

"No, no. I'm just a little on edge."

"I didn't wish to offend you. We'll talk about it another time."

"Yes, of course. Now I think I have to join Dan. He looks unhappy."

"No," the Russian said. "Dan's not unhappy. He always looks like that. Hey Dan," he yelled. "You unhappy."

"Not a bit."

"You have no reason to be unhappy. Eleanor says that she will come with me to Russia next month."

'What?" Trepin's anger showed.

"I did not," Eleanor stared at him.

The Russian broke out laughing. "A joke, just a joke. Why is everyone so unhappy? Look at what we've accomplished. Dan, you rule the roost. You have everything."

"Funny joke," Dan said dryly.

"Let's have a toast. To us."

It was all so foggy. The speeches, drinks, Cheppi walking out. And then, she remembered, that woman. Yes, that woman, it came into her drunken mind. As they left the dinner, there she stood, that detective. She blocked her path and said, "we found the dog. Evil *will* be punished."

She entered the darkened apartment and kicked off her shoes. "Cheppi?" she called. The bedroom was empty. "You here?" She walked around and called his name again. Exhausted, she dropped onto the bed.

Early the next morning he returned, walking unsteadily.

"Cheppi? That you."

"Who else would it be, your loverman?"

"Where have you been?" she mumbled.

"I've been out. Why should I tell you? You my boss."

She sat up. "You're drunk."

He laughed. "You are a smart woman." He put his hand on her breast. She pushed him away.

"So you don't like sex in la mañana."

"Sober up!" she said angrily.

He got into bed. "No, baby, I don't want to sober up." He leaned to kiss her, rum and cigars on his breath. She pushed him away. He pushed back. "You playing hard to get, or you tired of me now."

"Stop it," she yelled.

"You too good for me with your white guys and your school now and people loving you all over, so I'm gonna love all over." He climbed on top of her, and pressed his leg between her thighs. She slapped him. He stopped for a moment. "That's good, let's do it some more."

She grabbed his hair and pulled back. "Cheppi, I'm warning you. You rape me, you'd better never come back here again."

"I see. Now that you used me, you don't need me anymore. La Conquistadora is moving on."

"Get off me."

"Esperanza, she likes it like that." He pushed his mouth against her, forcing his tongue between her lips, holding her struggling head. She beat at his head, weakly. He pulled back and laughed. "You don't want to fuck me, I'll go to Esperanza. She didn't want me to leave anyway."

"Cheppi, sober up. You're drunk. I've never seen you so drunk."

"Yeah well, maybe you've never seen me." He stood.

She rose, her body shaking. "I can't believe it. Just another whoring drunk."

"Yeah, yeah," he slurred. "Another whoring drunk. Maybe you attract them. Your hubby, he drink too, I bet. You being so fucking superior."

"I'm getting out of here," she said.

He flopped on the bed. "Yeah, yeah. You go back downtown, Eleanor Rigby, where you come from. You done slumming now."

73.

Carmela Chan

———————————————————

S HE WALKED THE STREETS, found a small Haitian place filled with taxi drivers. Her head throbbed. She went to the bathroom. The toilet was blocked with paper, the sink leaked on the floor, an odor of urine throughout. She washed her face and wiped it with her sleeve. She returned to her table and closed her eyes.

The city awoke. The noise of traffic stirred her. The restaurant owner came to her "You OK?"

"Yes, thank you. May I have some more coffee and perhaps more toast?"

She was in shock. For once, she had let go, put her guard down and now this. Another cheating drunk in her life and that cop, that cop with the long scar down her face, she keeps showing up, reminding her of the past, calling her the devil. She was stupid to trust, Eleanor thought, to let go and allow passion to sway her. But as with Joey, her life was now intertwined with Cheppi. She needed to think. Here she was in this town, rich, but another drunk was in her bed and some cop still trying to get her.

"That's Cheppi," Carmela Chan said to Eleanor, shaking her head. "He's a man, what can I say?"

The two women looked at each other. "Look," Chan said, "Latino men they play around. That's what they do."

"I don't believe it. Not all men."

"Maybe not all men, but look at him. He's good looking, successful, real, you know how they say, "macho.""

"I don't believe it," Eleanor repeated.

"Listen girl. You're new here. You have no experience. *Nada.* You come to the *barrio*, steal Cheppi from Esperanza and you expect a life of love like in the movies."

"Cheppi said there was nothing between them anymore."

Chan smiled slightly. "I give you another little secret. Men lie."

"So what is it between these two? They married?"

"Married? No, not that I know. I'm pretty sure they're not. But you know, there's a *larga historia* there. Many years."

"He said it was over."

"This one will never be over. Sure, Esperanza has put on a little weight and she's grown into that age when men stop looking but still, for all his faults, Cheppi is an honorable man."

"How can you say that?"

"Listen, around this *barrio* there are guys who pick up chicas, go with them for a while, make them pregnant, and then they move on and if they pass 'em in the streets, they look the other way, and the chicas, they understand that after a while it's over. I mean they may cry and cry but these loverboys, they just keep doing their thing. Let me tell you, I know. But Cheppi's not like that. He's a good man for the man he is. He'd never look the other way. He's honorable.

"So he's still with Esperanza."

"No and yes. He's with you, Eleanor, but Esperanza? There'll always be something there."

"He got very drunk last night."

"Yes, I know."

"You know?" Eleanor asked incredulously.

"There was a celebration in the *barrio*. The sonofabitch who took over Samana and forced our folks up here, he died.

"You mean the General who chased Cheppi."

"Yeah, and everyone else. They killed him a couple of days ago."

"He told me about him."

"So Cheppi gave you that Samana story?" Chan shook her head.

"You mean it's not true?" Eleanor said.

"Who knows? I don't know what he told you, but he tells that story a lot. Impresses guys in bars and young girls. I'm sure parts of it are true. Did he have to flee the soldados? Or did he decide he just didn't want to work waiting on tables in some Gringo hotel? Maybe he just decided he had enough and abandoned his folks. Lots of people left back then for all sorts of reasons. Many brought their families up. Not Cheppi. If you listen to him, Cheppi is always the hero.

"And how did Cheppi and Esperanza come together."

"I don't know. Really. But the way I hear it, Cheppi got up here and couldn't make a go of it. He got into trouble and her family, good Catholics they are, took him in, gave him a place to stay. And she, young and hot and sexy, grabbed him like he was a sugar cone. They were together a good ten years, living together, until he started messing around."

"So I'm not the first?"

"No, honey. And, if you ask me, you ain't the last either. But I tell you this. He's loyal. I know that. Like a dog in the alley, he'll stray sometimes, find himself something on the side, but he'll come back home. If you'll have him."

Eleanor shook her head. "I don't know what to do."

"Look honey, I do real estate. That's all I know. I tell my friends and my customers, never leap before you leap. You buy something on a whim and you regret it for the rest of your life. You move out of your place that you love for all sorts of reasons, you better make sure you want to do that. Take your time. Talk with Cheppi. Maybe I'm wrong. Maybe he's changed."

Chan touched her hand. "You got so much to be thankful for. Look at what you've done. Nothing ever comes easy. I've been here thirty years renting little places, selling houses no one except the poor would buy and you come in and look what you've done. Don't think I'm not thankful for you. You've got a friend for life. I can retire now. So if you need me, you come on by, anytime.

74.

Dominoes

———•————————————•———

"I T'S GETTING SO, YOU CAN'T GET A CHEAP BEER." Crack!
"We'll have to bring it from the Bronx" Crack!

Cheppi and Eleanor walked to the park, distant from each other.

"Hola guapa," came a cry from the domino players.

Cheppi nodded quickly. "Que tal?"

"Saludos," one responded. "Que bonita la mujer."

"Gracias. He say you beautiful."

"I figured that out," Eleanor mumbled, looking to the river. A light wind blew across her face.

He put his hand in hers. She pulled away. "No, Cheppi, it's not that easy."

"I know, chica, I fucked up. You gotta forgive me."

They sat on an old bench, graffiti carved deeply into the wood. "Back when I was a child," she said, "they used to play dominos. In my Daddy's hardware store."

"We can play sometime if you like?"

"No, no. I really don't remember how to play. It's a game for men. Moving pieces around the board again and again, trying to reach the end, to "go out.""

That's the word they use. It's not a woman's game, is it?"

"Maybe not. But it's a game played all over. You go out to the boroughs, you see tables all over with guys smokin' and playing dominos. It's the thing they do. Better than drugs."

"Those men in my Daddy's store, they were friends. Customers. For years they came and just sat and played. They'd sit and move the tiles around, click, click, looking to see what's been played and what's not, talking a little, having a drink, probably like these guys here. Most times they didn't buy anything but my Daddy said, never mind, they're friends and if they need something, then they'll buy. Which is what they did, moving pieces around the table, day after day after day. I thought it would never end."

"Sounds like you didn't like it," Cheppi said.

She shook her head. "I didn't mind. Actually, never thought much about it. I was just a little girl. That's the way it was. Men sitting, drinking and talking, mixing up the pieces, over and over. I didn't pay them no mind. Had my own things to take care of. But this is the thing. One day, they stopped coming and the game stopped. Just like that."

"Why?"

"They built the big box stores out on the highway. Cheaper stuff, larger stores, I don't know. My Daddy said they were friends, townsfolk. But in the end, they were like everyone else."

"That's tough. Business is tough."

"Yeah, maybe. But my Daddy didn't take it too well. Took to drinking. Maybe it was those people. Maybe it was just my Daddy. But after the guys moved on and Daddy fell apart, our lives became hell. He would hit my Mom, scream at us, rant and rave, and then storm out of the house and disappear. We wouldn't see him for days. Mom just took it, she did, until she couldn't take it anymore and she threw him out. That was hard. I think she did it for us 'cause after that, she was alone and depressed. Went to church a lot, she did. But she wasn't the same."

She stared at Cheppi. "They stopped playing that silly game and went their way. You understand what I am saying?"

He nodded.

They sat quietly, looking out at the water. She said, "I'm told you like to play around. With other women."

"Who told you that?"

"Who didn't tell me that, Cheppi?" she said tersely.

He remained silent.

"I will tell you if we are together, we are together. If we're not, well, I'm sorry, really, really sorry, but you have to decide."

"I said I was sorry. I don't know what happened."

"And you ever ever, come in drunk like you did last night, I'll throw you out. I don't care what time it is. I am not going to live with another drunkard. Never again. And if you hit me or force me, I will kill you. Have no doubt."

He said nothing. They rose and walked towards the river on broken pavement. He put his arm around her. She pulled away. "I'm angry, Cheppi. You're going to have to give it time."

"Yes, of course."

She looked at him. "I really like you, but," she shook her head and turned away.

"You know," Cheppi said. "You wanted me to go to that dinner with all those white folks."

"You kept saying you wanted to be part of everything. Those dinners are part of everything."

"Maybe so, maybe so. But I have to tell you something. Those people last night are not my people. And even if I'm there, they talk to you and are polite with me or worse, they just nod and walk away. I'm like, how do you say it? Invisible. I'm not a part of this. You make your deals and I just come along"

"Yes," she said. "It must be difficult."

"Difficult? It is insulting. I am King in my restaurant and in this *barrio*. People look up to me. I walk down the street, and people nod their heads and ask how's it going? I go to your dinners and they ask me to go get 'em another bottle of wine. Or they say 'where are you from? I once went to a beach there.' Or they speak pidgin Spanish that I'm supposed to understand."

"I know."

"And the clothes they wear. I bet one of those dresses cost more than I made in a year. The food, the silver on the table, the fancy wine, and the flowers, do you know how many poor people live in this neighborhood? I look at that and I think about my *pueblo*. I just don't belong down there.

"OK. I'll try to be more sensitive."

"No, no. It's not your fault. It's reality. Rich white lady hanging out with the Spic. I can see it in their faces."

"I don't care about their faces and neither should you."

"Yeah. Well your Daddy cared about how he was seen and look what happened to him. I don't want it to happen to me. It's like the preacher-guy said, "different orbs.""

"I don't believe that. This is America. I'll try to understand more."

"No, there is nothing you can do, chica. This is something I have to work on." A breeze came up on the river. He put his arm around her. She moved close to him.

"Now there's something else I want to say."

"Yes," she said.

"Last night, I heard that this bastard who terrorized my town was killed, wiped out. The hijo de puta was responsible for me coming here in the first place and for lots of hurt. He's gone finally. So I think I want to go back home for a week or so. Visit the old place. Look around."

"Of course," she said. "Who will you go with?"

"Why, with you? Who else?"

"I just thought, maybe."

"No, chica. I want to show you my country. It is beautiful down there. Do you think?"

"Of course. And the restaurant?"

"Esperanza will handle it. Esperanza and Simon Bolivar, of course."

She laughed "Always Simon Bolivar. What is it with you?"

"Simon Bolivar controls his land. He prowls the basement, catches mice, and after dark he comes up," he moved his fingers back and forth across her neck, "chasing little beechos , cucarachas, ratones." She shivered. He laughed. "He makes sure that nobody gets in his way and he can rule his empire. Simon and me, we are Kings of our little place."

"Really."

"And if he does a good job, I give him a little breakfast like I do you, some bacon bits and huevos."

"You are both outlaws."

"Simon Bolivar was never an outlaw. Neither am I."

Part Five

75.

Hacienda del Coco

⸻

T HE GULFSTREAM JET GLIDED LOW OVER THE WATER. Cheppi looked out. "Yes, there it is, you see, down there, at the end of the cove. That's my town. And over there, that little island, that's where we used to go to play pirates."

"Looks beautiful," she said.

"It was once. Once a small town with small houses and now cement high rise hotels."

"I can't wait to see it all."

"Look at the color of the bay. Have you ever seen anything so beautiful?"

"No, really, no."

"Golfo de las Flechas, it is called, the Gulf of Arrows. Columbus came here and we greeted him with arrows."

"We?"

"And look at those green pastures and over there, the sugar cane fields on and on. Our families used to work those fields for the patron before the machines came in."

The jet rose up over the mountains and descended. A uniformed official escorted them to a land rover with official plates.

"How did you arrange all this?" Cheppi asked.

"You know. Dan has contacts all over the place. When I told him we were coming he insisted on helping."

"Helping, huh?"

"Come on, honey. You were impressed by the Jetstream."

"Yeah, maybe. But I get nervous when uniforms escort me to a car."

"Why? The return of the exile. You should feel triumphant."

"Nice jeep," he said.

They headed towards Samana. "Oiga, amigo," Cheppi said to the driver, "Podemos pasar al Hacienda del Coco?"

"What?" she asked.

"I want to go see the hacienda of the tyrant Vargas. Big fucking fortress. No one was able to get in. I mean we knew how to sneak around but not this place. If you ever got in, you never got out. Man, the stories they told about what went on there. They'd pick up little chicas from the city, I mean really young girls, have some fun, pay them off and throw them back home. They'd have slaves there too. Big black Haitians who made sure everyone behaved themselves. These Haitian guys came into town and they'd walk around like they'd owned the place. We'd throw pebbles at them and they'd just ignore it. Imagine that, Haitians, bossing us around in our own country. And if they caught us? Well, the word was, "They want you for a Hacienda del Coco vacation." And you knew you'd never come back.

The Jeep pulled to the entrance. The driver mumbled to the guard, shook his hand, and passed him some bills. "Nobody cares about this place no more," the driver said, in rough English. "Tourist attraction, now."

"What they going to do with it?" Cheppi asked.

"Quien sabe? Probably give it to another general. Or a German. Or a Gringo. Los ricos will take it one way or another."

Grass huts along the road. Purple bougainvilla and jacaranda dotted with yellow tabebulas. Women in loose dresses cooking dinner over rough wood. Children kicking a ball. Dogs barking, giving chase to the Jeep. A soft sound of waves sweeping onto the white sand beach. A large brick building overlooked the scene, an abandoned watch tower beside it. Workers in torn pants gazed at them as they past.

"This is amazing," Eleanor said looking out. "The water is so clear! And the beach! The sand! Listen to those birds! What a paradise."

"That's right," Cheppi said. "This son of a bitch killed and raped and tortured so he could have all this."

"But look at it," she said. "It's so perfect. So wonderful."

"Yes," he said sadly. "I think we should head on."

"We can't get out and walk a little?"

"We'll come back," he said impatiently. "Let's get to the hotel."

The car bumped along a broken, narrow paved road. Trucks laden with bags of rice and cartons of soap blocked their path. Buses cut in and stopped to discharge passengers. They crawled through the din, Cheppi becoming more and more impatient.

"You must be tired," she said.

"Look at this. There was a time when there was nothing. Emptiness. Now it is all noise and mayhem."

They entered Samana. Two lanes became four, with heavy traffic, dank diesel smoke, taxis cutting between lanes, horns honking and beggars on crutches walking the street. Meringue music blared from open windows. Crowds meandered outside small restaurants. Large neon signs advertised casinos, discos and tattoo parlors.

"Nice place," she said.

"Yes, for las turistas."

She looked at him. "You're not happy."

"This is not the town I left."

"Lots has changed here, Senor," the driver said. New people have moved in. Cubanos, Venezuelanos, Colombianos. They've all bought in."

"Twenty years," Cheppi said, depressed.

"Give it a chance," Eleanor said. "You've been gone for so long."

"Perhaps," he said. "Perhaps."

The doorman at the hotel greeted them in English "Welcome to La Buena Vista. I hope your stay will be enjoyable."

"Thank you," she said.

"You go straight to your room," the doorman said. "All the formalities have been taken care of. The Executive Suite. Top Floor."

"Dan has taken care of everything," Cheppi said in the elevator. "Is he going to sleep with you too?"

"Cheppi!"

"I'm sorry, honey. Bad mood. I'm really sorry. You know what I'd like to do, if you don't mind. I think I'll take a stroll, by myself."

"Sure, of course. I'll go to the pool."

"That's good. You relax."

76.

Pina Coladas

———————————————

"Y OU SHOULDN'T HAVE LEFT ME ALONE," she said playfully. "These two gorgeous guys sat next to me and offered to buy me a drink. They were quite handsome. And young, much younger than you." She lay in bed, her body only partially covered by a terry robe.

He said nothing.

"I'm afraid I've had a little too much to drink," she said. She turned and the robe fell open. "They make these Pina Coladas that are fabulous. I got you some sandwiches, over there by the couch."

"I'm not hungry," he said stiffly.

"You OK? Did you eat?"

He nodded.

She touched his face. "So, tell me, where did you go?"

He pulled away. He opened a beer. "I wandered around the old places. They're all gone, of course. Found some of the old crowd, a few cousins and neighbors. They fed me."

"That's nice. Will I meet them?"

He shook his head. "No, you don't want to."

"I don't understand. We came all this way."

"No, tomorrow we'll go back to Hacienda del Coco for a picnic. That should be nice."

"But I'd really like to meet your friends. Your family."

"They don't speak English."

"That's OK."

"No, it's more than that. The place has changed. It ain't what I thought. I mean, I thought I'd come back here and they'd all be happy to see me and all that but . . ."

"What happened."

"My friends from school, they're gone, some to the capital, to the States, some died and then some have vanished. And my primos, my cousins, they see me come from the north, they think I'm rich.

"You are."

"I know, Eleanor, I know. But it is a problem. I am not one of them, and they are living, how do you say, hand to mouth? They know I have the restaurant, that I am a leader of the community, and they think that I've made out big-time. I mean, they don't see me as family, as blood. They see me as money. That's the way they are. And they resent me as if I was Vargas. I haven't gone through what they've gone through, and here I am in a big hotel and they're trapped where they are."

"You can help them?"

"No, I don't think so."

"We have tons of money, surely we can ..."

"Baby, you're new to this. Up north there are loads of people who need money. All sorts of poor in the *barrio*. You don't see it 'cause, well, people don't wear their condition on their sleeve. Every day I see guys sitting at the counter for hours, sippin' that coffee. I give 'em refills. They don't have money. They got nowhere to go. No job. No future. They got their dignity and so they come and sit and sip. Down here, it's different. Everyone's cryin'. Shit, the whole hue puta country needs money. We are rich, I know, but,"

"Very sad."

"Yeah, sad. That's the word. Sad. It's not that I don't believe in helping people but when people are desperate, when people are just looking for handouts, then

I don't care what you do, it just won't work."

"Still, they are your family and you've been looking forward to…."

"No, we don't worry about them. They survived and they'll keep surviving. We came here to have fun. Tomorrow, we go to Hacienda del Coco and I'll show you real fun. I'll show you *la pura vida* not the bullshit that's going on here. What a shame. What a fucking shame."

"I'm sorry," she threw her arms around him and kissed his neck.

"We'll have some fun. Go swimming. Maybe a little fishing like the old days. Take a boat out. Make a barbecue."

"Yes, that would be nice."

"Then I think we head home. Back to where we come from."

"You sure?"

"I really wanted to come. I thought that the old life was left, at least some of it. I wanted to show you where I grew up. My school. My church. But the school is gone and the church is empty. No one there. I walked down the main street and saw hustlers and casinos, McDonalds, shops selling cheap souvenirs made in China, and hookers standing in seedy bars. The town is for the Germans and the Russians and the English and the Gringoes. Las Turistas." He fell silent and shook his head.

She pulled him to her and held him. "Shhh. Shhh. Tomorrow we'll go to the beach. We'll see what there is outside of this town. Trust me. I'm sure there is something to be found. Your country is just too beautiful."

77.

Mamajuana

———————————————

ELEANOR TIBBETT DID NOT HAVE A YOUTHFUL FIGURE. Still, a woman in her early 40s with slim hips and slight breasts attracted men's stares as she ran into the bay and jumped and laughed. Cheppi came after. She put her arms around him. He took her head and dunked her.

"That was not nice."

"Oh, Eleanor Rigby, you are a miracle. I forgot how fabulous this water is. In the city, you forget."

"Come, let's swim."

"No, I will just stand and watch you."

"Come, swim with me."

"No."

"Please?"

He turned his head away.

She laughed. "Ha, you can't swim, can you?" He said nothing. "I will teach you."

"You just go on."

"But why didn't you ever learn?"

"Too busy."

"Too busy?"

"Doing other things. Swimming is for los ricos. We people, we had to work. We wade and throw water at each other to cool off, but we don't swim. Only people in country clubs swim."

"I'll teach you."

"No, you go swim. I will go get us lunch."

She moved slowly through the water. Through aquamarine water she saw golden coral, bright blue and gold angel fish moved in and out of dark green grasses. A sea horse passed by. Then she jumped and swam to shore. "You won't believe it, I think I saw a shark."

"Possible," Cheppi said. "That's why I don't swim. It's dangerous."

"Do you think so?"

"No, probably a sand shark. They're all over the place here."

He handed her a sandwich of meat and tomato and a small glass. "Here try mamajuana."

"What is this?"

"Try it." She sipped and coughed. He laughed. "Put it in a Coke. This is why I never learned how to swim. I drink too much."

They ate and drank under the hot sun. She laid her head on his lap and dropped to sleep.

78.

Cocks

———————•———————

S HE AWOKE ALONE, LOOKED AROUND and said quietly "Cheppi?" Then she shouted. She stood nervously and looked up and down the empty beach.

A laugh erupted from the palm trees. "Scared you, I bet." He led out two horses. Three peasants stood beside them, hats in hand, staring at her.

"What's this?"

"We going on a trip."

"I, I don't know how to ride a horse."

"Anyone can ride a horse. Here, I brought you this old mare. She's slow but she'll do."

"I don't think . . ."

"Don't think. Put on your jeans and we'll go for a ride into la cordillera."

"I don't want to and, anyway, I have a headache."

"Yep, I bet you do. Here, take a sip of mamajuana. That will fix you. You got to come riding. I will lose face with my people unless you do."

They rode through palm trees into rolling hills, with small farms and cattle ranches, and into a field of sugar cane with a smoking trapiche. They entered a dense forest. A light rain fell. From tropical heat to moist chill. She shivered, holding tightly onto the saddle horn. He looked at her, smiling. "I think we've gone far enough," she said. "It's cold."

"Here, drink this." He handed her a flask of rum.

The mare struggled on the wet path slipping and sliding, its rider hanging on. It lost footing on the wet stones, saw a steep dropoff and slid to an abrupt halt, throwing her onto the forest loam. Cheppi broke out laughing, shaking his head. "La Gringa comes to the islands and falls on her ass."

"Not funny. Not funny at all."

"You OK?"

"Yeah, I guess so." He helped her back onto the horse.

"You don't hold onto the saddle. You hold the reins. The horse goes too fast, you pull them back. You keep your balance with your beautiful thighs. Hold them tightly against the beast."

"This is impossible."

"No it isn't. Children ride from the time they're born. You can do it."

"I think we should turn back."

He shook his head. "Nope. We're almost there anyway."

Cold and muddy, she followed him down the wooded path into a clearing. Cattle dotted the hillside. Small houses stood far apart, flagged with wisps of smoke. The sun warmed her body. They rode past a small cemetery ringed with hyacinths and a worn wooden fence and entered a cattle ranch. A circle of men stood around a corral, their white hats like candles on a birthday cake. An old woman walked between them handing out Coca-Cola bottles filled with rum.

"What is this?" she said.

"You'll see."

Two men edged through the crowd carrying hemp bags over their shoulders, opened them and two large white roosters fell out. They held them for all to see. "They are beautiful," she said. 'Are they selling them?" Cheppi said nothing.

The cocksmen pushed the struggling roosters to the grass and held them tight, their faces close together. They moved them back and forth. The agitated animals squawked and squirmed. The men withdrew and the fight began. The birds flew at each other, moving in and out, parrying and jumping and jabbing their claws. "Vamos," a man yelled. "Kill him" another screamed. "That one's dead" "Kill" "Kill" The small crowd grew more and more agitated. The birds stopped, parried, then attacked again.

Bright red blood shot out onto the white feathers. Eleanor strained to see, but the crowd jostled and pushed her aside. And then, in a moment, one bird fell back and the other flew on top. A loud yell echoed through the valley. A hand reached in and pulled the cocks apart.

She looked at the bloodied victim. "Is it dead?" she said.

"Might as well be. Soup."

"What?"

"Chicken soup. It lost and if it is alive now it won't be soon. That's the way it is."

A sharp cry interrupted. The crowd shifted and ran to the noise. Eleanor and Cheppi walked over.

"You don't have my money?" a peasant said to another who ignored him, walking away. A flash of steel. Blood spurted onto white pants and across the verdant grass. And then silence. The attacker rose and strode off, cursing. The others went to the fallen man.

"What's going on," she said.

"Machetes and mamajuana. Not a good mix. These peones, they get drunk. They bet and after the fight, it is time to pay, and when the loser is broke, what with the drink and all that, people get really angry." This crowd is too hot, getting edgy and now they're coming at us.

"Was that man killed?"

"Who knows? Probably not. A slice of an arm or a leg. He'll probably survive. But he'd better not show his face until he comes up with the dough. These guys are desperate. They're good, honest people, but a bet is a bet. And if you don't pay up, you deserve what you get. But let's get going."

"Why?"

"This is why." He pointed at three men, drunk and staggering and swaying towards them, staring at Eleanor.

They jumped on their horses. The drunks stumbled and followed. Cheppi struck Eleanor's horse in the rear. It leaped forward throwing her off-balance. He steadied her, took her bridle and pulled. A hand reached, grabbed her ankle and yanked her to the ground. "Cheppi," she screamed. The men laughed and surrounded her. She looked up.

A shot rang out. Cheppi pointed the pistol at the assailants. They froze and then moved towards him, holding machetes. "Don't you worry, we're just playing," one said, touching Eleanor's cheek. " Please, lady, we are broke, give us a little money."

Cheppi shot again, the bullet grazing the man's leg. "Basta! Enough! Get going, the next bullet goes here." He pointed at his heart.

The men stumbled away, Cheppi's hand still on the gun.

"Where did you get that?"

"In the countryside, you carry protection. I know these people. They are rough, honest and hard-working, but some are vagos, vagabundos, others are borrachos, drunks. They drink, they take a smoke or two and they get stupid ideas. The bad ones, they'd chop you in a moment if you have money. And the young ones, they're the worst, they think they can take whatever they want. That's why I have a gun. Came with the ponies."

"Horrible, horrible men. I'm surprised there are people like that in this world."

"No, chica. They are not horrible. They are men who rise before dawn, walk for miles to cane fields or cattle farms, machetes by their side, and then they work ten, twelve hours for pennies and they return home to huts filled with children. So here they are, looking for a little enjoyment in life, a few drinks, a bet on a cock, and then these rich people ride in over the mountain. These men are not horrible. They are God's children."

"They attacked me, Cheppi!"

"I'm sorry, really I am. But I wanted to show you."

They rode in silence, her body shaking. "You keep surprising me."

"I looked at you as the men came at us and I thought, you are really gorgeous. I know I shouldn't have brought you. You are too, too beautiful."

"Stop it."

"I mean it. It was too risky. But I thought you should see my island, the cockfighting and the beauty of the countryside."

"I don't like it. It is too barbarous."

"Maybe, but those cocks are better than any sport, better than boxing or football or whatever. It takes just one moment, one fleeting second, when they see each other and fly into a rage. And the one who is less fearful, he is the one who wins. That's life.

Her voice trembled. "This is not what life is back home, where I come from. This is another world. But Cheppi, I am happy we came. I am so happy we came."

79.

Pinas Coladas

———————•———————

IT WAS NOTHING LIKE I'D EVER IMAGINED. I WAS SO TIRED, *my legs ached from the ride. We returned to the room and ordered pinas coladas. They are so refreshing but seductive. Makes you want more and more. We drank and drank and laughed and jumped into the shower. He ran the soap up and down my body, pushed my head under the water, and scrubbed my hair, hard, digging his hands into my scalp. He turned me and soaped my breasts, my stomach, and my thighs down to my feet. He cleaned every part of me. I pushed into him, wanting him so bad. He toweled me dry and pushed me onto the bed. And then he stared. I stared back. He leaned and kissed my vagina and then tongued me, slowly, in and out. And then he mounted me.*

He entered me gradually. My body heaved, pleading with him to plunge deeper. So slowly he plunged and then faster and faster and my soul just quaked and I laughed and laughed so deeply and then I cried and he kept pounding and I kept pushing and it was like a birth, a feeling that never existed ever, ever, and then he moaned and we grabbed onto each other and rolled back and forth, back and forth, without control. We fell off the bed onto the plush carpet and my body ached and I thought, how many times can I fall in one day without breaking bones? How many times in my life can I do what I've just done? Never, never do I want this man to come off me. I have fallen.

80.

Diego Sanchez

———————————

A KNOCK ON THE DOOR. Then a pounding. "I think, I think, they've come about Bobby"

"What?" he said sleepily

"There's someone downstairs," Eleanor said. "I think they've come about Bobby"

"What you talking about?" Cheppi said.

She sat up with a start. "Oh, nothing. Nothing. Someone's at the door."

Cheppi rose and went to the door, naked. Two policemen stood outside.

"Yes."

"We need to ask you and your wife some questions."

"What time is it?"

"It's 6 o'clock."

"Morning or night?'

"Morning."

"Shit, can't you come back later?"

"I'm sorry. This can't wait."

"OK. Well meet you downstairs. If that's OK."

The dining room was opening. "You have breakfast?" Eleanor asked.

"Not yet Madam, the cook has not arrived. I'll see what I can scrape together."

The two young cops, one man and one woman, sat alone in the dining room. The man spoke sternly, as if to hide his youth. "I believe you were at Rio Naranjo yesterday?"

"Yes?" Cheppi said. We went for a ride and went by Rio Naranjo."

"Cockfighting there?"

"If you say so."

"I'm asking you."

"Yes, I believe there was cockfighting. We arrived and saw the fighting."

"How long were you there?"

"I don't know. Honey, what do you think, 20 or 30 minutes?"

"And you saw cockfighting."

"We saw one fight. We just happened to be there."

"You bet?"

"Did I wager? No."

"You speak to anybody?"

"What's this all about, officer?"

"Do you carry a firearm?"

"Officer, I need to know what this is about," Cheppi said.

"We received a report that a Dominican man and an American woman such as yourself, he nodded to Eleanor, were in the vicinity and shot a local resident. Not many tourists here this time of year. You were easy to track down."

"Really, did you also receive a report that three drunks attacked this woman, pulled her off her horse, and tried to rape her?"

The cop paused. "I'm talking about you. I don't believe you have a permit for a firearm."

"I see," Cheppi said. "And what happened to the man who was shot or supposed to be shot?"

"He went to the clinic. They called us."

"He dead?"

"No. He's OK. But every shooting…"

"And did they also tell you about the machete fight and the man who was killed, there?" Cheppi stared into the cop's eyes. "And the betting that went on. Was it in public?"

"I am concerned with you and no one else."

"What's your name, officer."

"Diego, Diego Sanchez."

"Diego Sanchez, eh? I once knew a Diego Sanchez."

"Sir?"

"Diego Sanchez was a good policeman You resemble him. Your father?"

"Yes. You knew him?"

"Of course, chico. We are cousins. His wife is my mother's sister.

"Really?"

"Diego died, I heard."

"Yes, when I was young. He was killed."

"I'm sorry. And your mother?"

"She went al Norte."

"They were good, honest people. Not like the scum that try to rob you. Your father was a good man."

The cops looked at each other, confused. "Listen," the policeman said, "I think it best you leave today. I'll take care of the rest, but you know . . ."

Cheppi threw up his hands. "I understand completely. And here, here's something for your family."

He handed each $20.

"No, Senor, I couldn't."

"Yes you can. I insist. We are primos, cousins. We are family."

The police left and breakfast arrived, toast, fresh sliced papaya, pineapple and mango. A bowl of yogurt and granola. A pot of coffee.

She devoured the meal. He nibbled at the toast and asked, "How do you keep so fit? You eat so much?"

"Breakfast is the most important meal of the day, I told you that."

"Yes, yes. Well, I think we should call for our plane. Time to leave paradise."

"I guess, but tell me, did you know his father?"

"Yeah, I knew his father. Worst son of a bitch who ever lived. Corrupt as cowshit. Worked with Vargas, of course. Informer. He used to beat up the putas, the whores, whenever he got a chance."

"You think his son knew?"

"Who knows? Police are police. We're cousins." Cheppi laughed.

"Are you?"

"Sure, down here, everyone's a cousin. That kid didn't want to take the risk."

"You lie easily, don't you?"

"Only when it is necessary."

"Do you think those men were going to rape me?"

"Not a chance. Too drunk. They only were after money and maybe a kiss or two."

"So you lied there as well."

Cheppi drank his coffee. "I want to tell you about his father. There was a beautiful girl I knew once. Her name was Rita, from the *campo*. She became a whore like many of them do. She was a nice girl, friendly. You ask her to do something, she'd do it. She was young, very young. Very innocent."

"I don't want to hear this."

"This Sanchez, the father, was always looking for favors. So he came by with his pals and they took her to the jail and gang raped her. Then they threw her into the street. But Rita was smart, country-smart, she knew the risks and all that, but she also knew that she had her own weapon between her legs. So one night, she went to the corner bar, standing near the door. She sees him and he sees that she sees him and he starts after her. She ran into the side alley. He followed. When he grabbed her, she knifed him in the groin, a deep stab, and she twisted that blade hard. She was strong that Rita, like all country girls, she moved that knife in him so that he would never ever fuck again and never do anything again. He hardly made a noise.

"And what they do to Rita?"

"They never found her. She disappeared, vanished, maybe to Santo Domingo or Puerto Rico or Miami or New York or Caracas or just down the road into the mountains. The cops looked but they knew, they knew. They went to her village, tore the place upside down and terrorized the peasants a little, but they knew. They knew. And after a while, they forgot. So you ask me why I lie. That's why I lie."

81.

Paradise

———————————————

H ER HEAD THROBBED. HE SUGGESTED A WHISKEY. The small plane
ran into turbulence, shaking from side to side, dropping and then
rising quickly. She moaned.

"I'm telling you. A little liquor will help."

"No more alcohol. Please. I think we've had enough to drink."

"Did you have fun?"

"Fun? I've never, never, well, you know."

"I know."

"So, anyway, what do you think of my idea?" she asked.

"I don't know. It would be interesting," Cheppi responded.

"It would be fitting justice."

"That it would be."

"So is it OK to talk to Dan about it?"

He looked out the window.

"It would create jobs. I think it would help the people."

"But what would I do?"

"You would run it. We would run it."

"Maybe."

"We could make paradise." She grabbed his hand and looked into his eyes. "We could set something up for us."

"Eleanor Rigby. You are a really interesting person. But you come up with the craziest things."

82.

Control

"**A**GAIN?" DAN TREPIN SAID. "Another idea. Out of the blue. You go for a weekend with your loverboy, and all of a sudden you're the fucking Marriott."

"Dan, I'm telling you. You should see this place. It's empty, virgin and the water, it's so gorgeous. Aquamarine. Fish all over the place. Views like you've never seen."

"I've seen them, Baby. Trust me. I've seen them."

"If we can grab the property now."

"Do you know how many beach resorts there are? You goin' up against Club Med? Sandals?

"No, not at all. This would be small. Exclusive. A hideaway."

"Small means expensive."

"Perhaps."

"I don't do small. I do big. Casinos in India with elephants. Hundreds of rooms. If you want small, do a bed and breakfast."

"Dan, just help me on this. Who can we call? I'll pay whatever it takes."

"And I suppose your loverman would run the place?"

"Stop calling him that. He's from there, speaks the language and has family. Why not?"

"Rule number one. Hotels are not run by natives. Natives run hotels they give free drinks to their brothers. They hire their wives' cousins. If natives could run hotels, you wouldn't have Marriotts or Sheratons. Sure, locals work at the places, but management, they go to hotel colleges, they're business folk, they come from London or Madrid or Miami."

"OK. OK. We'll get help. But he's got to have a lead role."

"Yeah, yeah."

"So?"

"If you hadn't been such good luck for me last time."

"And I still will. Hudson Hills is over. We've sold out everything. Time to move on."

"These banana republics. You got to pay the right people, and if the government changes, you lose everything."

"So?"

"I'll make some phone calls. But you gotta understand the rules. First of all, I deal with you, not with whatshisname. I don't deal with the natives."

"You're incorrigible."

"Why, I'm helping, no?"

"Just call him by his right name. Cheppi. His name is Cheppi. You should get to know him more. He's a really nice guy."

"No I shouldn't."

"Why not?"

"Cause he has what I want."

"Stop it"

He ignored her. "We'll need a local partner and not just whatshisname."

"Cheppi."

"Yeah. We don't do business except with the people who can make things happen."

"And on these hotel deals, we need foreign backing. We'll call in Raskolnikov. You've been getting close to him anyway."

She shook her head. "You're so jealous."

"Yeah, you've got this town running around for you. You flip a finger and the lights go on. Or off, as the case may be."

"Just making money for you, Dan."

"Yeah, anyway, you call the Russki. Go see him. He likes you. Maybe he'll do you a favor. You just don't let him get too close, though."

"Dan!!!"

"In the meantime, I'll make inquiries. The A-rabs might be interested in a piece of the action. Any room for a casino?"

"No, Dan. No casino. I want this to be a quiet place. Upscale."

"You can make lots of money with a casino. Don't have to worry about the room and food shit."

"No casino. Cheppi wouldn't like it, and neither would I."

"OK. We'll see." He shook his head. "Doesn't add up. Doesn't make sense. Small hotel. Perfect beach. Banana Republic. I don't know what I'm getting into."

"And," she smiled, "we've got to maintain control. That's the only way it's going to work."

"It will all come out in the deal, honey. It always comes out in the deal."

83.

Capital

———————————

Y OU HEAR? THEY CLOSED DOWN LEHMANN BROTHERS. *They're talk-ing about closing AIG. The suits are all over the place. Feds. The housing market is going into the shits. No, we don't have to worry about Hudson Hills. All that stuff has been hived off to Europe and Asia. We got out just at the right time. I thought something like this might happen. My father always said, "don't put your money in the deals, just profit from 'em. Take the fees and run." You know some of those buildings are probably goin' to go under. Yeah, they're so under water the Hudson is flooding their rooftops. Give it some time. We'll be able to move in and pick 'em up for 20 cents on the dollar.*

Yeah, yeah, everything's in turmoil and lots of people are gonna come running. The game's afoot. Now about Eleanor's hotel down in that place, what is it call Dominica? No that's another place Dominican Republic. She's love-drunk with that asshole. I want to help her out. I owe her a favor. We made so much from Hudson Hills I could buy the fucking country. No, I'm not fucking her and I resent the implication. I need for you to make the right contacts down there. Set up some meetings. See if we can get something going. We gotta do it fast. Prime property and all that. Make sure they know that if the price is right and the bank accounts well-guarded, they can all live pretty for the rest of their lives. Tell 'em I only have a couple of months. That I'm looking at Cuba. If that bearded fucker dies we're gonna move back there. Yeah, you tell 'em that. I miss Havana. Had good times when I was a kid. Take care of this for me. As a favor.

84.

Connections

———•————————————————•———

"So once again, I'm not involved."

"Cheppi, I'm trying to do the best I can."

"Baby. I give up. This ain't gonna work. You're running downtown day after day. I'm still flipping eggs."

"You like flipping. You told me yourself. God's work, that's what you said. That's where you have fun. You can stop any time you want. We're rich."

"I'm not going to sit here and watch you manage my life."

She threw up her hands. "OK. OK. If you don't want to do it, fine. I'll call up Dan but you got to hear me out first."

He said nothing.

She continued. "They think they've got the right people onboard in the government."

"The right people in the government?"

"Yes. The only way to get the property is to have a joint-venture with some locals in Santo Domingo. Connected with the government."

"That's bullshit."

"Yep. That's right. But if we don't do it, someone else will. Four Seasons is sniffing around and there's a Spanish company coming to check it out. We need to get a signature right away."

"Paying people off, I suppose."

"You know how it works."

"These are the assholes who destroyed my town."

"No they're not. These people were in kneepads when the dictator ruled."

"The agreement has a commitment to hire 80% local people at double the minimum wage. Local suppliers, too."

"And who's going to manage?"

"That remains to be decided."

"I see," Cheppi said tersely.

"You will be in charge. But we need to do a deal with some international management firm. We need a big name on the front to attract the big money. You will make the decisions."

"Sure I will."

"These people are pros."

"And I know nothing."

"Not about this business. No."

"El spic needs help."

She ignored him. "So, this is how I see it. If everything goes right, we design the hotel. I want a hotel that looks local. Small huts. Wood. Thatched roofs. Gravel paths. Modern baths with Jacuzzis. Nice meals. You'll take care of that. Especially breakfast. And we'll have a little house down the beach. Just for us." She touched his face.

He said nothing.

"We don't have to do this. But imagine, we'd have a place to live away from all this. You'd have your own business in paradise. And I could lie on the beach all day and read."

"Or we could stay here," he said. "And I could keep doing what I've always been doing."

"Yes. And that would be OK. But it's your choice. I will do whatever. Now, how 'bout some breakfast."

85.

Compromise

———————————————

"LOOK ELEANOR, WE'VE BEEN THROUGH THIS BEFORE. You know you have to compromise."

"There's compromise and compromise, Dan."

"I hear you. But how badly do you want this beach place."

"Look, if I can't do it with you, I'll just have to go off and do it myself."

Dan Trepin looked at her and nodded his head. "What if I just buy the place myself. I'll give it to you. How about that? All you got to do is ditch your friend and come be with me."

"Stop it, Dan."

"I don't mean sex or anything. I'm too old for that anyway."

"Stop, or I'm leaving. Why do we have to go through this every time?"

"Cause you're so irresistible." She stared at him. "OK, we'll put this aside for now. I was just kidding, you know?"

"No, I don't know."

"You can try to go off and get that property without me but I'm telling you it ain't gonna happen."

"I bet Raskolnikov would help me."

"Raskolnikov won't do shit without my say-so. You think he'd risk going against me for a little action even if he wants your ass?"

"Maybe I can do it myself."

Trepin smiled. "Honey, you're brave, I'll give you that. That's why I'm attracted to you. But if you think you have the connections and the experience, you go ahead. The locals will take your money, and you'll be left high and dry, or you'll be given the property and taxed to hell. You'll wish you never met your loverman, I'll tell you that."

"It really is hard working with you, Dan."

"I know babe. I'm just a property guy who has spent his whole life buying and selling, buying and selling. I've been screwed like you'd never believe. And I've screwed as well. That's why I've got lawyers, and why guys around the world are willing to work with me."

"So what's the compromise?"

"My people looked it over. I gotta hand it to you once again. You have a great nose. Absolutely right. Prime location, even some good infrastructure. Strong buildings, good protection, all that good stuff. And they're looking to lease it out, the government is."

"Lease?"

"Yeah, don't worry. Hundred-year lease. The law is you can't sell the beach. Crap like that you gotta deal with all the time. But I think we can grab it if we act quick before Club Med snaps it up. We've got a guy down there I used to know. Frankie Morazan. Good man and very well connected."

"And the compromise."

"We've got to expand a little. Build some other buildings and sell them as Condos. Not right on the cove but further away. There's lots of Venezuelan money coming through ever since Chavez took over, and there's always Raskolnikov's people. So it's got to be bigger."

"And who will run it?"

"We'll get one of the big hotel groups."

"That wasn't the idea. I wanted to buy the place for Cheppi and me, run it like a little resort."

"Yeah, I know but it ain't going to happen. Not a spot like that. Too valuable. We'll need lots of money to get the place, to pay off the right people, and then to advertise. That's the way it works."

"It'll ruin the spot."

"Nah, it will still be pretty. We'll make sure of it, you and me. But if this doesn't work for you, why not just go off and buy a little hut somewhere else? Or, if you're interested, one of the Condos we'd build."

"I thought Cheppi could run it." Her face fell.

"We can make it part of the deal. He can be the head of the place. Of course, we'd need to have our own people in place, the hotel chain and finance people."

"Let me think it over, Dan."

"Yeah, you do that. But get back to me fast. I've got a bunch of people hanging on this, and the walls have ears if you get what I'm saying."

86.

Frankie Morazan

A LINE OF CARS DROVE THROUGH A FOREST of bougainvillea gravel scratching underneath. They stopped short at the gate. This was the home of Frank Morazan, Frankie to his pals and customers, modest compared to the most powerful but still contained by barbed wire, security cameras and a platoon of security guards with strong, black German Shepherds. The setting sun gleamed off a light rain, sparking a symphony of songs of Hispaniola parrots, macaws and emerald woodpeckers, punctuated by screeching owls.

Frankie Morazan had survived dictators, criminal thugs, and American occupation. Frankie was no politician. Neither was he allied to any party, religious sect or ideology. Frankie was a deal-maker. A neutral intermediary, the man in the middle of all the action. Everyone trusted Frankie and Frankie made sure everyone got a piece of the action, the President, the General, the Archbishop, or the corporation. You want a deal, you went to Frankie. You want no trouble, you give him a call.

"I've known Frankie for years," Dan Trepin said. "He's famous in these parts. Difficult character, has his own way of doing things. But he's important. You want something done in the DR, he's the man. Dress well, will you? Suits and ties and gowns. This man was raised by Jesuits. He's as old-fashioned as Moses and as religious as the Pope. He's old, maybe past 80, but don't let that fool you. He's got his wits about him and has seen every trick in the book. When you enter his house, you go back a hundred years like into a museum, but that's the price you pay. You, Eleanor, you sit next to Carlota, his wife. Let the men speak. When we go out for cigars, you go for tea and chocolates or whatever the fuck she offers you."

Morazan stood erect, propped with a gold cane. His wife held his arm, and nodded as they walked into the vestibule. Trepin, the lawyer Galloway, Raskolnikov, Eleanor and Cheppi. The couple were a picture of aged propriety, strong and unsmiling, diminutive in stature, formal dress, and sculptured hair. They welcomed each in impeccable English except for Cheppi. "Bienvenidos," Morazan said to him. "Esta en su casa."

A stooped, dark-skin elderly woman served a modest dinner, roast chicken and rice and beans. A green salad. A Chilean chardonnay. A small chocolate pastel. "Thank you for visiting us," Frankie Morazan said with an English accent. "These days, not too many people come. They don't need our help much what with bankers and investors all over the place. They are mistaken, of course. They think times are different. but they are the same and they will learn."

"Absolutely," Trepin said. "The young people always think times are different until they find out differently." He laughed at his own joke.

"In Russia, times are different," Raskolnikov said. "A whole new world. The young businessman rules."

Morazan's head drooped as they spoke as if asleep. "I am not sure. My great-grandfather used to ship sugar to Odessa. I still have the receipts."

"That was under the Czars."

"Yes," Morazan said. "That's what they were called then. What are they called now?"

"Good point," the Russian said.

"Our estate is quite old," he said quietly, almost whispering, his head lowered. "My great-grandfather, he actually owned slaves. And his son had villages of peones living among us. Good, humble and honest people. Hard working and religious. We farmed our lands and traded sugar and molasses and rum all over the world including to your New York. Then the gringos came and took over the trade and there were labor issues and the government went from left to right to left and so we went into what we do now. But you know, I am not ashamed of my past. We fed our slaves and our peones lived good, clean lives."

His head rose and his eyes turned towards Eleanor. "I have learned not to make judgments. This poor island has seen tyrants and torture chambers, wars and wars, drug dealers and political scoundrels who pledged freedom and liberty and then stole this island blind. I make deals so that my country can survive."

"That is why I am talking with you all. I will work with you, play the percentage game, make sure that the Ministries don't get in the way, that the Casa Presidencial will, how you say it, give you cover as well. You'll get help from the police. I will do all that for my share of the take and make sure all the right other people get theirs. But I am not greedy. The shares I take will be reasonable, and you will not be unhappy. I don't like greed." He turned to Raskolnikov, "it is a deadly sin and produces trouble, and so I warn you if I find hidden benefits that do not accrue to me or if there is something fishy going on, I will close you down without warning. You can write all the contracts you want, but if I feel cheated or I hear that drugs or prostitution or any other filth is going on, you'll be out of here."

"No problem, Frankie," Dan Trepin said.

'Perhaps. Perhaps."

Carlota Morazan looking at her husband, paying close attention, her cracked face showing not a bit of emotion. A brief silence. She touched Eleanor's sleeve. "We raised our children here," she said. "They're off around the world now, in China, New York, and Paris. They are doing well for the family firm, except for little Pedro. He is a writer, you know."

Frankie Morazan shook his head. "Writers in Paris. He thinks he is Hemingway."

"He is doing what he wants," Carlota said, quietly.

"Yes," Frankie said. "They are all doing what they want, but I'm afraid they are forgetting their homeland." He turned to Cheppi "Usted me entiende? Do you understand what I'm saying?"

"Yes, of course," Cheppi said, in English.

"I would like to read your son's writings," Eleanor said.

"I'm afraid you won't like them," Frankie said brusquely. "Everything is politics. The bad old days. Los indios muertos. These new writers, I'm afraid they don't understand the world, like Borges or Vargas Llosa. You know them, Dan?"

"I'm afraid I don't. I don't have much time to read," Trepin said.

"The old values, our history, our soul, it is very important. We understand that," Frankie said.

"Yes, of course," Trepin said.

"I admire them," Eleanor said.

"You've read them?" Carlota said to her while staring at her husband.

"Of course. They are quite wonderful, though those who have come after ..."

Frankie waved his hand. "Enough of books. Two centuries of books and what have they given us? Let us go smoke. Good Dominican cigars. Good Dominican brandy."

The men headed towards the verandah. Eleanor sat with Carlota. "Madame Tibbett," Frankie turned, "would you please join us?"

Carlota smiled. "This is very interesting, my dear. Frankie never deals with women. He is either going senile or is smitten with you."

"So you see, dear," Frankie said to his wife. "I am not the dinosaur you think."

"No, you are very modern," she said with a sly wink. "My dear," she turned towards Eleanor, "I hope everything works well for you. I will give you my son's books. I'd like to know your opinion."

87.

The Way of the World

———————————————————

So THIS IS WHO WE DEAL WITH? *He is the enemy. He is the man who I fought against all these years, the guy behind the, how do you say it, curtain. The banker? The dealmaker? The fucking devil himself? 'Neutral? No judgments?' You've got to be kidding me. This is the same old bullshit. This is 'the way of the world.' So this guy and his rich friends are gonna make everything work for us, gonna pave the way for Trepin, for that Russian, and for all those rich ladrones who steal from their countries and need a nice place to stash it? This is what you want me to do, Eleanor? This is the price we have to pay?*

I don't think you realize how much I have given to make you happy. We destroyed my community. I sold them out. You say that's 'the way it is.' That's the way of the world.' Someone else would do it. But I did it and now you are asking me to make a deal with the devil. Can't you see this fellow is evil? He may not have a big mansion or drive a Maserati. He may go to Church every day and stay close to his old lady, but that makes no difference. His deals, his greasing the wheels, makes it all easier to bring in the soldados and fuck the people.

And I have to tell you, as I sat silently at that table with that viejo and his old lady, as I listened to his mierda, the tension in me built and built. I wanted to say "fuck you," stand up and walk out. And on the verandah, as we smoked and drank and he was so familiar with me, tu-tuing me this and tu-tuing me that, as if I were his son, my skin crawled. Like one of those horror movies, here we were in the middle of the forest with this fiend, making a deal with the devil.

Why did I do it? Why am I doing it? I don't know. For the money? For the power? So that I don't have to finish my life in the back of a diner flipping burgers? No, I don't think so. I did it for you. Eleanor. Yes, that's it. I did it because I was infatuated with you. Overwhelmed by you. Imagine me, Cheppi, taken in by a rich gringa. I can't believe it. I can't fucking believe it.

I need a shower. A drink. Maybe a little hierba, some grass, maybe some coke.

88.

Cindy Williams

———————————•———————————

"I DON'T BELIEVE IT, THAT DEVIL, that killer, and look at her now," she threw the NY Post onto the desk.

"You really should let it go Cindy. It's finished. A beautiful girl like you should be out getting a guy."

"That's what my Auntie May told me. She said that you can't solve everything, that bad men may succeed on this earth, but they will roast in hell forever."

"Your auntie was wise. I say tend to your own garden, and let the others do what they may. White people get away with murder every day."

She ignored him. She had lost track of Tibbett some time back. The doorman building was a dead end. She had staked it out, but Tibbett never showed up. Then she went to City Records and had discovered an Eleanor Tibbett corporation but with the address of some downtown lawyer.

The devil kept popping up in her face, in the newspapers and then, as if God himself had willed it, at that bar where she had been doing security, walking out with a bunch of high and mighties. She had grabbed a cab and followed the limo to this place uptown. Hudson Hills. Another doorman building, another, "sorry I can't help you" and another dead end.

Then, to the precinct house. "I'm telling you she's a killer," she had said to the officer behind the desk.

"Look, I said I would see you 'cause you security guys work with us all the time, but I looked over the file and I gotta' tell you, she didn't kill her sister."

"She's a serial killer, I'm telling you, her husband, that dog and her sister"

"Miss Williams, I don't know anything about her husband. Not our jurisdiction. And there is not a hint of foul play from the witnesses in Joan Tippett's death. Reckless driving, that's what is written here. Nobody mentioned anything about someone being shoved. Now I'm not saying it didn't happen the way you said, but a traffic violation ain't homicide, if you get my drift. I mean witnesses, there are ten here in the file, at the corner of a street where everybody minds their own business, talking on their phones, looking at the sights, and waiting for the light to change. What you're saying is pure conjecture.

"She is evil and must be stopped."

"Look, I'll look into it if you wish, Miss Williams. You free tonight? I thought maybe you and I could have dinner to discuss it."

She knew what that meant, another guy with dreams in his pants. And then, the devil had done his work again. That Tibbett woman disappeared from Hudson Hills. She sat in the park, on a worn wooden bench, waiting for her to come out, but she never appeared. She pulled out the old newspaper picture of Tibbett and Trepin and showed it to a bunch of old guys playing dominoes.

"You know this woman?"

"Si, of course," one of the guys said. "Come, sit with us. Have a beer. You know how to play?

"No. I got to get to work, but when did you see her?"

"Oh, pretty lady, some time ago. She was with this guy Cheppi, but I don't think they got along too well. They argue too much. One day they were here, the next they were gone. Isn't the way it used to be I tell you. People got married, had kids and stayed in the *barrio* forever. Now they make love and move on. You sure you don't want a beer?"

"Where you going, pretty lady? What did I say? Did I insult her?"

"You never were good with girls, viejo. And this negrita, she too high class for you. Now are going to play?"

89.

The Club

———————•———————

Welcome to Club Hacienda del Coco, *the newest luxury resort in the Caribbean for those who enjoy privacy, golden sands and crystalline, turquoise waters. Traditional Caribbean architecture reinvented for modern living. Take your choice of one of 35 beautiful private villas, each discreetly hidden amidst a jungle of palms, each designed by a world-renowned architect and each with access to the most private, secure beachfront in the region. Modern interiors, with hardwood floors, gracious baths, Jacuzzis, and a host of options. A world-class marina.*

A Trepin Resort.

In the mornings, Eleanor and Cheppi met with builders, the Germain Management Group, and the local staff. Garden paths should be secluded, away from the road and the beach. Each cottage with a Jacuzzi? How large a TV? Will there be a library? A kitchen? A bar? A spa, perhaps? The condos were to be around the cove, away from view, and run separately.

After lunch, they relaxed with a horseback ride into the countryside or a dip in the soft bay or a fishing cruise for *huachinango*, red snapper that Cheppi grilled with garlic and onions over an open fire. A bottle of wine or two and later a night of love making.

After a while, as the hotel took shape, more free time. Eleanor took Spanish lessons. She volunteered at the village school teaching English. She read. Long walks in the sugar cane fields.

"Why 'Club'?" Cheppi asked. "Why not simply Hotel?"

"They're aiming at high spenders."

"How much they charging?"

"Depends. Hasn't been set yet. Somewhere between $500 and a thousand."

"A month?"

"A day, honey, a day."

"Chinga."

"It gets better," Eleanor said. "They're selling shares. Venezuelans, Argentines, Russians, Israelis, some Arabs. They see this is a good, tax-free investment. This is what Dan brings to the picture. They know and trust him."

"Tax-free? They don't pay taxes?"

"We got a tax holiday from the government. Thanks to Frankie."

He shook his head.

She touched his arm. "And the thing is we've promised Frankie double minimum wage, health benefits, housing and schooling for the employees. Most important, we'll preserve the environment. There were other bidders who wanted to come in and carve the place up, put in large hotels and casinos. I think that's what sold Frankie on us."

"Frankie, huh."

"He liked you. He really did. We told him you'd be upfront, the manager, running the place with the Germain group"

"I don't know, all these rich people."

"You'll overwhelm them, honey. You're a natural. That's if you want. If you don't, we'll just stay in our villa and have fun. All you'd have to do is cook breakfast for me."

"I don't know."

"You deserve this. You've worked your entire life, and now here's the chance to live a little."

"I don't know."

"It's up to you, really. Whatever you want."

90.

Love

———•———

THE TALE IS NEARLY OVER. Or so you might think. Eleanor has a new man with whom she is deeply in love and a home in paradise. She is rich and her own woman. Hubris, that's what the Greeks called it. Overwhelming pride defying the gods, under a hot, blinding tropical sun.

There she is lying on the beach, her tan body at rest. She sips a pina colada, reading the latest Martin Amis or Annie Proulx. The maids have changed the bedding, vacuumed, dusted and placed new towels on the rack. They lowered the air conditioner and lit a spice orange candle for her return. La *pura vida*, that's what they call it. Her shield, that protective guard from her childhood, which hardened and protected her from the tragedies of later life, that guard was relaxed.

A moment of hubris.

Life isn't a beach resort, is it? Brochures and movies offer love, warmth, good food and escape. "What we promise our clientele is total, complete relaxation," the Germain Management Group promised the Hacienda del Coco consortium. "We provide anything our guests might wish from music to massage, from fine food to fun and games, and we train our personnel to protect our guests against any and all intrusions."

But life is not a sales pitch and the realty principle is not the reality principle. First, a slight warming tropical breeze cools the skin and next a Caribbean hurricane sweeps in from the Atlantic bringing rain and wind and flooding that destroys homes and lives in a matter of minutes.

Neither is it a perfect love affair. Life has ups and downs, wins and losses, sort of like a game of dominos. You are given your tiles and you play them out. You might win. You might lose. Then the tiles get tossed into a pile and mixed up, black and white thrown around, add some outside force, be it the gods, God, the fates, a Hurricane wind, whatever, you get a new hand to play. A prudent woman, one who has suffered life's vicissitudes, will look at the new hand and keep playing.

91.

Carlota Morazan

———————————

HACIENDA DEL COCO WAS THE BIGGEST SUCCESS of any hotel in the Caribbean. Prices soared. First, $500 a night, then a G, then 2G, the jewel in the crown of the Germain Management group. Those in the know said it was the place to be, small but luxurious, secluded and discreet. Private, oh so private. Secure, oh so secure, with high tech security taken from the previous owner.

A perfect place to take your mistress or lover. Food to die for and the breakfasts, the best ever, no old croissant and bagels or warmed-over eggs or tired buffets, but luscious local bacon, fresh eggs with delicate rice and beans (who ever imagined?). "What is the recipe?" was the refrain. "Ask Cheppi. If he likes you, he'll tell you."

Reservations three years in advance. Russian oligarchs took the place for a month. American bankers, French politicians and Chinese moguls, they all demanded rooms. "Perhaps in four years' time, if we can fit you in."

If Cheppi gave the resort its soul, Eleanor provided the spark. "You must meet her, she's quite some woman. You need anything, just ask her. Give her my name (they always said), and she'll give you special attention. "

Over dinner, Eleanor moved from table to table, meeting and greeting. If invited for a drink, she sat and talked, responding naturally to the guests be they large obese Russian millionaires, swarthy Colombians or withdrawn Chinese officials. The girl from the hardware store stool knew how to smile, respond, and charm.

Looking back, the tragedy was predictable. The resort's guests, rich and powerful men, insisted on telling insensitive jokes, directing the traffic, giving orders, especially to this Dominican guy with the funny American accent. Imperiously, they would drop their Mercedes with the doorman, usher their girlfriends or wives or business associates into the lobby, brush by Cheppi or worse: "Chico, make sure my luggage gets to my room, will you?"

"Ignore it," Eleanor counseled. "They're just guys trying to impress."

"Yeah, I know. But it makes me feel like shit."

"So why bother with them. Enjoy yourself. Let's go horseback riding or fly back to New York for a couple of weeks."

"I gotta do something. I've worked all my life and now you saying I should just play. I can't do that."

Eleanor's life was full. Spanish lessons, then a visit to the local school to teach English, and socializing with the guests. Her friendship with Carlota grew. Weekly lunches at the Morazan mansion, sharing books, trips to the old capital, to museums and art galleries. From time to time, Frankie Morazan joined in, clearly attracted to the American woman.

It was a warm afternoon. They sat in the garden, sipping sherry quietly. Carlota nodded off and Eleanor rose. "You're not leaving?" Carlota mumbled.

"I thought . . ."

"No, please stay awhile" she said, under her breath.

Eleanor sat.

"I didn't want to marry him," Carlota whispered, her eyes closed. "They forced me, my parents. I fought and fought. I loved someone else, a boy so beautiful who made his living building fishing boats with his own hands, mind you. I'd sit and watch him craft the wood, sanding, bending, and forming a keel, varnishing the body, adding the fixtures, and ensuring that the vessel was so watertight. He was such a serious boy, concentrating so much on his work, not paying me any mind until later when he looked at me with the same, how do you say, attention, as to his work. And he was so strong, his arms so muscular, and his hands so tight. When he hugged me, I knew I was protected. He swept me away."

"They wouldn't allow it, my parents. Different times, you know. And maybe they were right. Practicalities. Frankie? It was a marriage of convenience. It was the depression, times were tough, and we were going to lose our land. Frankie was not much to look at back then, skinny, awkward kid, smart, sure, but full of himself, so full of himself. I don't know to this day whether he really wanted me. He says he did but he is a polite man. A gentle man. I came to respect him over time and love him."

"It is not an easy life for Frankie and me although it seems that way. You have to be careful of everything and everyone. Drug dealers, politicians, policemen, bankers, and foreigners. Every year, there's a new threat, communists or gangsters or crooked bureaucrats. He fends them off with money or deals or even threats.

"Our family is a noble family. We even have a crest. We are members of the most elite club on the island. But we are the target. It makes Frankie into a stern man, a defensive man. He is not that with me, but with the rest of the world . . ."

"Our children are so far away. They call, come back from time to time, but this is not what we wanted. We wanted a house filled with noise, people yelling, grandchildren playing and getting underfoot. Instead, we are rich and powerful and lonely. I hope you will be our friend."

92.

The Golf Course

———•———————————•———

T HE SUN FELL OVER THE BAY, casting a long shadow on the balcony. Eleanor read, a drink at her side, turning the book to catch the failing light. A bright blue tunic partially covered her swim suit. She spotted Cheppi walking down the beach, his arm around a member of the staff, a young woman in charge of the pool. The couple laughed. He looked up at the house and waved to Eleanor.

"She's quite pretty," Eleanor said as he came in.

"Yes, but not as pretty as you."

She put her book down. "Now you know that's not true."

Cheppi kneeled and kissed her knee. "She's just a kid."

"Yeah, yeah, just a kid."

"Don't be jealous."

"You coming with me to the Morazans tomorrow?"

"Again? No, not this time."

"O.K., I'll go by myself."

"You don't mind?"

"Sure I mind. We were going to discuss an expansion."

"Expansion, of what?"

'Of this place. Frankie thinks we should put in a golf course."

"You've got to be kidding me."

"He also wants to set up a clinic, plastic surgery. A quiet place for the foreigners to have their faces cut."

"Gee, I hear a clinic, and I think doctors for the villagers."

"We can do that as well. Why don't you come to discuss it?"

"He's playing you."

"No, he's not," she said angrily.

"Yeah, yeah, he's playing you. They're both playing you and you want to be played."

"Why don't you just come and say that to him."

"I got better things to do."

"I bet you do."

"Better than golf courses and face treatments."

"I don't understand, Cheppi. Why is this such a big problem?"

"No, you don't understand. We build apartments in New York, a beach resort down here, and you're not satisfied. Enough is enough. You got to keep buying and selling, buying and selling. I don't get it. I thought we were going to hang out and have fun."

"It's just an idea."

"Yesterday," Cheppi said, "I went for a walk down the road towards town. When I returned, the guard at the gate asked me where I worked, in the kitchen, the laundry or maintenance. He wanted ID. So we stand there for a half-hour, waiting for some guy to come, and you know what that guy says, 'he's OK, let him in.' He didn't say, 'I'm sorry sir for the inconvenience.' Nope, I was just another peasant. And then it hit me, we turned El Coco from the estate of the tyrant to the estate of many tyrants.

"That's not fair."

"Isn't it? Sure, no torture, but just the same, guards and walls. We've lost our land. Again. I'm going out. I need to get some fresh air."

"Cheppi, please!"

He stormed out the door, jumped into a Jeep and skidded down the road.

The next morning she ate breakfast alone, boiled eggs and a stale croissant.

She tried his phone. No answer. She left a note on the bed and drove to the Morazans. When she returned that evening, he was asleep. She shook him awake.

"I told them that we didn't want the golf course and the clinics right now. They understood."

"Right now, huh?"

"Yes. I couldn't say absolutely no. They'd go off and build it themselves."

"So why don't they? They can do anything they want."

She fell quiet.

"So why don't they?" he repeated.

"They wanted me to set it up, be on the board and be the front man."

"You've really gone over, haven't you?"

"Over?"

"To the otro equipo," is what we say.

"Excuse me?"

"When a straight guy goes gay, we say he's joined the other team. When an ally becomes a traitor and joins the other party, we say the same thing." He rose.

"I did what you wanted."

"No, you just postponed the inevitable. They want to build a golf course, they'll bring in the tanks, knock down the villages, throw them into cement slums in the city, and plant grass so that some thieves can play. Do those gringo golfers ever think about what they're playing on? They think grass, I see old farm land or villages dispossessed."

"It's not a done-deal," she said. "If you're against it, forget it then."

"It's a done-deal. With you, you have an idea and somehow or some way, it's done. It's always "if we don't do it, someone else will," as if there is some great power out there, some god of bulldozers, knocking down peasant houses and building condos and resorts and golf courses." He dressed.

"What are you doing?"

"I'm going out."

"And leaving me?"

"I'm not leaving you, you're leaving me."

93.

Anger

●━━━━━━━━━━━━━━━━━━━━━━━●

DOMESTIC VIOLENCE IS WORSE THAN CRIMINAL, they tell us. A guy cheats you, you mess him up a little, your wife cheats on you, well, the jails are filled with wife murderers and beaters. The closer you feel to your loved one, the more you let your guard down, throw away the caution built through life. And when betrayal comes, anger surges, violence ensues, hateful felonious revenge, or worse what they call displacement, when hate takes other forms, injuring everyone.

The pattern was set. Cheppi, out all night, weaving home, crashing into bed.

"I told you," Eleanor said to him. "I won't live with a drunk. This has got to stop."

"Yeah," he mumbled into his pillow, "you won't huh? Well get the fuck out of my house and go live with those old fuckers you hang out with."

It happened so fast, Cheppi's anger, his resentment and drunkenness. She was in shock, paralyzed, caught in her island paradise. Management complained about his late night loudness. He no longer worked at the hotel, quietly replaced with a Mexican hotelier from Cancun.

"We should see a marriage counselor," she suggested.

"We're not married."

"Get help from someone."

"Get help? I'll tell you what help you can get. You can get the hell out of here."

She tried another tack. "Let's go back to New York for a while. Try to sort out our lives."

"You go back to New York. I'm finished with that town. I'm back where I belong. Doing what I should be doing."

Midday, after lunch, she was in the dining room, talking with a Brazilian family. "Mrs. Tibbett," a waiter interrupted. "There's someone to see you."

The small woman in the lobby wore a plain, wrinkled dress, her face scorched from the sun, her arms strong, a worker. She spoke in Spanish with a mountain dialect, clipping the ends of the words, haltingly, about her "nin," she mentioned Chep and then her "nin" again and then "drog." Eleanor caught the words or thought she did but not the meaning. Eleanor looked about and called to the waiter. "Would you help me?"

The waiter listened and touched the peasant's arm. "I'm sorry, Senora," he said. "I really shouldn't hear this. You get someone else."

"Please?" Eleanor said. "I need to know what she is saying."

"Someone else, Madam, someone else."

She looked around. The peasant stared at her, trembling, with tears in her eyes. Eleanor led her to a bench. "Sientese aqui," she motioned. She called Carlota and explained and handed the phone to the peasant. "Aqui," Eleanor said. "Habla aqui."

The peasant shook her head. "Policia?"

"No, no policia," Eleanor said. "Una amiga mia. Hablale."

Nervously the woman took the phone. Her voice was weak, interrupted by sobs and nervous glances. She handed the phone back to Eleanor.

"Carlota, what did she say?"

"Eleanor, dearest. This is a conversation not for the phone. We should talk. Tomorrow, here."

"Why can't you tell me?"

"Trust me, dearest. Come and we'll talk."

That evening, Eleanor told Cheppi about the incident. "What did she say?"

he asked.

"I don't know," she said. "I really wish you were there to help."

"Yeah, well, I got more important things to do," his voice slurred

"But Carlota will tell me."

Cheppi stared at her, his eyes blazing. "You just remember this, baby. We're in this together. Whatever happens to me, happens to you. You just be careful."

"You threatening me?"

"You just remember. This is my island. My people. And you are my guest."

94.

Drugs

———————————————•

THEY SIPPED TEA IN THE GARDEN, Frankie and Carlota Morazan and Eleanor, the pungent odor of rotting tropical leaves all about. A flock of parrots announced their presence overhead, cacawing in a blaring chorus.

Frankie spoke. "Eleanor, my dear. There are good people in this island but many are frustrated. They watch television or movies and they see all these people, sex symbols, rock stars, and famous celebrities, and they envy. It is the illness of the age. Tradition and understanding one's place in the world have vanished. Everyone wants to be someone. And the illness is fueled by drugs."

"Excuse me Frankie, what are you saying."

"That woman yesterday, she told Carlota that Cheppi was with her daughter."

"I see."

"It is much worse. Her daughter is not yet 15. And he and she are both using."

"Using?"

"Coca. Cocaine."

Eleanor said nothing but stared ahead. Fury surged through her veins, harkening back to the dark days. The outward, gentle and cordial face remained, masking anger, a hardened shape of reactive smiles.

"You didn't know?"

"Of course not."

"The woman says that her daughter is not the first," Frankie continued. "That other girls are involved too. He lures them to the resort, plays around with them, and then . . . Remember what I said when we first met. Any trouble, I'll take action. I've got a lot riding on this place, and there will be a lot of angry people if this gets out. I cannot let that happen"

"Yes," she said quietly.

"Once drugs take hold, they don't let go. I don't think you can handle it."

"That's enough," Carlota said angrily. "Dejale en paz. Leave her alone."

He looked at his wife, blankly. "Mi vida, would you please get us a little sherry."

His wife rose passively. Frankie moved next to Eleanor, and took her hand. "My dear, I'm told that you are tough. Your New York friends say they trust you to do the right thing."

Eleanor nodded.

"I'm an old man. I served in my country's army and, I've run corporations none of them were pure. There were always people doing what they shouldn't. But I've always handled problems directly. I've made sure my investments and those of my associates were safe. Nobody likes these things, and I'm not proud of some things I've had to do. But messes happen. If you are to live in this world you get hold of them and clean them up before your enemies do. Before the press gets wind. You understand what I'm saying?'

She turned and stared at him. "Yes Frankie, I do."

"I know, affairs of the heart are difficult."

"This is not an affair of the heart," Eleanor said stiffly. "That is gone."

"I cannot have messes."

"I will take care of it," she said. "I promise you."

"With haste, Eleanor. With haste."

Later, after she left, the elderly couple remained in the garden finishing their sherry. "I love spending these afternoons with you, Frankie," Carlota said.

"They are peaceful."

"Just as the mist rolls in and the birds sing, and we sit here in contemplation, it is my favorite time."

He said nothing. "So what do you think?" Carlota asked.

"I think she will handle it."

"I don't know. I wish you weren't so hard on her and used a little more diplomacy. She's just a young woman. I think you should have dealt with it in the way you do. She doesn't know how, I think."

"My dear," Frankie said. "You didn't see her face? She will do something."

"But what if it's the wrong thing."

"Then we get rid of all of them, call our friends in the Ministries, and take over the place, but I don't think that will happen. She's a smart woman. Something in her is very hard. I understand her. She has learned the lesson, been bitten by love you know, but who hasn't?"

"That's why I don't trust her," Carlota said. "She's a woman in love. You should have handled it. Get rid of him once and for all."

"Time to go in, my sweet. It's getting a little chilly. You'll see. I am a good judge of human nature. She has become us."

95.

Contracts

————————•

"YOU'RE MY LAWYER, DAVE?" Eleanor said.

"I'm Dan's lawyer," he responded.

"But you drew up my contracts," she said.

"Yes, in those cases, I am your lawyer."

"So we have attorney-client privilege?"

"Yes, in those cases."

"So tell me, in the event one of us dies, Cheppi or me, what happens to the corporate shares?

"You ill, Eleanor?"

"No."

"Cheppi?"

"Please, Dave, answer the question."

"What is this about?"

"Cheppi has a drug problem. It's getting worse. I don't know if he's going to make it."

Galloway reviewed the agreements. "The way I wrote it, actually the way Dan Trepin and I wrote it,"

"Dan?"

"He insisted. Didn't trust Cheppi."

"Dan is always a problem, isn't he?"

"Maybe. But he has your best interests at heart. He's your guardian angel. Anyway, you control everything in your corporation. Cheppi has a minority share, but if for whatever reason he is not around, all rights pass to you."

"And the other way around if something happens to me?"

"Your rights pass to the Church."

"Dan, huh? Doesn't seem like a guardian angel to me."

"You are here today because of him. Don't you forget."

"Maybe."

"And he is forgiving. He may be rough and tough but like a guardian angel, he is forgiving. When the time is right, go to him."

96.

Yachts

———————•————————•———————

J UAN CASILLAS HAD KNOWN THEM ALL, but this guy took the cake. Here, in this Puerto Rican port, rich guys come with their teenage mistresses, gays party through the night, drunken vets go fishing and vomit through the day, and co-eds go naked. They fish in the Caribbean, and they dock with headaches, sunburns, and ODs. He just smiles and complies in his broken English, keeping his eyes astern. The cash was great. Large tips, a few bottles of booze, and an easy life.

Casillas hosed down the deck as the sun fell. A short, stocky figure walked toward him. He paid him no mind. "I like your boat," the figure said.

"Gracias." He picked up a rag and dried the hardwood railings.

"How much?"

He stopped cleaning. "For a day, five hundred, fuel, gear and drinks not included."

"No, how much to buy?"

"Buy?"

"Yeah, buy"

"No, senor. This boat not for sale."

"OK, I go someplace else"

"OK, Hasta luego."

The man turned back. "Tell me, that boat over there. the thirty-footer with the big Evinrudes, really shining and good-looking, with the For Sale sign, you know that boat?" The man spoke English with a thick accent, not Spanish, that was for sure.

"Yeah, I know that boat. It's Paco's.

"How much do you think he wants?"

"Paco? He'll take forty."

"Forty? That seems a fair price."

"Yeah, he can't make the payments. He thought the tourists would go for all that chrome."

"Forty, huh?"

Casillas nodded.

"I tell you what. I give you 50 for your boat and you go buy Paco's and you keep the change."

Casillas looked at him. "Why don't you buy Paco's?"

"I like your boat. Not Paco's. Chrome never did it for me."

"I gotta think about it."

"Tomorrow morning. I meet you here. We go to the bank."

Casillas looked at the guy. Tough, scarred, not young but tough enough. Could be Mafia. Could be Russian. He had a strong smell about him though. Not unusual on dogs, but this guy really needed to wash. Casillas moved upwind from him. "You into drugs?"

"No. No drugs, no smuggling, no immigration shit. I give you my word."

Casillas shrugged. "Your word, huh. You running from something?"

"Nope, I like your boat, I just want to take it to Miami. Here, I'll show you my passport. He flipped it open. It was his picture. His hand covered the name. Too dark in any case.

"Sixty," Casillas said.

"Now you're getting greedy. I told you fifty and that's it. I tell you what. I give you five more to cover your costs. That's it, 55. Otherwise, fuck it, I'll go talk with Paco."

97.

Seabound

———————●———————

MARTA WAS YOUNG, VERY YOUNG, with dark, budding breasts and slight hips, short jeans tied tightly. "Cinnamon and clove," Cheppi murmured. He touched her cheek and brought the glass to her lips. The Bacardi was almost gone, the ashtray crammed with butts and lime rinds.

"Tengo que irme," Cheppi rose from the bed. "It's late. I have to do some stuff tomorrow."

"Vienes manana?"

"Seguro que si."

"Tomorrow," she said into her pillow, "siempre manana. Don't you forget, more of the good stuff."

"Don't you worry. We'll have a real party tomorrow." He threw her a kiss and drifted out onto the dark hotel path, wandering unsteadily through palms and flora. Dim border lamps marked the way.

"Cheppi?" A voice called from behind.

"Si," he turned awkwardly.

A blow to the head. Then another. He crumpled to the ground. He felt a hood pulled over his head. Then another blow. Then another.

The figure shoved his body into a black bag and dragged it slowly onto the beach. He heaved it onto a dingy, retraced his steps and brushed the sand, removing all traces. He pushed the dingy into the mild surf and rowed to the waiting fishing boat. He hoisted the dingy onto the stern and jumped on.

The motor purred quietly as the vessel pushed slowly away from land. No running lights. The figure opened a beer, turned on the autopilot and drank. He walked to the stern and kept his eyes on the dingy.

In the dark, Cheppi opened his eyes, confused and dazed. He moved his legs. Blood stung his eyes. He wrestled to clear them and saw nothing. "Que quiere?" he shouted helplessly. "What do you want?" No answer. "What do you want with me," he said louder. He heard a chain, then felt it being wound around one leg and then the other. "What are you doing? Wait, let's talk. I'll give you money. Anything. Please."

He cried out. "Man, you hurting me. What do you want?" The figure ignored the protest, picked him up and threw him into the sea. Cheppi rolled back and forth but the chains held. "Por favor, no mas, no mas."

Darkness. Water. For only a second did he understand. "Eleanor," he whispered, "Eleanor Rigby." The boat moved slowly and quietly in the dark, dragging him into the deep. Cheppi struggled futilely. He gasped for air, inhaled the sea water and gasped one last time.

The boat returned to the bay in a quiet crawl. Early morning house lights surrounded the vessel on three sides. A slight moon declined on the horizon. The figure leaned across the stern and pulled the bag in. He removed the chains, opened the bag, removed the corpse, and placed the body gently into the bay. An incoming tide carried it towards the beach. The boat moved out to sea.

98.

Receptions

———•———————————————————•———

THE TRIP TO SANTO DOMINGO WAS NECESSARY. Frankie Morazan was holding a reception for the Provincial governors and their wives. They were to discuss the new golf course and meet with the Chief of Police to discuss security. "Don't worry," she had told Cheppi. "I'll be OK. You enjoy yourself as you usually do. I'll be back tomorrow." When she had entered the Mercedes, Cheppi had moved for an embrace. She pulled back. "You be good," she waved goodbye.

The evening had gone well but it had been a long night. She enjoyed Carlota with her stories of those who had come through in the old days, Satchmo, Sinatra, even Elvis. And she agreed with the Minister of Tourism on the latest brochure. Yes, she might be interested in serving on some Boards, but she'd have to wait and see, she told them. The hotel comes first.

She didn't like Santo Domingo, in particular, faux-French tourist restaurants and the island's newly rich. Flaming desserts and cognacs for men who once cut cane, false laughter and little flirtations. Men whose parents starved for rice and beans argued over their new investments. Their cousins were important in the Ministries, or so they said. They had an "in" at the bank. They all had plans for getting rich. "Y Senora Eleanora, quiere participar? We should work together."

Eleanor Tibbett was tired this night, too much talk and drink and too much smile, the smile of the girl on the stool too late into the evening. But one does what one must for business.

In the early morning came the knock, first a faint knock then stronger before the chirping of birds, before the tropical sun lit the drapes. She was deeply asleep and so the knock came louder and louder. She stirred first, moving just enough to wake Cheppi. But Cheppi wasn't there.

99.

Esperanza

ESPERANZA SIGHED AND WALKED DOWN THE COUNTER. "Ya!," she said, "la hora." The few remaining coffee drinkers closed their newspapers and wandered out. "Hasta manana," she waved to them. A young man cleaned in the rear.

Carmela Chan entered. "You heard?"

"Sure I heard," Esperanza said, shaking her head. "What a shame."

"Terrible. They said someone killed him."

"Bound to happen. He had too many enemies. Hurt too many people."

Chan took her hands. "You two were so good together."

Esperanza looked away, tears in her eyes. "I knew. The moment that woman came in that door, I knew she'd be trouble. But would he listen?"

"Chica, he was long gone from you."

"I know, I know, but to la gringa and all that money."

"He cleaned up with her. Stopped using. Stopped selling. He became a new man for a time."

"He wouldn't clean up for me. Every night, going out, hustling drugs, snorting that shit, getting laid, chasing women like they were chickens in a coop and drifting back in the morning as fresh as can be, his body filled with that shit. He just couldn't stop, could he?"

"He did with her."

"Yeah, and he made some money. You know he kept sending me money to run the place. Wasn't the same though, without him. And the guys, they've been drifting away to Duncan Donuts and Starbucks."

"I see you've got a nice pretty boy slinging in the back."

"Jesus, yeah, he's a good kid. Cousin of my neighbor. Isn't carded yet, so we got to keep him under lock and key. Don't know what I'm gonna do now Cheppi gone."

"I remember," Chan said, "back in the old days, when he pranced down the street, like he owned it, making moves on all sorts of women. He'd have a roll of cash in his pocket, and we'd never know where he'd got it. He was into everything and he seemed like he ruled the world."

"Yeah," Esperanza said, "the good old days. And, you know, I resented that gringa but I really thought she had changed him. I guess I fell for her too. We latinos always think whitey is so strong and powerful. That they know something we don't. But people never change, do they? I mean the boy was just bad. Just bad."

"He loved you, you know that."

Esperanza said nothing. She turned to the boy in the back. "Vamonos. We're closing up."

"Listen," Chan said, "When you're done here, when you've had enough, you let me know. I got a buyer and he'll pay top dollar, much more than you can get from anyone."

"Who would pay for this dump?"

"You'd be surprised with all the gringos coming uptown. It's a prime location."

"Don't know. Don't know where the guys would go. They need a place to sit and spend their days, read their papers, and have their coffee."

"You're a good woman, Esperanza, but if this all is too much, you let me know. I'm pretty sure I can get you enough for the rest of your life."

100.

Dan Trepin

———————•———————

FLOCKS OF SEAGULLS FLEW OVER THE BEACH filled with white tents, and a sea of balloons. Husky men in tuxedos wandered Dune Road, bulges in their armpits. Musicians, straight from Las Vegas gigs, gathered on the temporary stage. Long limos brought the rich and famous. The anointed reporter was there as well. It was the wedding of the summer. "She really is my lucky charm," Dan Trepin told Raskolnikov. "And she has suffered so much. I need her."

"You do what you have to do. We Russians are fatalists, we love and kill and live passionate lives. I salute you." Raskolnikov, now close to the elderly titan, urged him on. "You can afford it. Go for it."

Pastor Wainwright presided, speaking about how wonderful that two people were so fated to come together after all these years. "God's will be done," he said.

As we all know, sometime after the wedding, Eleanor was named head of Trepin Enterprises, and a year later Dan Trepin was judged incompetent. Lawyers attacked and the media went wild: "She took advantage." "If the old man is bonzo now, he certainly was bonzo when he married her." "There oughta be a law." Commentators proclaimed that Tibbett was a symptom of a wider, national disease of greed and disregard for the poor. Headlines and recriminations.

The article in the *Daily News* created an overnight sensation. An "unnamed source" provided the News with background on this gold-digger, Eleanor Tibbett, how both her husband and sister had died under mysterious circumstances, how her youngest son had run away from home and now was being kept hidden, and how she went from rags to riches by kicking poor people out of their housing and selling condos.

The networks picked up the story. Her old mid-western neighbors were interviewed. They were amazed at the controversy. She may have been strange or withdrawn but a murderer, that was not possible. Her husband was a drunk, it was a tragedy, and why, they asked, was the press dredging this up now?

An enterprising reporter found these four old Latin guys up at Hudson Hills who claimed to have known her. He published a human interest story on how these old guys had been playing dominoes at the same place for thirty years and that not even Eleanor Tibbett could move them. A few beers from the interviewer and they opened up, "She was a nice woman," they said. "But she didn't speak Spanish."

The *Post* ran an "exclusive" story, based on interviews with the Police Chief in charge of the investigation of Joey Tibbett's death. "Was it bungled?" the headline read. A special state prosecutor was named to investigate the charges.

In the meantime, Eleanor Tibbett kept silent while her attorneys handled the press, attacking those who would slander his client, that there was nothing to the charges, that she was a victim of those who would try to destroy her for political purposes or out of envy. Her life was an open book, one of tragedy. Did they know that her other son had died a hero in the Gulf? She had suffered enough.

And then quickly, the issue died down. New investigations proved nothing and, despite the efforts of the press, nothing more was uncovered. There was a new war in the Middle East. And elections were coming. Anecdotes came across the transom, one about a dog she supposedly killed, and another about her missing son, but they were filed away in the archives.

In the meantime, the Trepin estate was divided, confidentially and with no leaks. The children, Trepin's long-gone offspring, were given a few condos.

They had no right under law after all, Eleanor was his wife. But to end the fight, she gave in. The commercial real estate remained with the company under her control. And then, when the market crashed and real estate holdings crumbled, the children found their buildings laden with mortgages, mortgages they could not pay. The agreement was clear. They had signed it. Trepin Enterprises exercised its right of first refusal and reclaimed the buildings. Inscrutable. That's what people say about Eleanor. Wherever she is seen, in meetings or out, day or night, she wears those large, dark sunglasses which have become her trademark. It began after Cheppi's death, at the funeral and then the wedding, then at Ciprianis for those big charity events. The dark glasses were always there shielding her eyes and her thoughts.

Since she took over, the business expanded considerably, her name as famous as Trump or Buffett. Russians, Arabs and Chinese came seeking partnerships. Eleanor Tibbett meets and greets investors courteously and then turns them over to her associates. "She doesn't like meetings," they are told. "Don't worry, we'll handle it."

Her lawyer, Dave Galloway usually sits alongside Sergei Raskolnikov, recently appointed to the board. And there is a guy on the phone, a strange almost quirky fellow, who takes part in all the meetings and never shows his face. He is the great mystery on Wall Street, this telephone voice with a strange Slavic accent who doesn't say much but when he does, it is like a knife cutting across an issue.

Of her personal life, little is known. Her office at Trepin Associates sits high above New York harbor where boats and freighters glide past Miss Liberty. The office has changed. Long and tall shelves now line a wall crammed with books. There is a small gap in the middle for a bar. Above it, are pictures of the two founders, the corporate namesakes Dan Trepin Senior and Junior. In the corner is an easy chair and a small table holding an elaborate reading lamp with copper tubes twisting all about and ending at three bulbs. This is where she spends most evenings, reading and thinking.

101.

Security

——————•——————

IN THE HR DEPARTMENT OF TREPIN ENTERPRISES, a beautiful, tall
African-American woman is being interviewed to become Chief of Security.
She has poise and experience in Detroit, as a Detective, and in New York, se-
curity work. She comes with perfect recommendations. She is a college grad.
She is earnest. She takes notes in a little red notebook.

She would need to be trained, of course. She would begin learning all the
security systems, the cameras, entrance procedures and financial controls, the
codes to the most confidential areas of the company. Then she would take
over the corporate file system, making sure they were safe from snoopers and
business rivals.

She is a perfect fit for a huge, multinational corporation, the interviewer
thought, a perfect fit.

102.

Petra

———•————————•———

S HE CLIMBED UP AND OVER A ROSE-COLORED HILL, Bedouin tribes-men at her side. The sun was blinding but the dark glasses shielded her eyes. In the distance, high on the surrounding hills, guards sat on camels, their heads down and rifles at their side. It was hot in this desert nation and she gasped for breath.

"You cannot visit Petra through the main entrance," the Prince said. "It would not be convenient what with your fame and the tourists. You must go through the back via Wadi Musa where the tribesmen live. They will accompany you and provide everything you need. You are our honored guest.

Cautiously, she walked up the stony path to the peak. "The idea," she told the Prince, "is to set up small and secretive resorts near the world's greatest historical sites. These days, tour buses come and visitors walk about for a few hours and leave. They spend nothing. We want to create a world-class facility where the wealthy stay in a safe and secure environment, lounging in spas and around pools, eating in world-class restaurants and touring historic sites with world-class experts. We are setting up Tibbett Resorts throughout the world, at Anghor Wat, Tikal, Macchu Picchu, and we want the Petra site to be our flagship resort. For me, it would be a place not only to invest in but where I might live for a time, maybe even establish a residency.

"Safe from authorities, I assume," the Prince said.

"Perhaps," she said, ignoring the implication. "I thought we might build at *Ain Musa* near where Moses struck the rock for water. That would be a wonderful draw for the Jewish and Christian faithful to relax where our civilization was born."

"We would not be opposed given the right arrangements."

"Of course. The royal family would be given a major share, and we would insist that the local Bedouin profit from our enterprise. But I must say, a feature of Tibbett Resorts is that we have women managers in all our facilities. I hope that would not be a problem."

"Not at all. Jordan is a modern country and we encourage opportunities for all."

She reached the hilltop and then looked down, into the valley of Petra and the hundreds of caves, temples and tombs, carved into pink sandstone. "We were once the center of the world," a voice said behind her, "thousands of camel caravans passed through here bringing goods from Asia and on to Egyptian pharaohs and Roman Caesars."

"It is very impressive."

"We did not rule the world, but the world needed us for their salt and pepper and spices and cloth. Goods from Petra made their way to England. We were very much like your New York, today.

"But it is the valley that is important, the homes cut into rock high up where we retreated when enemies invaded. They came to conquer the best fortress in the world, a valley with defenses at each end and our havens were impossible to reach. We were untouchable and so we were never conquered. We were great, but it is all gone. Trade has gone elsewhere. We are but just a memory.

"It is still overwhelming," she said.

"Yes, you know two thousand years ago, myrrh and frankincense passed through this site and on to the three kings and your baby Jesus. Our trade was there at the beginning."

She nodded. "If you don't mind, I'd like to sit alone for a while."

"Of course. Of course."

The Bedouins withdrew and kneeled in a circle around her. From behind her dark glasses, she stared down at the ruins of empire. She sat quietly and passively. And said nothing.

THE END

www.ingramcontent.com/pod-product-compliance
Lightning Source LLC
Chambersburg PA
CBHW030408180626
46812CB00005B/1976